Sirens and Grey Balloons

Peter Hurdwell

Sirens and Grey Balloons

Copyright © 2011 Peter Hurdwell. All rights reserved.

Peter Hurdwell has asserted his right under the Copyright Act 1976 to be identified as the author of this work.

Photographs and images are the copyright of the author unless otherwise identified. The photographs of "Chingford bomb damage" are sourced from the book "Chingford At War" published by Chingford Borough Council in 1946, whose copyright is acknowledged.

Published in the USA.

Typeset by Chargan My Book Publisher Pty. Ltd.
Level 18
152 St Georges Tce
Perth, WA, Australia 6000

www.chargan.com

ISBN 978-1-4478-3286-7

Dedication

To Wendy – my wife and closest friend.

Acknowledgements

Following my retirement from full-time work I was approached by a large Sydney insurance company to work on a month long project. One project led to another and my sojourn at that company was to last for the next seven years.

It was my good fortune to work with other employees who were naturally many years my junior but we soon built up a great rapport with each other to such an extent that every fortnight we would repair to the local pub after work and yarn about life in general which naturally touched upon our previous experiences.

As I related details of my early life, my fellow workmates appeared to be fascinated by some of the unusual events which I related, doubtless viewing these experiences through the prism of young people living in the twenty-first century. Often they would say "Write it down, Pete".

When I finally retired in 2009, three of my closest friends at work presented me with a fountain pen, suitably inscribed, telling me that the pen should be used in the writing of my book.

Thus, I wish to acknowledge the inspiration of Helen Warren, Sotheary Tin, Chris Carter and Adam Bevan without whose prompting my experiences would have been lost in the mists of time.

I also wish to thank Alan Jones who would regularly read my proofs and offer suggestions as the episodes of my book took shape. His comments were invaluable.

About the Author

Peter Hurdwell was born in London in 1937 and as with many children of that era experienced the traumas of living in war torn London during World War II.

After leaving school he joined the office of a London insurance broker before being conscripted into the British Army in 1955 where most of his army service was spent in the British Zone of post war Germany.

During that time he developed a keen interest in military history and has read widely about the various theatres of the two world wars.

1964 was to be a watershed in his life when he joined his two brothers and sister-in-law to drive from London to Kathmandu in a 1942 ex army Willys Jeep and an old Bedford van purchased for fifty pounds. After a journey lasting over six months they eventually arrived in Australia where they all settled.

He remained single for the next thirty years but had the good fortune to meet Wendy, his future wife during a short trip to Toronto, Canada. They were married the following year.

Since then he has visited the battlefields of Gallipoli and in 2005 trekked the Kokoda Track. More recently he spent time on the Western Front where he and a friend managed to find the place where his grandfather had fought almost a hundred years before.

He and Wendy now live in Sydney but make annual trips to stay with family in Toronto.

Peter Hurdwell

CHAPTER I EARLY DAYS

Although our family home was in Chingford, Essex, both parents were country people having been born and raised in Surrey.

My father was born in Camberley, Surrey in 1908 and christened 'Reginald Ernest' and at the time of his birth was the second of two surviving sons.

The eldest son, Thomas, had been born in 1903 but died three years later from tubercular meningitis. Apparently, he used to say grace at meal times but after his death, the family never said grace again. Doubtless they felt that the ritual would have reignited their earlier sadness.

After attending Camberley Public School both my father and his brother Ray went to Farnham Grammar School where my father excelled at sport but his brother Ray, excelled at all things intellectual, with sport not seeming to have been high on his list of priorities. Thus, upon leaving school, Ray won a Boot's (Chemist) scholarship to Nottingham University where he obtained a degree in pharmacy, whilst Dad applied for a position as a cadet reporter for the local Camberley News. Although he was selected over other applicants for the position, his family could not afford for him to take the job, as the family budget was stretched with Ray at university and the starting salary at the newspaper being insufficient for the family's needs. Ray eventually ran a pharmacy in Portsmouth which sadly was demolished by German bombing early in the Second World War.

However, my father did find work at the local garage and started to take a particular interest in motor bikes, which, as it turned out, was quite an advantage later on. Thus, at the age of fifteen he purchased a 1910 Rover Motor Cycle. I have actually seen the very same model in recent years and it was a revelation of antiquity, having a 500cc four-stroke single cylinder motor, swept back handle bars, wide leather saddle with massive coil springs but with clutch and gears being notably absent from its design. The rider was required to paddle the contraption to start the engine and apply a compression releasing valve lifter to bring the machine to a halt. Fortunately there were no traffic lights in those days and riders were not obliged to take a driving test or have a Drivers Licence.

His family lived quite close to a hill off Park Street, Camberley and to facilitate the starting of the Rover he used to push it to the top of the hill and free wheel down the other side until the monster struggled into life. Coming home, the Rover lacked the momentum to negotiate the entire hill leaving him no option but to dismount and push it the rest of the way home.

One day he overheard his mother saying to a neighbour "Reggie must love his motorbike. He pushes it all the way to work and all the way home!"

As work was hard to find in the early 1920's he was employed in various jobs on building sites including being a plasterer for a couple of years. However he later applied for and was accepted as a trainee in the London Metropolitan Police Force completing his training at Peel House, London in 1928.

It was, apparently, a great relief, given the depression and the vagaries of employment in the late 1920's, that my father's intake at Peel House had produced young men who had not only graduated into the London Metropolitan Police Force but who had also entered the ranks of those fortunate enough to have attained not just an interesting occupation but also the prospect of a safe and steady income.

Thus, upon graduating, this intake of budding Police Constables found various ways of celebrating their passport into new found employment. Most graduates headed for the nearby London pubs which abounded in the area but Dad, being a non drinker at the time, remained within the precincts of Peel House for the evening whilst the revellers sank the odd pint or two nearby.

However, he and a fellow newly appointed constable made the evening a memorable one by filling a chamber pot with lemonade into which they proceeded to launch a somewhat oversized gherkin into the sea of soft drink. Having left it on the dormitory landing they retired to their beds.

Needless to say, the newly appointed guardians of the law returned to Peel House in various stages of inebriation only to trip over the jerry, spilling its contents over the floor. I was unable to ascertain even in later years whether Dad and his fellow abstemious friend had ever owned up.

After working as a Policeman in Stoke Newington and Enfield, he finally became PC 254 in J Division, stationed at Waltham Abbey although after a couple of years he became a permanent fixture at Chingford Police Station. By then he had been selected to be one of twenty Police Motor Cyclists, in the Metropolitan Police, the first such 'speed cops' in Britain.

Although my father was a little short of six feet tall (nevertheless well above the average at the time), he was larger than life in so many ways. He had a jocular sense of humour, not of the bottom slapping uncle variety but somewhat of a more subtle hue in that he could appreciate the humour in a multitude of situations and manage to relate them to others in a picturesque fashion with slight embellishment but little exaggeration. He also had the ability to enjoy a laugh at his own expense which is so seldom the case these days. Many a time we kids would listen, spellbound by his narratives of some humorous episodes which had crossed his path during his duties as a policeman, but more of those later.

One of the most endearing aspects of his personality was that he was a good listener and his heart would go out to anyone who was in distress and one incident which he told me of in our many walks later in life showed his warmth and humanity, not to mention his considerable courage under trying and emotionally stressful situations.

During the depression in 1936, whilst on police duty, Chingford Police Station received a 'phone call advising that at a nearby park a man with a knife had been seen chasing a woman' and accordingly my father had been instructed by the station sergeant to attend the incident.

When he arrived at the park he managed to apprehend the man and when the situation had simmered down he endeavoured to find out what had transpired. He found that the couple were actually man and wife and happened to live in a house backing onto the park, thus allowing him to accompany the couple to their home nearby to ascertain the facts of the situation.

Sirens and Grey Balloons

It appeared that the husband had been thrown out of work and, although having applied for a number of jobs over a substantial period of time, had been unable to obtain employment. Adding to his woes was the fact that he had loaned his car to somebody but the borrower had failed to return it or pay for its hire.

In a fit of depression he had decided to end it all and put his head in the gas oven (there were no safety devices in those days), intending to commit suicide. At that moment his wife returned home, the husband panicked and in his rage picked up a kitchen knife and chased her out of the house and into the nearby park.

What was my father to do? He questioned the couple about their personal lives and asked them how long they had been married and it transpired that they had been together for many years and that their relationship had been a happy one, in fact, his wife said that "they had never had a wry word in all that time".

Dad explained that the penalty for attempted suicide was up to seven years gaol (in those days) and that attempted murder attracted a similar term of incarceration. He told them that if he carried out his duty as a policeman to the letter, the husband would be facing the possibility of a long custodial sentence if convicted in a court of law.

He then told them that he could return to the police station and register the incident as only a domestic argument with, hopefully, no further enquiries. He pointed out that if this course were taken and another such incident occurred between the couple, he would lose his job with the Police Force. This would affect not only himself but the livelihood of his wife and two year old son at home.

Much relieved, the couple promised that such a circumstance would not occur again and the 'domestic argument' duly appeared in the Police Station's 'Incident Book'.

Six months later, whilst on duty in the area, Dad walked into a cafe and saw the man in the corner having a cup of tea. The man looked somewhat embarrassed but upon enquiry told my father that shortly after the chase in the park episode, he had found employment and that both he and his wife were managing quite well. He mentioned the incident on one of our many walks through Epping Forest during one of my visits from Australia where I had migrated some years before

My mother was born in 1910 in a flat rented by the family overlooking a barber's shop in Lightwater in Surrey and was christened 'Mercy', a name which she always disliked, so much so that in later years she insisted on being called 'Mary' by her friends. Although Lightwater was only about 15 kilometres from Dad's home in Camberley, they had somewhat differing childhoods. My dad's father was in his 40's when military conscription was introduced into Britain during World War I and, as a consequence was not called up to serve in the military. Thus, the family was not separated from their father and he continued his normal occupation as an insurance agent and was never called upon to become cannon fodder during the long years of the conflict.

However, my mother's father, who at the outbreak of war was operating a thriving retail grocery shop, being of military age, was called up in November, 1916 and served for the remainder of the war in the Queen's (Royal West Surrey) Regiment where he remained Private Percy George Gorton, Regimental No G/39184. He, like hundreds of thousands of young men was called upon to fight battles planned by imbecilic British generals who often spent much of their time in chateaux away from the action seldom venturing out to take a firsthand look at the results of their rampant stupidity.

Having completed his basic training he was sent to an infantry base in Etaples in France after which he finally ended up with the 10th Battalion Queens Royal West Surrey Regiment.

In July, 1917 he took part in the large Allied offensive known as the Third Battles of Ypres, more commonly referred to as Passchendaele.

As the First World War drew to a close the 10th Battalion was sent to France where he was subject to a German mustard gas attack in the area of the Somme. After recovering from the ordeal his battalion was involved in heavy fighting from March to September, 1918, the March battle in which he was engaged taking place in the Thiepval area at a village called Bucquoy.

Sirens and Grey Balloons

At the conclusion of the battle a shell exploded in his trench which resulted in the death of his companions. He was eventually found wandering in No Mans' Land, very shaken up.

In 2010 I visited the scenes of the battles in which the 10th Battalion fought. It was a very special experience for me to tread the soil on which the battles had been fought and to wander across No Mans' Land as he had done in 1918. Little could he have imagined at the time that nearly a hundred years later his yet unborn grandson would visit that very spot?

Although he survived the war he died of Parkinson's disease at the early age of 61, doubtless having some connection with the gas attack. I say 'early' with some conviction as his father lived to be ninety-four and his siblings shared similar longevity.

Life in the United Kingdom and elsewhere in Europe during the First World War was extremely difficult for all families but particularly for those whose traditional breadwinners were away fighting the war for 'the King's shilling'. Mum, her sister and their mother were certainly no exception and with malnourishment and winter cold, their resistance to illness must have been very low. Thus, just as hostilities on the Western Front had ground inexorably to their close, so the force of nature dealt another blow to the struggling masses with the advent of the 'Spanish Flu' pandemic. Unfortunately all three fell victim to the flu although, unlike twenty-two million others, they recovered. I recall seeing a photograph of all three of them just after their recovery and they looked more like skeletons than human beings.

After leaving school at the age of fifteen, Mum, like so many other country girls, went into service, taking up a position as children's nanny in the household of the British Army officer, Sir Rob Lockhart who in later years was to become a general in the Indian Army during World War II eventually becoming Commander in Chief of the Indian Army after that War.

My parents first met at a church function in Camberley, when Mum was fifteen and Dad eighteen. They soon became quite involved with each other but Mum's father wasn't at all pleased at her having a regular boyfriend. However, when Dad was invited to tea at the Gorton household in 1925, her father took an immediate liking to him and he also met with the approval of the whole family.

However, when my mother took up the position in the Lockhart household in Gloucester, their courting was confined mainly to meetings in London with each of them travelling by train to London from their respective places of abode and commuting back to their homes later in the day.

My mother was very happy working for the Lockhart family and always said that they were very kind and considerate to her at all times and, in fact, when Sir Rob received word of his posting to India, he asked Mum if she would be prepared to go with them. However, she felt that Dad was the one for her and they decided to marry as soon as they received the consent of Mum's parents.

Eventually, on 20 June, 1931 they were married but not before Dad had applied for and received permission from the Commissioner of the Metropolitan Police. The couple were married in Camberley Baptist Church with the wedding reception, (dry of course) being held in the Anglican Church Hall, Lightwater. Ironically, they spent their honeymoon at Margate in a small rented cottage called 'Katoomba', the irony being that thirty-four years later their three sons were destined to drive overland through Europe and Asia ending up in Australia where they settled, all within eighty miles of Katoomba in the Blue Mountains of New South Wales.

My father's first posting in the London Metropolitan Police Force was at Stoke Newington Police Station, situated a few kilometres to the north of central London, which, at that time was regarded as a typically working class area of the great metropolis.

Early in his career at this police station he encountered a circumstance which presented the opportunity for him to use his innovative skills as a young 'copper' on the beat. Late one night, after patrons had been ushered out of the many local pubs at closing time, he chanced upon a woman renowned by the locals including the police, for her regular over indulgence in liquor, in fact, on this occasion she was in such an advanced state of intoxication that she had stumbled on the pavement where she remained in a drunken coma.

Sirens and Grey Balloons

What was this newly appointed policeman to do, bearing in mind that there were no radio controlled vehicles or mobile phones during those days. He needed to get her to the safety of the police station but how was he to do it?

He had a brainwave. In those days, if a member of the police force needed to transport a deceased person to the nearest police station, there was available a coffin-like box mounted on a low slung trolley built for the purpose. Thus, Dad went back to the station, pulled the manual hearse to where the woman lay prostrate, placed her in the box and started on the return journey to the police station where it was intended that she remain until her release in the morning. However, shortly into the journey, the motion of the make-do hearse must have awoken her from her drunken stupor and she started screaming, much to the surprise of passersby, not to mention my father as well.

On another occasion whilst on duty, he came across his long lost Aunt Annie whom he hadn't seen or heard of for several years. Annie was his mother's sister and her disappearance from the family home in Camberley had been a quite tragic affair.

Annie Sadler was one of a number of children in the household ruled by their didactic father William, in an autocratic manner typical for those times. He was also a leading light in the local Baptist Church. Unfortunately for his son and daughters, the Sabbath was supposed to be a sacrosanct day with activities restricted to attendance at church and bible reading. However, by all accounts, his children were a somewhat high spirited brood whose attitudes and desires were inevitably at odds with his precepts, particularly on the Sabbath when their behaviour was constantly watched over by their sanctimonious father.

Annie was certainly no exception and, whilst compliant with her father's authority at home, she certainly enjoyed the freedom of life outside the family and sometimes returned home at a later hour than required by her father.

Thus, when she returned home late one evening he reprimanded her severely and made an example of her by banishing her to a home for fallen women. One imagines that her father also had one eye on what others in the congregation would have been thinking of his erstwhile daughter and was as much influenced by the judgment of his peers as those of his spiritual Master. Doubtless what Annie didn't know about life during her cosseted days at home, she would certainly have found out shortly after residing with the other 'fallen' women.

However, this may be a rather stern assessment of my paternal great grandfather as he was popular at his local place of worship and was, by all accounts, an interesting raconteur, possessing a very sharp wit, a gift which he harnessed to great effect at the local Dunmow Flitch trials in Camberley.

The Dunmow Flitch Trials entailed contestants proving as eloquently as possible, that they and their wives had not had a harsh word during the previous year and a day. The trial also involved rigid cross examination by their peers who made up the jury. The winner of the trial ended up with a flitch of bacon from Dunmow in Essex, which apparently was where the most succulent pigs were bred.

By all accounts the old boy, armed with his lightning wit and casuistic gymnastics, allowed him to tie up his interrogators to such a degree that he won the flitch of bacon on many occasions. However, I imagine that he really did have an unfair advantage over the other contestants as his wife was as deaf as a post and would never have been privy to any of his comments at home, whether complimentary or otherwise.

WALTHAM ABBEY.

When my parents were first married, my father was posted to Waltham Abbey Police Station, having spent the earlier part of his career at Stoke Newington and Enfield Stations prior to that time.

Waltham Abbey was a beautiful country market town nestling amidst the Essex countryside and surrounded by lush farmland but still within reasonable travelling distance of Central London.

The Abbey itself dates back to the eleventh century and was established before the Norman Conquest in fact King Harold was reputed to have been buried within its precincts although, as yet, firm evidence to this effect has not been verified.

On trips back to UK from Australia I loved driving to Waltham Abbey and often gazed in wonder at an old oak tree in the abbey churchyard which had been mentioned in the Domesday Book. It had survived for almost a thousand years and its demise was only quite recent.

Not far from Waltham Abbey runs the River Lea. In my father's later years we used to drive to Waltham Abbey, have a drink at the English Country Gentleman pub overlooking the river and, suitably sustained, would walk along the banks of the river, often discussing Izaak Walton's book 'The Compleat Angler'. Whilst we did not commence the trip at Hoddesdon as Walton's three characters had done, we nevertheless passed meadows and fishing holes along the way south towards Tottenham Hale, as did the Angler, Falconer and Hunter on their way to their final destination three hundred years before.

With the pages of the book in mind we tried to imagine the spectre of a peaceful pastoral scene; a fresh dew-soaked morning, long, lush, succulent grass upon which a lone carthorse stood munching his breakfast in contented verdant solitude. How could the poor creature have possibly imagined that on the other side of the hedgerow an angler was taking an extravagant interest in his wellbeing? Nothing strange about that one would have thought except that one of the angler's requirements was a long hair from his tail for use as a fishing line. Dad and I compared vivid mental pictures of the angler creeping up behind the poor unsuspecting creature without a care in the world, only to have a long hair yanked from its tail. It presented even more of a challenge had the angler required a second hair for fishing in deeper water.

One would only hope that the angler could restrain himself from stealing a hair from a horse whose owner was delivering milk in a nearby lane. Our minds ran riot as we pictured the horse rocketing along the country lane at high speed with the angler in hot pursuit trying to avoid the churns of milk as they rolled off the dray.

However, back to 1931 and my parents' move to Waltham Abbey.

Only a hundred or so metres from the Abbey is situated Monkswood Avenue and it was here at number twenty that my parents took up residence in a small two storey, red brick house built probably at the beginning of the twentieth century.

My parents thoroughly enjoyed their early married life and Mum, in particular felt a wonderful sense of freedom. Being a housewife was very satisfying for her, particularly as she had given up work and could concentrate on being a home maker. This sense of freedom derived mainly from the new found experience of coming and going as she pleased, where previously, when living at home with parents, restraints were placed on the amount of time girls were allowed out of the 'family home, in fact she, like most of the girls of that era had to be home by 9.30 sharp or otherwise incur the opprobrium of their parents.

When my father was on late turn' duty, they often used to meet at a pre-arranged point on his beat and keep each other company as he continued his rounds on foot.

Whilst they had little money to spare they did manage quite well, even stretching the budget to visit the cinema when a good film was being screened. Alas, in the 1930's the financial storm clouds were gathering due to the great depression, culminating in wage cuts for most workers including those in public sector. Thus, London Metropolitan Police wages were severely reduced and my father's wages were cut by ten shillings per week, quite a sum in those days.

Unfortunately, there remained no alternative but to speak to the landlord and request that he reduce the rent by five shillings a week. He eventually agreed and their tenure at Monkswood Avenue was able to be maintained and it was at this address that in 1934 my elder brother, Gerald (Jerry) was born.

It was whilst my father was stationed at Waltham Abbey that the Marshall of the Royal Air Force, Lord Trenchard, became the newly appointed Metropolitan Police Commissioner. One of his first innovations was to found a new Police College at Hendon which sought to produce an 'officer class' into the force.

Having heard of the new college and as a young married man wishing to enhance his career prospects, my father applied for and was duly granted an interview for a place at the college.

He and another young constable from the station were subsequently summoned to Scotland Yard for an interview before a panel of senior police officers. It soon became apparent during the interview that these top brass officers were not at all interested in whether candidates were well versed in policing, police procedures or even the law which they had been charged to uphold and enforce.

He was asked where he had met his wife, at which school he was educated, what newspapers he normally read and was even questioned about 'the classics'. Other questions were thrown in which were not even remotely connected to the police force.

It appeared that the newly created officer class were required to have emanated from good British stock and to have been the result of 'good breeding'. Needless to say his application was not successful.

CHINGFORD

Shortly after my brother's birth, my father heard of a vacancy at the Chingford Police Station and my parents became very interested in a posting to that area as new and fairly affordable housing developments were under way in that part of London. Thus, my father applied for and was accepted as a police motor cyclist at Chingford Police Station.

Chingford, situated only twenty kilometres North of London, but still in the county of Essex, had been just a small village in mediaeval times and, as it was surrounded by magnificent forest land, kings and queens of England used to hunt deer in the surrounding Epping Forest, the most famous of them being Henry VIII and Good Queen Bess. Legend has it that Henry VIII was hunting at nearby High Beech when he and his party heard the cannon at the Tower of London signifying the beheading of Anne Boleyn, a deed which eventually led to his being able to marry Jane Seymour, something he had been contemplating for some time.

The Royal Hunting Lodge at North Chingford, which is now a museum, was used by Queen Elizabeth I who is reputed to have ridden her horse up the stairway to her room. However it is doubtful if the horse ever emulated the antics attributed, wrongly one would hope, to Catherine the Great's stallion, although most historians have dismissed that legend as pure fantasy, even though Catherine was noted for her unusual sexual proclivities.

Charles II was also a great hunter and used to spend days in Epping Forest hunting deer and was said to have spent some time in a lodge in Chingford, less than a kilometre from Queen Elizabeth's Hunting Lodge. Apparently, on one occasion after an exhausting days hunting with his courtiers, he was relaxing after drinking a mead or three when a loin of beef was served. The king, in recognition of the appearance of the mouth watering loin, bestowed upon it a knighthood, pronouncing it Sir Loin', a name by which we now recognise as a particular cut of beef. It was probably not the only loins in which the king displayed more than a passing interest, particularly when Nell Gwynne was around.

It took my parents some time to scrape up the deposit for a newly built home but in the interim they were renting a small, old style house in Willow Street, North Chingford. The convenience of the location to the Police Station was somewhat outweighed by the age of the home and its dampness which created more urgency for my parents to find a new home to buy. Thus, in the following year having hunted around every affordable building site in the area, they finally set their hearts on a 'chalet bungalow' at Chingford Hatch.

Fortunately Mum's mother gave the young couple five pounds, quite a sum by my parents standards, which enabled them to put a deposit on their house at number 7 Blackthorne Drive.

By all accounts, the mortgage of six hundred and twenty pounds seemed like an enormous commitment but, for the first time, they could genuinely look upon the house as their very own domain, together with the Woolwich Equitable Building Society which would hold an interest for the next twenty-five years until the mortgage was finally paid off.

They moved into the empty house in the December, 1935. At the time they possessed no floor coverings, the only furniture being a bed, table and chairs, Jerry's cot and some armchairs Dad had made himself. Mum used to recall how cold it was that Christmas for although they had lit a fire in the dining room, the house was like a butcher's cool room as the brickwork and mortar were damp and still in the process of drying out.

The greatest attribute of their new home was undoubtedly its location for, at the time, the housing estate was situated in a semi rural area with fields and woodland where cattle grazed a few hundred metres away.

Sirens and Grey Balloons

When I was a small boy, I recall that cattle which had been grazing in nearby fields and woodlands, having grown tired of the same old fare these locations offered, used to wander along Blackthorne Drive, blundering into people's gardens consuming flowers, plants and any greenery they could find, like a plague of sumo locusts leaving behind them gardens stripped of their greenery but enough cow dung to guarantee a new crop for their delectation in the coming spring.

The semi detached house itself was interesting to say the least and bore credence to the obvious fact that it must have been designed by a consultant whose experience in architecture had been limited to the design of sub standard barns and public conveniences.

There were only two rooms upstairs, both bedrooms, the rest of the living area being below on the ground floor. There was no bathroom or toilet upstairs which posed the inconvenience of being compelled to make the journey down the steep stairway should the urgency of a pee overtake anyone during the night. Chamber pots were somewhat out of vogue at the time.

The house, like most others of that era, had both a front and a back door, the only difference being that with this house neither door faced either the back or front of the building. They were both at the side of the home facing north, inviting the sub zero north wind to pay his unwelcome visits at all times on wintry days and nights.

The toilet was also quite interestingly located, being sited adjacent to the front door where, inevitably, anybody knocking at the front door could well be greeted by a thunderous fart from within by Dad or, if my mother was on the throne, a somewhat more refined twinkle. At all events it did have the effect of advertising to all and sundry that someone was definitely at home when they called.

My very first memory was, as a child, in May, 1939, being taken by my mother, accompanied by my elder brother, Jerry, in a steam train to visit my father in Whipps Cross Hospital, which was situated between the electoral boundaries of Walthamstow and Woodford. Strangely, the local member for Walthamstow was Clement Atlee and the member for Woodford was Winston Churchill. Both areas were but a few miles from

Central London but in those days a social universe apart from each other.

Dad's ward was situated on the ground floor of the hospital complex with Dad residing in the third bed on the left as we proceeded into the ward. He was dressed in white pyjamas which boasted a wide blue stripe with parallel stripes of less forceful hue. At the end of his bed was a hospital trolley on which I now presume must have been instruments and medicines although at that age I was obviously no judge.

In later years, a certain sad irony struck me in that the first memory I have of my parents together was at this hospital. Many years later we farewelled my father in 1991 and my mother in 2005 in the very same hospital.

Although we lived in Chingford, on the border of London and Essex, I was actually born in Hackney at the Salvation Army Mothers' Hospital which, of course, automatically made me a Cockney by birth, having been born within the sound of Bow Bells (the bells Of St Mary-le-Bow in Cheapside). However, due to Bow Bells having been destroyed during the London Blitz in 1941 and not being rebuilt until 1961, I was, at least for a while, in rather select company, the supply of Cockneys having dried up in the absence of the bells for a period of twenty years.

Another stroke of good fortune lay in the fact that I was born in a hospital with attendant professional care, (my other two siblings being born at home, as was quite usual in those days). My good luck lay in the fact that during the birth I managed to become entangled with the umbilical cord although fortunately professional medical help was on hand. I was also born in a caul, a membrane or bag supposed to bring good luck and to be an infallible preservative against drowning. The 'old salts' superstitions must have well been infallible as, here I am at the age of 72 years, writing this account, having lived in Sydney, Australia for over forty years, and very close to the sea. My mother, on being asked if she wanted this icon preserved for good luck was not at all interested and the item was discarded.

But my greatest good fortune in my life was to have been born into a loving family with my parents being the soul of kindness and understanding with barrels of humour and laughter thrown in for good

Sirens and Grey Balloons

measure. As children these qualities were often taken for granted as being the norm and it was only later when observing the lives of others, the realisation dawned on us as to how lucky we were. This lesson was yet to be learned.

CHAPTER II SECOND WORLD WAR

The next memory I am able to recall was only three months after our visit to see my father in hospital where he was recovering from an appendix operation. This recollection was to occur on one of the most significant days of the twentieth century. The 3rd of September, 1939.

Although I do not remember the journey down to Camberley where we stayed with my paternal grandparents, I do remember the hustle and bustle interrupting what should have been a quiet Sunday when our weekend visit was cut short, and we made a hasty retreat back to Chingford. As is now common knowledge, Britain had declared war on Germany following that country's invasion of Poland and my father assumed that he would be required back at Chingford Police Station as soon as possible.

Mind you, prior to the outbreak of hostilities, local police forces in most areas had been rehearsing duties which would be required following possible enemy air raids. Sadly, some of these drills hadn't quite gone exactly to plan.

Dad told me of one such drill being undertaken in his area, the scenario being that several people had been injured by a bomb dropped by an enemy bomber. On that occasion the police had called for volunteers to act as victims of the air raid and some poor unsuspecting soul had decided to become a person injured by the bombing.

Whilst the volunteer was lying prostrate on the ground, one of the burly policemen, kitted out with various wartime accoutrements including steel helmet and gas mask, looked down at the injured man, whereupon his steel helmet fell from his head breaking the volunteer's nose. Panic ensued as these guardians of the law commandeered a van which acted as a makeshift ambulance. They placed the injured volunteer on a hastily made up stretcher and shoved him feet first into the van. Unfortunately the van wasn't quite long enough, as the police found out to their dismay when they slammed the door of the vehicle, causing further injury by way of concussion to the hapless volunteer

On that fateful Sunday we returned home to Chingford by train via Waterloo Station and arrived in Blackthorne Drive just as darkness was

Sirens and Grey Balloons

falling and the first task for the family was to check the 'blackout curtains' which had already been installed. Tape had also been stuck in strips onto the windows so that in event of a bomb blast shattering the window, shards of glass could not travel in all directions. The only remaining task was to remove the light bulbs in all the rooms where there were no blackout curtains. Globes from the sitting room, bathroom, toilet, hallway and bedrooms were removed and we were given torches to guide us around the darker parts of the house.

I recall that just after dark I accompanied my father out into the back garden to test the blackouts to ensure that there were no chinks of light escaping into the blackness outside, thus denying enemy planes the opportunity of seeing civilization in the town below and the opportunity to drop their bombs.

On that day the lights went out in the United Kingdom and Europe and were to remain dormant until May, 1945 when victory over Hitler's Germany had been finally achieved. By then over a hundred civilians in our suburb would have been killed in the bombing with many more suffering serious injury and only ten per cent of homes escaping damage from enemy bombing.

Fortunately for our family our house suffered little damage losing a couple of doors and having windows blown out plus broken tiles and ceiling damage. This was in spite of seventeen bombs exploding within a radius of 500 metres from our house. These bombs consisted of 13 high explosive bombs, one parachute mine, an oil bomb and doodlebug (V 1 flying bomb), plus various small incendiary bombs.

When the family moved to Chingford, the town was still set within the precincts of semi rural surroundings with a relatively small population but by the time the war had commenced, Chingford had grown considerably, mainly due to the migration of young couples buying the newly built houses which had become available, in fact in 1939 the population had grown to about 30,000 residents.

Whilst there was still evidence of the depression around, there were many factories and business enterprises in the vicinity providing welcome employment. However, at the outbreak of hostilities, many factories were turned over to making products for the war effort. In addition the nearby Enfield Small Arms factory naturally increased production of war materiel, a nearby company making bakelite products switched production to wartime communications equipment and a local furniture manufacturer turned its attention to the construction of the wooden wings for the renowned Mosquito fighter bomber. Added to the list of nearby wartime manufactures was an ammunition factory in the Waltham Abbey area some fifteen kilometres away.

Thus it was that our area provided reasonably rich pickings for the attention of enemy bombers although they may have been wary of the North Weald RAF base about twenty kilometres east of Chingford.

Whilst we were not as vulnerable to the saturation bombing experienced by residents in Central London and its environs, Chingford was nevertheless, quite an attractive enemy target as we were to find out as the war ground on.

Life in the initial stages of the war did not appear to have changed very much and certainly there was no German bombing in our area for several months which was just as well as we had no air raid shelters in which to take refuge. However, rationing was introduced early in 1940 and was reasonably severe at first becoming more stringent later, impacting on Jerry and myself on a personal level when the sweet ration was cut down to 2 ounces per week, but more of that later.

RATIONING

A cross section of the rationing per person per week when first introduced is as follows.

Butter	2 ounces	(50 grammes)
Cooking fat	4 ounces	(100 grammes)
Sugar	9 ounces	(225 grammes)
Bacon or Ham	4 ounces	(100 grammes)
Eggs	1 egg per week or 1 pack of dried eggs per month.	
	(1 pack =12 eggs)	
Tea	2 ounces	

Sirens and Grey Balloons

Milk	3 pints	
Cheese	2 ounces	(50 grammes)
Jam	18 ounces	(450 grammes) every two months

Also rationed were clothes, shoes and sweets, the latter being of a top priority to a young kid of three years of age.

I recall going up to London with my father to the Metropolitan Police clinic where he was to have some dental work done. It was a great day out for me as I had Dad all to myself but also I had my first experience of London and the River Thames. I rode in a tram along the embankment for the first time and when we got off, I looked across the mighty river for the first time and to my amazement witnessed the sight of a steam tug boat whose funnel was too high to go under a low bridge, but as I set my imagination for a collision between its tall funnel and the bridge, the tug lowered its funnel and disappeared from view through the gap.

However, as rationing had only just started, I was given a penny by my father and told that some of the chocolate vending machines still had chocolate in them. I had visions of penny bars of Nestles chocolate buried in their bowels ready to disgorge their confections for my delectation. After a few vain attempts at extracting the treasure, one machine managed to cough up a much sought after slim bar of chocolate which delighted me no end.

My mother was issued with a ration book for each member of the family by The Ministry of Food, each book bearing the name of the individual family member complete with their address and ration book number.

Purchase of these rationed items was strictly controlled although a household could exchange their jam ration for extra sugar with which to make their own jam. My mother used to avail herself of this facility and we used to spend afternoons picking blackberries during the summer months and with the apples from my grandmother's garden, she used to make many jars of jam for our family.

Similarly we gave up our meagre egg ration in exchange for 'balancer meal' which, when mixed up with household scraps, was used to feed the chickens in our back garden. The chicken manure wasn't wasted either as it was used by my father on his allotment, a small piece of ground about a mile from our home which could be hired from the local council for a peppercorn rent. The vegetables produced went a long way in supplementing our rather bland diets. Even the allotment was bombed but fortunately Dad' vegetables were spared and we were thus not treated to chunks of shrapnel encrusted in our potatoes.

At about the same time that rationing was introduced, I recall a person from some Government Department knocking on the door and fitting us up with gas masks. There was always a fear that Hitler would use gas on civilians but, fortunately for all the combating countries, the fear of retaliatory gas attacks remained a sane deterrent and none was ever used. It was quite good fun trying on these masks and I was delighted with mine because it was a red 'Mickey Mouse' model. Having donned the mask, I could blow hard and the little red nozzle made a funny noise not unlike a high pitched fart. The only trouble was that if I tried to blow and emulate a fart, the Perspex goggle used to fog up. Jerry's mask was of much more sedate affair than mine being black and a bit larger, as was the one issued to Mum. However, Dad, due to his occupation and exposure to more dangerous situations, had a huge respirator with a flexible hose going down to a filter cylinder. It was most impressive and made him look like the cross between a deep sea diver and an elephant. When my younger brother Rob came along, my mother was issued with a most peculiar contraption designed for babies. It looked like a padded cylinder in which the baby was placed, the top being battened down leaving the person in charge to induct air by way of a tube attached to a manual pump. It looked for all the world like a snub nosed miniature sub marine. Heaven knows what deep psychological scars would have been visited upon the poor unfortunate child had it been subjected to a session in one of these chambers.

AIR RAIDS.

Up to this time the war seemed to have been somewhat of a non event but in 1940 this all changed and I was, for the first time in my life, to experience real fear and that was the first bombing raid in our area. My father was on night duty and had left the house at about 10 pm. leaving Mum, Jerry and myself at home.

Sirens and Grey Balloons

Shortly afterwards, the air raid sirens started to wail which was not in itself a new experience but, apparently, there had been a BBC newsflash to warn people in the London area of an impending raid, although the intended target was not known. However, my mother gathered us up shoved us into the cupboard under the stairs where we cleared a space by jettisoning a couple of my father's boots and a few items of outer garments. It was rather cramped as the cupboard housed the coin-in-the slot gas meter as well. In the absence of an air raid shelter it had been noted that when houses collapsed after being bombed, the stairs usually managed to stay intact, making this area the safest place in which to shelter.

This night was particularly memorable as we started to hear the drone of German bombers in the distance at first but then coming nearer and nearer to the place where we were hiding. We then heard them overhead and we could hear the anti aircraft guns pounding away at our unseen assailants and the thunder of bombs as they exploded nearby. In the midst of all this I recall the clatter of what was probably a machine gun, and a couple of minutes later a large thud giving rise to the hope that one our fighters had downed a German plane. I also remember being worried about my father being out in all this in pursuit of his police patrol duties.

Air raid sirens were to become a common sound in our early childhood and even to this day, when watching a war time film or hearing the wailing of an air raid siren, my scalp still contracts and my hair stands on end.

Obviously it took some time for civilians to become accustomed to living their everyday lives in the shadow of hostilities which were starting to invade their very homes. As the bombing increased, my parents, along with thousands of other families in the London area, decided that we should seek the relative sanctuary of a country town or village, away from the bombing. This was to become known as 'evacuation'.

EVACUATION

Thousands of children from all over London found themselves deposited on railway stations with small satchels, suitcases and, of course their gas masks. They were waved off by their mothers to areas in rural

England which many of them had never heard of, to be cared for by strangers they had never seen of even spoken to. Many of these children were looked after by kindly country folk and can recall fond memories of their lives in the peace and tranquillity of a British country village. However, many experienced little joy in their new environments as it really was a matter of the luck of the draw. One thing most of these children had in common was that they were away from their parents and this great chunk taken out of their lives made for difficulties in readjusting to life with their parents when they were finally reunited in 1945. Many of the children had fathers whom they could not remember; fathers who had left home to fight for years in far off theatres of war, only to return home and be looked upon by their children as intruders or strangers.

We were much more fortunate as our father was in a 'reserved occupation' which meant that he could not be called up for military service. My mother, having two young children, could not spend time away at work, as most unattached women did, and therefore our family life was not initially disrupted to any great degree.

As the bombing in our area intensified, more and more houses were being lost or damaged, it was decided that Jerry, Mum and I should be evacuated to a safer haven away from London. As my parents had been brought up in Surrey, we headed for the Camberley area where we would be able to keep in contact with all four grandparents and my father would be able to travel by train to see us when the opportunity arose. Thus it was that Dad found a small cottage just off the A30 London Road between Bagshot and Camberley called Lamb Foist.

We didn't stay there very long and I am unsure as to why we left this house but I have a vague recollection that it was a little remote and to leave the house to access the main road necessitated going though someone's private land which apparently caused some problems. I did get the impression that evacuees weren't very welcome there.

However, the next home we moved to was at Yately, still near to the A30 Main Road and only about five kilometres from my paternal grandparents' home. If our previous temporary abode was primitive then this small cottage could be described as prehistoric although in reality probably dating back to only the mid nineteenth century.

YATELY

To describe the cottage as being primitive would have been, even in the mid twentieth century, flattering in the extreme. However, it did have the advantage of being bounded by very pleasant surroundings. Although there was only a tiny village nearby which housed but a few shops, we were, nevertheless, not far from the larger town of Hartley Wintney. One side of the house faced a small strip of forest, mainly of fir trees which exuded a very sweet aroma whilst the front bedroom of the cottage confronted a large stretch of sandy soiled common land which was occasionally used by army tanks practising their war time manoeuvres. We used to watch them roaring up sand hills and over ditches with their steel tracks crushing everything before them and sounding like mechanical prehistoric monsters rejoicing in their new found freedom as they trammelled the surrounding vegetation.

The one shop in Yately which commanded Jerry's and my attention was a confectioners shop run by a very gentle and kindly person called Miss Stevens who showed great patience as we chose our weekly halfpenny stick of toffee. I'm sad to say that she appeared to be an exception, for unfortunately it wasn't long before we came to realise that we were not at all welcome in the neighbourhood. Jerry, who had been enrolled in the local junior school, became the victim of the local kid's invective. It was commonplace for us to be walking near home whilst being followed by the local boys shouting "Go back to London you 'orrible vacuees". Even at that tender age I felt confronted and uncomfortable and my mother had to endure school children such as Harry Pithers yelling the same insults but ending up with calling her "Ole mother turd'ole", not that I knew what a 'turd 'ole was at that tender age.

The one redeeming feature for my mother could have been the nearby pub 'The Cricketers' but she was not able to appreciate its fellowship or libations it sold as she was, like most of our family at the time, a teetotaller.

The tiny cottage was settled adjacent to 'the big house' where doubtless the gentry of pre war times would have lived, although during the war it was unoccupied and used as a furniture warehouse. Presumably our temporary home had once housed members of the lower classes whose work involved service with the big knobs next door. Although the big house had all the trimmings of opulence, our little cottage was devoid of most creature comforts including even electricity, being illuminated instead by gas which sadly did not extend to the stove which was a wood fired Kitchener. On this ancient stove Mum had to cook, boil water and keep warm in winter.

In years past the only source of water must have been supplied by the well situated in the garden of the big house next door. On the first day at the cottage our mother took us to the site of the well. It had a deep narrow shaft whose access was secured by a wooden lid on top at ground level. We were instructed that under no circumstances were we to go anywhere near the well. Realising the gravity of her instruction we promised faithfully never to go near it.

The cottage had two bedrooms, one of which was used by Mum and the other shared by Jerry and myself. The local old style Baptist Church was next door and the graveyard came right up to our wall in fact if we opened the sash window of our bedroom we could touch the headstone of the grave of one Eliza Newman. Over sixty years later I visited the home but although I found the cottage I was unable to access the churchyard as it was by then fenced in and the gate was locked. I was very disappointed at not being able renew my acquaintance with Eliza.

Our abode did not boast a bathroom and we washed ourselves in the kitchen sink and on bath nights my mother heated up buckets of water on the stove but only after my father had managed to clean the soot from the blocked chimney using the wispy branch of a nearby fir tree. As regards a toilet, the only remnant left was a commode style lavatory seat in a nearby outhouse under which resided a half empty bucket, adding a nasty smell enough to dissuade use by even the most desperate of diarrhoea sufferers. Fortunately during our stay I do not remember either Jerry or myself having an attack of the squitters. Every evening, Mum used to take us to the big house by the light of a torch and in the darkness Jerry and I would do our 'number two's. The vast, dark empty house seemed very scary at the time as though haunted by the ghosts of the aristocracy of yesteryear.

Sirens and Grey Balloons

There wasn't much to occupy the minds of two small boys in our new environment and apart from the occasional walk into nearby Hartley Wintney our activities were mainly confined to amusing ourselves playing hide and seek in the woods or wandering in the garden. It was thus inevitable that the temptation to look down the well became akin to the serpent's temptation in the Garden of Eden.

Eventually we succumbed to the ultimate mortal sin. Jerry lifted the lid from the top of the well and we both peered down into its cavernous interior.

That evening I was so worried about the incident that I was unable to eat my supper. My mother became so worried she asked if anything was wrong and I blurted out that we had looked down the well. Mum was aghast as she got up from the table, grabbed Jerry and gave him a walloping with the back of her wooden handled hair brush, blaming him for the incident as he was the eldest and "should have known better".

The atmosphere was somewhat strained that night as Jerry and I shared the same bed next to Eliza Newman.

In the absence of electricity, my mother used to keep up-to-date with the news and world events by listening to a radio powered by a wet cell battery which required re-charging every week. This entailed a walk of several miles into Camberley where we always called on Granny and Grandad Hurdwell, my father's parents. We loved seeing Granny as she spoilt us as only grannies can and we looked forward to bread and honey, the honey being produced by the bees from several hives our grandfather kept at the end of the garden.

I feel genuinely sorry for children who have never experienced the joy of having grandparents either for reasons of geographical distance or whose grandparents died too early to have been able to leave an endowment of fond memories and fun. It was always a wondrous experience for me to glean from my grandparents' snippets of what my mother and father had got up to when they were my age.

Granny Hurdwell was everything that a model granny could be although in that era, anyone even a few years older than my parents, seemed to me to have belonged to a bygone era, which when comparing living in

Queen Victoria's reign as opposed to George VI's reign, probably contained an element of truth.

Granny started life in 1880 as Elizabeth Sadler and carried the nickname of 'Cissie' throughout her life. She was the youngest daughter of William Sadler, previously mentioned as being a luminary of the York Town Baptist Chapel in Camberley and who was noted as a strict enforcer of authority at home, particularly when it came to his three daughters, Rhoda, Annie and Cissie. It was William Sadler who had been responsible for consigning his daughter Annie to the home for 'fallen women' when she came home late once too often.

Although the daughters were spirited girls, they dared not cross their father although their brother the young William Sadler locked horns with the old man at fairly regular intervals, particularly as he had been endowed with a spirit of adventure coupled with a perverse sense of humour. Thus, he was the victim of his father's vituperations on countless occasions.

The Baptist Chapel was sacrosanct to William Sadler Senior but young Will, by all accounts harboured little reverence for the House of God.

One hot summer's afternoon his father advised young Will that there was to be a baptismal service in the chapel that evening and that he required the large pool at the front of the chapel, near the pulpit to be filled with water. At baptismal services those wishing to be baptised were fully immersed in water, being symbolic of the washing away of their sins and the commencement of a new life. Young Will dutifully went about the business of filling the pool with water but as it was a hot summer's afternoon decided he would partake of a short swim to cool down. Unfortunately his father returned to the chapel a little earlier than Will had anticipated and one can hardly contemplate his father's wrath when he confronted his son almost naked in the baptistery.

One would have thought that he would die of apoplexy at that moment but the old boy soldiered on until he was eighty-nine, but maybe The Almighty wasn't ready to take him until then.

.

Sirens and Grey Balloons

On another occasion Will's mother decided to make a large supply of broth and to do this she placed various vegetables in the copper (usually where the clothes were boiled on washing day) together with water and a pig's head, the idea being that when the fire under the copper was lit, it would, over a few hours of simmering, produce the required stock. As the family was going down to the chapel for the evening they left young Will in charge of the copper with strict instructions to not let the brew boil over and to generally keep an eye on it. After quite some time he lifted the lid of the copper and to his surprise found that the pig's head had risen to the surface but not only had it floated to the top but a turnip had floated into the pig's mouth as well. Will, not one to be lost for a word, ran to the church and in the middle of the meeting announced to his parents that the pig was eating the vegetables.

Young Will eventually 'escaped' to the comparative safety of the Colonies, ending up at New Plymouth on New Zealand's North Island and it was from Will's daughters, many years after his death, that I learned of his many escapades. I felt sorry that I never met him as I think we could have sunk the odd jar or three listening to his life story which also included a stint on the Western Front during the First World War.

However, back to Granny. After leaving school she went into service at the household of Major Samuel Rudge (Retired) at "The Whins" in Frimley Road, Camberley. Many young girls in the Camberley area became servants to army officers and retired army personnel as Sandhurst Military College was situated nearby. At the age of twenty, she married my grandfather James Thomas Hurdwell.

She was a truly lovely person with a bustling and jolly temperament and I gather from my father and those around her that she appeared to have possessed no malice at all. She shared with all the Sadler family members a shortness in stature, a slim build and a wiry aspect which belied her remarkable strength. Whilst I was in her scullery one day I recall her taking a large cast iron saucepan, scooping up boiling water from the copper and effortlessly taking it over to the sink. She could also walk for miles and miles without showing any effects of weariness. Her face was quite round but in no way pudgy but one rather dominant feature was her large front teeth, a family genetic which I was unfortunate enough to have inherited. Her thick long pepper pot grey hair flowed down her back but was gathered up in a bun, as was the custom then, and was fastened by a large hat pin with a coloured bobble at one the end.

Granny was extremely intelligent and apparently when a radio programme called "The Brains Trust" was on air, she knew many of the answers to the questions put to the pundits who included Professor Job and Commander Campbell, but on the rare occasion that my grandfather answered correctly, she used to say "clever Daddy" as she absolutely adored him.

Her husband, my paternal grandfather, whilst not as quick or jolly as his wife, was nevertheless quite accomplished in so many ways, being a great gardener, and also adept at making bee hives, picture frames, upholstery etc. He also fashioned leather items by hand sewing them and quite unusual for the male of the species at the time, knitting. I can picture both grandparents sitting in front of the Kitchener coal stove during the Second World War, knitting scarves and balaclavas for the British troops, with Grandad peering over his steel rimmed glasses with a hand rolled 'Tom Long' cigarette in his mouth, though seldom alight. However, one of his more recognised talents was that of a marksman with the rifle, quite odd one would have thought for someone who was a confirmed pacifist. He used to shoot at the British Marksman Competitions at Bisley and his normal shooting partner was a woman whose name I cannot remember but who did manage to carry off the cup on more than one occasion. Apparently she used to have tea with my grandparents quite often, arriving on her Levis motor bike.

My grandfather, James Thomas Hurdwell had been no stranger to difficulties particularly in his early years, when, at the age of twenty-one, his father, who was employed as a forester, was killed in Bagshot Park when the bough of a tree broke off and struck him. Thus, my grandfather found himself in the position of having to provide for his mother and siblings. Although he continued his work as a gardener at Broadmoor Lunatic Asylum in Crowthorn, which entailed walking seven miles to work, but he also supplemented the family income by calling in at Sandhurst Military Academy on the way home to polish the boots, gaiters and Sam Browne belt of an army Major. Apparently his mother used to relate how, when he arrived home from a long day's work he was almost sleep walking.

Sirens and Grey Balloons

Grandad was born only four days before Winston Churchill at Somerton near Oxford in 1874 which, strange to relate, is not far from where the great World War II leader was born. However that is where the similarity ended. Tom was a pacifist and Churchill was quite the reverse. Thus at the time of the First World War he was too old to be conscripted into the forces which was fortunate for him given the brutality which was sometimes meted out by the British Army to persons of conscience.

He was only a little taller than my grandmother, thicker set but certainly not fat by any means but whereas Granny had strong thick hair, his hair had started to recede although as with many men of his era he had cultivated a thick moustache. Having a broad Hampshire accent he came across as being quite homely and showed affection to his doting wife.

My grandfather never struck me as being particularly athletic although he had been quite a cyclist in his time, in fact when Will Sadler migrated to New Zealand in 1902, my grandfather cycled all the way to Swansea to farewell him which was no mean feat given that bikes in those days lacked the multitude of gears modern cycles are able to boast. However, at the time I knew him he had been afflicted by double inguinal hernias which he refused to have operated on, preferring to be fitted with a double truss whose straps and belts were adjusted by brass buckles. You always knew when he was around as the buckles jangled when he moved, making him sound rather like a trotting pony at a harness race meeting.

For some reason he did not believe in immunisation or vaccination either which proved to be almost fatal for my father who, at the age of eleven, contracted diphtheria. Dad was nursed at home by his mother and was apparently navigating the rapids between life and death for some time before finally overcoming the potentially fatal disease and making a full recovery. Fortunately my grandparents were spared the tragedy of losing two out of their brood of four boys.

Thus it was that we, as children looked forward to our visits to our grandparents during the six years of hostilities.

We lived at Yately for less than a year and it was not the happiest time of our lives by any means. There were, however, some bright intervals, particularly our weekly visits to Camberley to have our radio battery re-charged and to call on our grandparents. Whilst at their home I used to be fascinated whenever the milkman called in his horse and cart. The milk was not supplied in bottles or cartons but was measured out in different sized ladles and poured into china jugs Granny had left on the living room window ledge, complete with muslin netting weighted down with beads to keep the flies at bay during the summer months.

My father used to come to see us at Yately as often as possible and we were particularly excited one day when he arrived astride a 'Coventry Eagle" two-stroke motor bike, loaned to him by a friend. We took it in turns to ride pillion but I was quite scared, as my feet had no chance of reaching the footrests as I clung on to Dad's waist like a limpet

The winter of 1940 was very severe, and we always felt cold, an experience exacerbated, perhaps, by a fairly restricted diet coupled with the fact that the cottage, whilst only small, was terribly cold. The only heating was provided by the Kitchener woodstove which Mum would stoke up in an effort to encourage the beast to squeeze out a few more calories into the draughty room. We used to sit in front of the stove, oven door open and with our feet within its very jaws, trying to keep warm. At bedtime, our mother used to fill stone hot water bottles with boiling water for us but as the night progressed, the bottles and our feet cooled down and we began to feel as cold as Eliza Newman resting six feet below us on the other side of the bedroom wall.

The weather did have its compensations particularly when the snow arrived in January. Dad came down one weekend and made a couple of toboggans for us. Jerry had his own but because I felt the cold so much my father fashioned sled runners upon which he affixed a large wooden box with a bench seat inside. It was wonderful being pushed along at speed across the nearby common and being sheltered from the wind and cold and it must have resembled a supercharged sedan chair. However I became a little apprehensive when he let the toboggan go and I hurtled down the slippery embankment and onto a frozen pond where other kids were enjoying the pleasures of an ice slide.

CHAPTER III RETURN TO CHINGFORD

With the passing of winter in 1941 my parents decided that although the German bombing of Chingford and its environs was continuing unabated, it was preferable to live under those conditions than by being split up as a family. My mother wasn't happy to be away from home and the unfriendly atmosphere we had encountered whilst away must obviously have been taken into account. Also, Jerry's schooling was suffering as he had already attended five separate schools up to that time and his education was starting to resemble a patchwork quilt but without any common thread with which to produce a real education. By the end of the war he had attended no less than nine schools including two government funded private tutorials when access to his current school had been prevented after it was damaged in an air raid. Thus, by the spring of that year we were back in Chingford which had altered considerably in our absence.

An Air Raid Precautions Post (ARP) had been built not far from our home which housed volunteer Air Raid Wardens whose job it was to patrol areas in the neighbourhood and to make contact with those families affected by the bombing. Their duties also included patrolling the streets to ensure no shafts of light escaped the cloak of the blackout curtains. On odd occasions one would hear a voice bellowing "put that light out"! They also monitored areas where bombs had been dropped and advised the Fire Brigade accordingly.

Following the war I heard of a very humorous incident involving a well known and highly respected American newspaper journalist who at the time was posted to London to send back despatches on the London Blitz. Ed Murrow made a habit of travelling around with local London Fire Brigades in an effort to gather information for his newspaper in the United States. On one occasion he witnessed a three storey tenement block on fire as the result of German bombing and upon his arrival found firemen at the base of the building holding a large sheet and entreating an old man on the third floor to jump to safety, the fire stairs having been demolished.

The old man repeatedly came to the window before dashing back into the flaming tenement again. The firemen yelled out that he should hurry up and jump as the building was in danger of collapse but the old boy shouted that he couldn't find his false teeth whereupon one Cockney fireman retorted "Dad, they ain't droppin' cheese sandwiches yer know"!

Not far from the local ARP Post the government had constructed a huge concrete above ground water storage tank which held thousands of litres of water to be utilized by the fire brigades in the event of the existing water mains being damaged or demolished during air raids. It was possible for older children to bunk up their friend so that they could peer into the water. On one occasion, Donald the son of Dad's police colleague Matt Purvis, managed to drop his spectacles into the water whilst having a look. It was galling enough for his father to have to retrieve them under normal circumstances, but it was the end of November and the water was icy cold. Poor Mr. Purvis had to don swimming trunks and as my father shone the torch into the pool, the irate Mr Purvis slipped into the freezing water and managed to fish them out. I could imagine that poor PC Purvis had quite a lot to say to his 'dear Donald' when he handed the glasses back.

Dotted about various suburbs were a large number of grey intimidating looking barrage balloons. These huge gas-filled monsters were not new inventions in fact similar models had been used on the Western Front during the First World War when observers were hoisted up above the battlegrounds to observe the enemy emplacements and also to direct artillery fire. Needless to say the attrition rate of the observers was extremely high.

It was not generally known until recent times that London and some home counties were very severely bombed by Germany during the First World War, first by Zeppelin airships and later on by the massive Gotha bombers which had four or sometimes five engines and a wing span of forty-two metres. So severe was the damage these bombers caused that the British hoisted barrage balloons at about the height that a bomber would fly to release its bombs, the idea being that the massive steel hawsers which anchored them to the ground would prevent low level bombing or, with luck, sever a bomber's wing if it flew too low. Thus, it was a usual sight for us to see grey barrage balloons dotted around the countryside during the Second World War.

Sirens and Grey Balloons

During our absence at Yately a new 'Anderson Shelter' had been erected where our garden shed had once stood. These shelters afforded considerable safety during air raids except in the event of a direct hit by a large bomb. Their construction consisted of a large trench about four metres long by three metres wide and about ninety centimetres deep. The trench was lined with concrete above which a thick semi circular sheet of corrugated steel had been affixed and embedded in the soil. At one end was bolted a flat sheet of corrugated steel with a similar piece at the other end but into which a doorway had been cut. The door was usually quite small and made of very thick timber allowing the occupants to squeeze in for safety.

After construction earth could be shovelled over the roof and rear of the shelter to cushion the blast generated by exploding bombs, particularly high explosive devices. The blast effect could be quite significant and during air raids we always placed our hands firmly over our ears to prevent the suction from the blast affecting our eardrums.

Unfortunately our shelter had a propensity to fill with water during wet weather and as it was always damp, we used to seek safety in our next door neighbour's more comfortable shelter. Her husband was away in the Falkland Islands and she welcomed having company during the bombing raids.

GERMAN BOMBING

1941 was a year during which there was heavy bombing in the Greater London area with Chingford and its environs being no exception. In retrospect, the family's returning to London was not well timed. Although we would have preferred to sleep in our own beds, all too often we were awakened by the haunting wail of air raid sirens which prompted our mother to gather us up and take us through our back gate and into our neighbour's garden, finally ending up in Mrs Davies' Anderson shelter.

Although the shelter afforded a feeling of comparative security, it was nevertheless permeated by a general air of dampness inevitably accompanied by an aroma of musty concrete. Having jumped about ninety centimetres onto mattresses in the base of the shelter, the thick timber door was secured. We would lie there and listen to the sound of anti-aircraft guns as they followed the incandescent rays of the searchlights stretching out across the sky like voracious octopuses in search of their prey. Quite often we would hear the muffled sounds of explosions as the bombs from the German aircraft hit the ground, and in fact during that period, two high explosive bombs and one oil bomb were dropped within a hundred metres of our home in addition to numerous incendiary bombs which were normally released in clusters of seven. These bombs consisted of about three kilograms of solid magnesium with a striker pin igniting the missile as its nose hit the ground. To facilitate the flight of these bombs, they were encapsulated in a flight case which resembled a rather rotund dart. Quite often the bombs would escape from their flight case which would drop to the ground in one piece. Jerry and I often played with these little cages of metal before taking them to the local ARP Post together with shrapnel from anti aircraft shells we had also picked up, to be re-used for the war effort.

At this stage of the war, most enemy bombing took place at night as the Luftwaffe had an aversion to daylight raids which meant that children were still able to keep up attendance at school. Thus, each day we would set off for school with our gas mask satchels strung over our shoulders, each school having been provided with an air raid shelter should a daylight raid occur. We also had strict instructions not to pick up anything resembling a child's toy as it was rumoured that the Germans dropped toys which were booby trapped. This of course was totally incorrect and was doubtless a tool in the propaganda armoury of the government.

There were also air raid shelters dotted around the suburbs in case of emergencies although they were almost invariably damp with many having pools of stagnant water on their floors and evidence of recent habitation such as discarded newspapers, cigarette ends and other rubbish. In later years a friend told me of an amusing incident he experienced when returning to London during shore leave whilst serving in the Fleet Air Arm aboard the aircraft carrier HMS Victorious.

One night as he was walking home to his parents' house in Fulham he heard the air raid siren warning of the arrival of the enemy and shortly thereafter he heard the unmistakable drone of German bombers and anti

Sirens and Grey Balloons

aircraft guns. Hastening his step he came across a public air raid shelter in which he sought sanctuary and in the darkness he gingerly fumbled his way along its contours until he found the entrance, thence into the set of convoluted walls until he reached the safety of its inner sanctum. As the searchlights above sought out their prey and the anti aircraft guns opened up, he started to feel quite relieved until, looking up he found to his dismay that the shelter was only half completed and the reinforced concrete roof had yet to be installed.

As the bombing became more intense during 1941, my parents decided to take Jerry out of his school in Chingford and deposit both of us with our paternal grandparents in Camberley which pleased me immensely as I loved being with Granny Hurdwell although it must have been very unsettling for Jerry to add yet another school to his post alma mater compendium.

It was whilst we were staying at our grandparents home that we received some stunning news. One day Jerry and I were busily occupied slithering down a makeshift wooden slide we had erected at the garden gate when Granny appeared with a couple of sweets (always most welcome) and told us that we now had a baby brother. We had received no advance warning of this event and were at a loss to understand why this had come about, particularly as we had been quite happy with the current arrangement. Moreover, when Mum came down to Camberley a few days later with Rob, our newly acquired brother, I happened to wander into the front parlour where Mum was seated on a blue chaise lounge breast feeding Rob. I was chased out like a vagrant peeping tom. In retrospect I suppose that in those days it must have been regarded as unseemly for a sibling to have witnessed such an intimate but natural event.

Meanwhile, back in London the Germans had intensified their bombing on London, culminating in the Battle of Britain which, as it transpired, became one of the great turning points of the war in Europe. With the decimation of the Luftwaffe Hitler turned his attention to the Eastern Front. Although there was still some bombing in Chingford and the surrounding districts, the skies, if not exactly tranquil, were at least the subject of less frenetic enemy activity. Thus, later in the year we once again returned to Chingford.

The comparative tranquillity over the English skies happened to coincide with my reaching school age, although it was not the first time I had attended a school. A year before, when I was aged three, Jerry and I were staying with our maternal grandparents (more of them later) and Jerry was attending the Windlesham Primary School. Probably to get me out of her hair and grant her some peace, Gran spoke to the school principal and it was agreed that I should accompany Jerry a couple of days a week to the school. The School principal was a lovely lady and I think she must have taken a liking to me as, at that time, I was very small for my age and had angelic blond hair and blue eyes, in fact she often used to invite me to her office where I used to play with an armchair which I was able to adjust by altering the position of a rod which supported the back. This chair held a fascination for my young mind.

However I was soon allowed to attend lessons with Jerry in the school's only classroom and on that first occasion witnessed a little boy having the leg of his shorts rolled up to his thigh to receive what I perceived to be a heavy smack which made him howl. This was enough for me and I walked out of the classroom and about half a kilometre back to Gran's house. She wasn't very pleased to see me and took me back to the principal the next morning where I was told that I could stay in her office and play with the chair. However, I was adamant that I would not return to school. That was the conclusion of my first foray into academia.

PRIMARY SCHOOL

One year after this traumatic experience saw us back in Chingord where I was enrolled at New Road School, the school in which Jerry was now a student. I suppose that most children have vivid memories of their first day of school and I was no exception. I can still feel the sense of loneliness as I was committed into the care of complete strangers for the first time. First I was taken by my mother to meet the headmaster in his study. Mr. Grattan seemed to be quite a kindly man although history through the eyes of more senior students would have painted a picture totally to the contrary.

I was then ushered into a small classroom and deposited amongst the other students, after sadly saying 'goodbye' to my mother. The teacher, whose name I am unable to recall, then gave us plasticine to play with and generally tried to put us at our ease. However, for one little boy her ministrations were to no avail as he screamed and howled, unsettling the whole class, many of whom started to howl as well, redolent of the kennel scene from 'Lady and the Tramp'. Fortunately I was not one of them, my whole being seemingly numbed by this totally foreign environment. My first day seemed to last an eternity and it was a huge relief when my mother finally arrived to take me home.

The next day was little better than my first day at school although the teacher and the howler's mother did make an attempt to gradually immerse the howler into accepting that the idea of school wouldn't just go away like a bad smell. Instead of depositing her charge into the teacher's care, his mother stayed with him for quite a while, hoping that this would give him confidence and perhaps encourage an interest in class activities. Alas, this ploy was a complete failure for, as soon as his mother left the classroom, the howler yelled and bellowed so much that he became ill and vomited all over his desk. I have no idea what happened to him subsequently but after a few more similar episodes of daily pandemonium we saw him no more.

Unfortunately for me, shortly afterwards, I also quit the school having contracted pneumonia which caused me to be away from school for several months. My first attack of pneumonia, whilst being serious, was not all that severe and my mother was able to nurse me at home, under the guidance of our local doctor. I occupied the upstairs bedroom all on my own and even enjoyed the luxury of having an open fire in the room which was very unusual given the rationing of coal at the time.

Eventually, after a lengthy absence, I was able to go back to school where I resumed my education under the watchful eye of Mrs. Morris. It was in this class that I met a boy of similar age who was destined to become a lifelong friend, in fact, as I pen this narrative we are still in regular contact almost seventy years later. We often recall events of yesteryear over the odd ale when I return to the United Kingdom for visits.

Alex used to arrive at school each day dressed in his normal grey short trousers, grey shirt, socks and pullover over which he had donned a loose fitting pair of Royal Air Force dungarees. Mrs. Morris, for whatever reason, used to call him to the front of the class and divest him of this outer garment each day.

Like all school kids we enjoyed playtime which usually involved ruining our shoes kicking a tennis ball around the playground, much to our parents' annoyance not merely because the cost of new shoes but also the fact that shoes, like other clothing, were rationed. During one playtime Alex produced a piece of string and proceeded to tie me to the school railings but, unhappily for me, when the tambourine was sounded for the resumption of lessons, Alex was off like a startled gazelle, leaving me manacled to the railings. Fortunately, a fairy godmother in the person of a little old lady saw my plight and managed to release me from my bondage.

Unfortunately for me, the bout of pneumonia had made its mark on my overall health and I continued to traverse the long road of ill health, prone to any predatory infections which stalked the community. Thus I was pronounced as be a very 'chesty' boy and a willing guinea pig for any new fangled or patent remedies, effective or not, that were currently doing the rounds.

Whooping cough was the next malady to which I succumbed and as there existed no immunisation for this exhausting illness, I went down with it and took some time to reach the road to recovery.

Boils, now almost unheard of, were during our early lives a constant and painful menace to both the adult and the younger members of the population of Britain. For no apparent reason they appeared on the more fleshy parts of the body and manifested themselves initially as small spots on the skin, gradually morphing into mini volcanoes with deep seated subcutaneous cores which, in time spewed out their white pus through a small aperture in the skin. They were extremely painful and one boil on the arm could render the limb totally useless until it had finally run its course.

Ironically, the cure, presumably dreamed up by some mediaeval apothecary, was often more painful than the disease itself and subjected the sufferer to excruciating pain during treatment. To treat the boil, a poultice was made by heating a glutinous mass of kaolin (china clay) and

Sirens and Grey Balloons

when really hot, placing a splodge onto a piece of pink lint which was then placed upon the offending boil in order to draw out the poison. There were usually three applications per day and to remove the spent poultice required either prising or whipping off the poultice plaster which had held the lint in place, to the accompaniment of the screams of anguish from the sufferer. Even worse than boils were carbuncles which were really a larger version of a boil with more than one core. I recall having a carbuncle on my leg which, I suppose was the upmarket model, boasting no less than five cores. I still have a large scar on the back of my knee as a reminder of that experience

Being a 'chesty' boy, my parents' minds were fertile ground for any of the many remedies which abounded at the time, whether they were recent discoveries or merely old wives tales. The 'tallow poultice' being one such remedy made its way into my life and onto my chest, finally ending up on the playground floor. It must surely have been either the figment of some lunatic's imagination or a scheme dreamed up by a local abattoir to stimulate the sales of sheep tallow. I watched with a mixture of apprehension and incredulity as my father prepared the poultice which he had been assured, would remedy my latest cough.

First of all he laid out a piece of brown paper and cut out two rough outlines of my chest upon them. He then tied a shoe lace at each corner of the two pieces of brown paper so that they resembled two baby's bibs. He then cut several pieces of tallow and placed them onto the 'bibs' and put them in front of the fire. When the tallow had melted and was still hot, he then whacked one of the bibs onto my chest and one onto my back, securing them with the shoe laces. I went to bed looking very much like a speedway rider, feeling very uncomfortable as these attachments had a propensity to stick to my chest and back, not to mention sounding like the rustling of a paper bag when I decided to turn over during the night. I then had to wear these appendages to school for a few days, but when my mother came to meet me at the school gate the poultices had usually come adrift and were languishing on the ground in the school playground. I might just as well have rubbed the sheep's dag on my chest for all the good it would have done me.

Gradually, when my health seemed to be improving, I came to the conclusion that school was an inevitable fact of life although I have to admit that the age old adage that 'school days are the happiest days of one's life', if not a downright lie, was certainly over rated and never found a comfortable niche in my ever questioning psyche. In those days, attending school appeared to have changed little since the days of Charles Dickens' and events portrayed in his novel Nicholas Nickleby. Education was not tackled by the authorities as an interesting journey from childhood to adulthood with thrilling revelations en route. Rather it was a laborious grind of learning by rote with the ever present threat of corporal punishment thrown in for good measure. In fact, it wasn't until I progressed to high school that this method was to some degree abandoned as adulthood beckoned from the horizon.

Thus, Jerry and I used to set out each morning, gas masks slung over our shoulders, to walk the mile or so to school. By now, enemy bombing was more sporadic than before and was usually at night time. Also, there was little traffic on the roads, as much of the male population was away fighting in various theatres of war and the severe rationing of petrol. In those days ownership of cars was a luxury reserved for the well-to-do segment of the British population.

Most of the motorised traffic consisted of service vehicles such as buses, trucks, fire engines and ambulances whilst bread (unwrapped), milk and many daily necessities were delivered by horse drawn vehicles in an effort to conserve petrol. Regarding the latter, if we were lucky enough to witness a horse having a poo within the vicinity of our house, we would quickly scoop the steaming trophy into a bucket for use as manure on the garden or for Dad's allotment.

During the war the duties of a London policeman were not just restricted to normal policing duties. Policemen and women were sometimes required to help rescue injured civilians from wrecked or damaged dwellings and were quite often called upon to break the news of a military fatality to a serviceman's next of kin.

One day my father returned home from his 'early turn' shift carrying a pistol complete with leather holster. Naturally Jerry and I were more than a little fascinated by this accoutrement and asked if we could hold it. The Browning semi-automatic pistol was extremely heavy for a small child to lift and quite impossible to hold in one hand.

Sirens and Grey Balloons

A week or two later he came home with another hand gun, this time a revolver similar to the ones we had seen on the cowboy movies at the cinema. We started to look on cowboys in a new light and marvelled at how strong they must have been to be able to draw such a heavy instrument from its holster with one hand and shoot a 'baddie' within a split second.

It eventually transpired that on several occasions he was directed to attend the British RDX factory at Waltham Abbey where bombs and other explosive devices were manufactured. His duty as a police motor cyclist was to escort large trucks carrying dangerous ordnance which required him to be armed. It was never quite clear how a police constable would ever have been able to guard a truck carrying tons of high explosives armed with a six gun.

However, on one occasion he did have an opportunity (not taken up of course) to terrify the enemy. As he was riding his motor bike some distance behind the truck a German plane swooped down to view the truck. Whether from fear or just plain commonsense Dad maintained the same distance from the truck and resisted the temptation to fire his pistol at the enemy. Doubtless the pilot of the plane was also relieved not to have been apprehended by the local constabulary.

The routine of going to school in the morning, returning home for lunch and thence back to school in the afternoon continued on through the autumn on 1941 and well into the spring of 1942. However, it was on a spring day in 1942 that upon returning home one lunchtime a boy from a couple of streets away, one Donald Godbold, started wielding his gas mask satchel around and unfortunately struck me on the head with some force.

A short time later as I was about to tackle my lunch, I started to feel decidedly unwell and quickly developed a headache and fever which worried my mother to the point that she contacted the local doctor who lived nearby. He called, took my temperature and advised that it was 104 degrees Fahrenheit and that I should go straight to St Margaret's Hospital in Epping where I was duly diagnosed with another dose of bronchopneumonia, thus confirming my mother's worst fears.

My first day at school and being left in the care of people I had never met before had been, as with all children, an emotionally difficult experience but under those circumstances there had always been the prospect of returning home to parents and siblings at the end of the school day. However, being transported to hospital in an ambulance and finding myself alone in a cot on the ground floor ward engendered a feeling of utter desolation and loneliness.

After a troubled night with the odd nightmare occasioned no doubt by the high fever, I woke up to my first full day of hospital routine. I recall seeing a doctor walk from cot to cot, but was unable to fathom what he was doing although by the time he arrived at my cot it had become obvious that my fears of this white coated Dracula taking my blood actually manifested itself. However, he seemed to be a very kindly man and I don't recall feeling any pain as he siphoned off some of my blood and gave the vial a thorough shaking before handing it to the nurse who was accompanying him on his rounds.

Obviously I am now unable to remember everything which happened on a day to day basis but some memories and incidents have remained with me including the kindness of the nurse who was often on duty in our ward. Her name was 'Sister George' strangely enough. Whenever I dropped a toy soldier or other toy through the rungs of my cot, she seemed always to be there to retrieve it for me. I can still recall the radio loudspeaker on the wall at the end of the ward and remember Richard Tauber singing the song 'Dearly beloved' on so many occasions.

After I had been in hospital a few days there was a sudden flurry of activity around my bed. After some prodding and thumping on my chest by several doctors I was taken from my cot, placed into a wheelchair and pushed into the X-ray area where I was instructed to hold a square silver plate to my chest before they carried out X-rays of my lungs. It was not until many years later that I was told by my parents that I had been diagnosed with tuberculosis and that arrangements were to be made for me to go to a hospital at Black Nockley in Essex as I had a limited time to live. Fortunately for me (and my worried parents) the diagnosis had been incorrect and the shadows on my lungs had been, in all probability the result of the first bout of pneumonia. Presumably, patients' records in those days were just as haphazard as they sometimes are even in today's computer age.

Needless to say, I was delighted to finally leave the hospital and I felt very important as we drove home to Chingford in a motor car which Dad had borrowed from a friend. I was also very thrilled with the cardboard cut-out soldiers my parents had bought me for a returning home present although I had no inkling as to the degree of relief they would have been experiencing at the time.

To enable me to rest and be away from the London bombing, my maternal grandparents suggested that I go to stay with them at their home in Windlesham in Surrey and I was soon on my way, having been collected by my Uncle in his car and delivered into Gran and Gramp's care.

My maternal grandparents were always very special to me, not only at the time I undertook a protracted stay with them but throughout the following years until their deaths. In my grandfather's case it was a premature demise caused in all probability by his being a victim of a mustard gas attack in 1917 during the First World War. He died of Parkinson's disease in 1948 at the age of 61.

Gran, (who was born Florence Harding) and Gramp got along very well together although the more overtly dominant character in the partnership was Gran. She was of average height with a figure well rounded but not matronly and a countenance suggesting a disposition of energy and perception. Her hair had been dark and was still to a certain extent although flecks of grey had started to infiltrate, as would befit a woman who was fifty-three years of age at the time. Her light green eyes betrayed a sparkling sense of humour, always near the surface, often bubbling over with unfettered laughter, usually at someone else's expense or minor misfortune. I loved my Gran and always looked forward to our visits to Windlesham and was happy to be left in her care from time to time.

My grandfather was of a quieter disposition and often used to hum or whistle to himself when alone with his thoughts. He was a fine looking man, quite tall, with finely fashioned nose under which nestled a short moustache which was as fair as his the thick carpet of hair with which his head was thatched. His overall appearance was that of a person with an attractive winsome personality although he gave the impression of being somewhat more self effacing than his wife.

Photographs of him prior to 1914 seemed to display a light heartedness in his aspect. However, the suffering and hardship visited upon the ordinary soldier during the First World War, directed by unintelligent generals with a voracious appetite for casualties must surely have left its mark. How could it not be so? Following the end of the war, my maternal grandparents faced the daunting task of rebuilding their business which had foundered in his absence.

By the time we grandchildren came into the world they had, by dint of initiative and hard work, attained moderate success in their business ventures. My Gran initially took in washing and ironing and after a while had the good fortune to come into a legacy of one hundred pounds, quite a sum in the early 1920's. This helped them start a small laundry, eventually burgeoning into becoming the 'Lightwater New Model Laundry'. Gran initially looked after the physical running of the laundry and Gramp used to drive around the districts drumming up business. The area was apparently fertile ground for such a venture as many quite well off military personnel had retired to the Windlesham/Camberley district.

In the 1930's, whilst still keeping the laundry, they purchased the Windlesham Post Office and the freehold land and building in which they continued to live until their retirement, which sadly coincided with my grandfather's death in 1948.

Thus, my Gramp ran the laundry and Gran was in charge of the Post Office, having employed a wonderfully vibrant young Irish girl of sixteen to run the day to day business. Kath was a real character and epitomised every humorous aspect with which the Irish are blessed, including a very sharp wit.

WINDLESHAM

It was the Windlesham Post Office that I was destined to call home for the next few months, my stay being interspersed by visits from by my parents and brothers from London and an aunt and uncle who lived in nearby Bagshot.

It was during one of these visits that our father decided to take Jerry and me to see our maternal great grandfather who resided in nearby Woking. I cannot recall what expectations, if any, we had harboured of our great grandfather but our visit was certainly a memorable one.

It was a warm day as we entered the front door of his cottage and proceeded up the hall which led through an open doorway into his sitting room where we beheld what could only be described as a living apparition. Great Grandfather George Gorton was sitting in an armchair close to a window which overlooked the garden, wearing a whitish flannel shirt and a dark waistcoat and probably wearing a benevolent smile. However, his head was a mass of long silver hair which had somehow run amok like steroid propelled bindweed cascading like a waterfall down to his neck. Jerry and I took one look at the figure before us and dived under the dining table. Dad's entreaties for us to withdraw were to no avail and our visit was thus curtailed.

Apparently he was a very likeable man and I am sure that had Jerry and I been a few years older we would have learned to enjoy his company, particularly as he was known to have loved children.

Looking back it is strange to think that we are able to remember a meeting, albeit it a very short one, with a relative who was born in 1861, particularly as during his lifetime the Crimean War had only just ended and Britain still carried out public executions. However, we can draw some comfort from the fact that we did inherit the gene which propagates thick hair into old age although I have to say that we do seem to manage to discipline our thatch with greater success than our great grandfather.

The Post Office building was of red brick and was situated within an acre or so of land which had originally started out as an orchard prior to the erection of the current building around the 1880's. The orchard was still intact and I was able to enjoy an array of fruits which abounded in the garden including apples, pears, plums, gooseberries, damsons as well as walnuts and almonds. Many of these items I had never encountered until that time and certainly had not seen in any quantities in war ravaged London.

Within the confines of the old orchard was a reminder of a bygone era as, entering the garden one was confronted by a croquette lawn which came into view when descending the steps from the veranda. There were still a few old croquette mallets and balls hanging around but unfortunately all other implements required for the sport had been pensioned off many years before, probably along with their previous owners. However Jerry and I used to love hacking our way around the lawn which in better days would undoubtedly have witnessed more skilful exponents of the game than two small boys.

At the end of the garden, chickens roamed within the confines of a very large run and I was never in want of the nourishment of health giving country victuals.

The old house was a revelation to me particularly having come from an environment where serried ranks of terraced and semi detached houses abounded and the gardens were, by comparison, rather like segments of patchwork quilts. Apart from the post office on the ground floor, it also accommodated a spacious lounge and dining room which led into the garden via the french windows. Two objects in the dining room fascinated me, one of which being framed prints of the hunt complete with gentlefolk on horseback accompanied by a pack of hounds, although the fox was nowhere to be seen. It would be many years before I was to read Oscar Wilde and agree with his description of fox hunting as being in 'the unspeakable being in pursuit of the inedible'. But the item which fascinated me most was a beautiful wooden clock which depicted Old Father Time sitting above a huge rock under which various scenes were depicted, including peasants returning from the fields and a fox arriving at its lair with a chicken firmly fastened between its jaws. It was apparently handed down to my grandfather's side of the family and had been carved by a university student but after my Gran's death in 1963 I never saw it again.

The kitchen and scullery on the ground floor were also of commodious proportions and even boasted a separate room which was used for a larder, its inner cavern spreading under the winding staircase leading to the floor above. As very few people possessed refrigerators in those days, there was to be found on the pantry working top, an ice box in which Gran kept butter, cheese and milk, plus, of course a large block of ice resting upon a shallow grille. Melted ice used to drip its way to a small tap at the base of the ice box for drainage.

Having mounted the curved staircase to the upper floor, the first feeling one had was that of space and light, particularly when the doors to the five bedrooms were left open during the day. When the house had been built, there would have been six bedrooms but having reached the landing, the first room on the right had been renovated and converted into a huge bathroom where the bath seemed almost to have been an afterthought, so large was the rest of the room. As with many bathrooms and kitchens in those days, the walls were painted with gloss paint with the lower half of the wall being of pea green hue and the top part up to the ceiling being dark cream with the almost compulsory delineation being a thick black line about two centimetres thick. Hot water was no problem here as the coal fired boiler on the ground floor propelled hot water to a large tank in the bathroom where it was stored for distribution to other areas throughout the house.

Venturing further along the wide landing were another five bedrooms, my room being the smallest one situated opposite my grandparents room. Next to my room and adjacent to the road was Kath's bedroom from which the sweet aroma of perfume permeated the surrounding air. I sometimes used to sleep in Kath's room and if she had been out of an evening she often used to bring me home a small gift, usually a couple of pieces of chocolate although on one occasion she gave me a tie pin in the shape of a butterfly.

The other bedrooms were large and palatial and even the upstairs store room used for the storage of jams and other preserves seemed to my young eyes to have been enormous. I recall most vividly some years later, helping my Gran wrap Cox's orange pippin apples in newspaper to be stored for future use, particularly for Christmas treats. To me this was a wonderland and a universe far removed from a London suburb, so peaceful that it gave the impression that the war had either passed it by or had never existed. Nevertheless in war torn London air raids, albeit more sporadic in the suburbs, were still a constant threat and the interminable queues for non rationed items which only rarely became available, were still part of everyday life.

Although my grandfather supervised the running of the laundry and Kath was in charge of the day-to-day running of the post office, he was also called upon to deliver telegrams within a radius of about fifteen kilometres of the post office. Whilst we in the twenty-first century take speedy communication as the central foundation of our daily lives and think nothing of 'phoning and emailing to all parts of the globe, in the 1940's most people did not have access to phones but placed a great amount of reliance on telegrams. Kath used to take down the messages on the phone (phone number Bagshot 42) then wrote them down on a telegram sheet before handing them to my grandfather for delivery.

Gramp usually asked me to accompany him on his delivery runs and it was always a pleasure to climb into the seat of his blue Ford Prefect and drive around the countryside, in fact it was a pastime tailor-made for the rest and recuperation which I was apparently in need of.

One rainy afternoon he was called upon to deliver a telegram to an address on the London Road quite near to Sunningdale railway station and, leaving me in the car, he walked to the house which was situated at the end of a long driveway.

When he returned to the car he found that a Czech army lorry had run into his parked car, the impact having flung me from my seat and into the windscreen. Such was the force of the impact that not only was the car badly damaged but the lorry had skidded sideways and ended up in a ditch by the side of the road. The soldier in charge of the vehicle tried to comfort me but to no avail, as he spoke no English.

Although the car was badly damaged it was still driveable so we drove home to a somewhat alarmed household. My grandparents had been trying to ensure that my sojourn with them was to have been free from stress only to find that hazards more likely to occur in places like London often made visitations to unwary country village dwellers as well.

Sirens and Grey Balloons

Just when it appeared that life was once again settling down to some semblance of peaceful equilibrium, another circumstance arose which was even more serious than the motor accident.

On some occasions I accompanied Gramp to the laundry where I took a great delight in sitting at his desk, playing with his candelabra phone and his pop up address book which held a certain fascination for me. The ladies who helped run the laundry machines or carried out the ironing (with heavy solid cast iron flat irons heated on a coke burning stove) used to make quite a fuss of me, especially my favourite lady called Daisy. Daisy gave me a small clay pipe and often used to mix up a bowl of soap suds to enable me to blow bubbles from the pipe.

One afternoon, Gramp and I were at the top of the laundry garden picking blackberries when I heard Daisy calling out that she had just mixed up some suds for me. I immediately left my grandfather and hurtled down the hill towards where Daisy was standing. When I was only a couple of dozen steps from the laundry building I heard my grandfather shouting and as I looked round I fell into the large well used to gravity feed water for the laundry, hitting my head on an iron cross bar and ending up unconscious in the water below.

After being fished out of the water by two laundry employees I regained consciousness and was dried and placed in a blanket to be taken back to my grandparents' house where the village nurse was summoned to dress the gash on my head which I had sustained during the fall. So much for a quiet environment in which to recuperate!

Kath was a great asset to my Gran and she soon became an integral part of the family. She adored my grandparents and as far back as I can remember always called them Mum and Dad. It was obvious to me even as a child that her affection for them was truly reciprocated as their eyes lit up whenever she came into the kitchen when taking a quick tea break from her duties behind the post office counter.

She was a slim girl, wiry in stature and standing no more than 160 centimetres tall. Her hair was dark but it was her eyes that were her outstanding feature. When she spoke they seemed to dance as though some humour-packed circumstance was about to erupt before our very eyes. She was, by all accounts, a super efficient worker and got on well with almost all of the customers who crossed the threshold of the Windlesham Post Office. I say 'almost all customers' because several years after the war she related a situation involving Field Marshall Bernard Montgomery.

Sometime after his retirement from the armed forces Monty called at the post office to collect his old age pension to which all British persons were entitled after reaching pensionable age. Kath apparently made some off the cuff comment to the effect that she was surprised that he would bother to draw the old age pension, an observation to which he took great exception and demanded to see her superior. He felt that she was somewhat of an upstart who needed a thorough dressing down and made his feelings known to my Gran accordingly. Although Monty had been a very brave lieutenant in the First World War and a tenacious commander during the Second World War, particularly in his fight against Erwin Rommel, he could hardly have been described as a picture of frivolity or a barrel of laughs. Rather he was a self made man who worshipped his own creator with the love of himself somewhat exceeding the adulation of others. However, my mother's sister who had been his children's nurse during Monty's time at Sandhurst Staff College did have a very high regard for him as an employer whom she found to be kind and very considerate though very direct in his dealings with people.

In spite of the various mishaps which befell me at Windlesham, I managed to survive the 'serenity of country life' with my grandparents and fully recovered from pneumonia, a car crash and falling down the laundry well. Thus, in the autumn of 1942 I returned home to Mum, Dad, Jerry and baby Rob.

By this time my parents had developed high hopes that I was well on the road to recovery but, alas this was not to be for having returned to New Road School for a couple of months I again succumbed to yet another attack of pneumonia. I have no idea whether it was due to the onset of winter (which I had come to dread) or my low resistance to multifarious maladies which plagued the lives of weaker children, but I again started to feel ill, ran a high temperature and late one night found myself a patient at nearby Wanstead Hospital.

Sirens and Grey Balloons

Upon arriving at the hospital I was examined by a couple of doctors who peered into my ears with a conical shaped torch, thumping my chest as though it was a snare drum and generally making me feel uncomfortable. In the midst of all this the air raid sirens started to wail their warning which added to my worries until it became apparent that the bombs were dropping quite some distance away. The bed I was in had earphones attached to a bracket and I was able to put them on and listen to a radio programme. I thought how neat they were as I had never come across earphones before.

Fortunately for me, medical science had come up with a new wonder drug for the alleviation of fever. Previously the pneumonia sufferer's temperature would rise until reaching its highest point called 'the crisis' and then the temperature would gradually recede back to normal. Such fevers were, for me, accompanied by the most grisly nightmares imaginable where the walls of the room, pink in colour, would advance in ever enlarging circles until almost upon me, at which time I would wake up in a hot sweat. Apparently, after the drug had been administered I slept for a day and a half and made a very speedy recovery.

The drug in question was at the time referred to only as M and B as it was discovered by May and Bakers, a prominent drug company. Since then I have found out that its full name was M & B 693 its main constituent being Sulphapyridine and was discovered in 1939. Winston Churchill had a severe case of pneumonia at the same time as me and I remember my mother showing me a photograph in the Daily Express of the Prime Minister dressed in his dark dressing gown after his recovery which was put down to his treatment with that drug.

Whilst a patient at Wanstead Hospital a strange incident occurred which I could not comprehend at the time and could throw little light on afterwards. One morning I was told by a nurse that I had an aunt in a nearby ward who wanted to see me. I was placed in a wheelchair and pushed along several corridors until we arrived at the ward where my 'aunt' was waiting for me. Although she looked ill and had a gaunt look about her, she smiled and reaching forward asked me to select a couple of sweets from a tin of goodies. I needed no second bidding and selected the two largest sweets in the tin, both being star shaped and made of solid icing sugar. She then gave me a hug before I was deposited back into the wheelchair and transported back to my own ward.

In retrospect I can only imagine that my 'aunt' was very ill or dying and had little or no family of her own and sought the company of a small child to ameliorate her loneliness at her darkest hour of need. Nevertheless this incident did make an indelible impact on my mind, even though I was only five years of age. When I returned home and related these happenings to my parents they could shed no light on the occurrence at all. Almost seventy years later I am still none the wiser.

Once again I was able to return home to my family after my three weeks stay at Wanstead Hospital but as I was too weak to return to school I was again taken to my maternal grandparents in Surrey but not before I had been able to master the knack of maintaining my balance on a two-wheeled bike, in this case Jerry's fairy cycle.

In the middle of the twentieth century the term 'fairy' had somewhat a different connotation to that which prevailed some fifty years later. The fairy cycle was a small two-wheeled bike which was the size of a child's tricycle but smaller that a bicycle and was designed to bridge the gap between the two, there being no training wheels at the time.

Having witnessed my somewhat unsteady but promising prowess on that machine, my father promised that he would make up a bike for me if he could scrounge some spare parts and find a small enough frame for the purpose.

I used to enjoy the journey down to my grandparents as we travelled by train. It was therefore a thrill to arrive at London's Waterloo Station and board the Southern Region's electric train to Sunningdale. This train struck me as being very modern for it was silent and clean compared with our local LNER (London & North Eastern Railway) trains whose workhorses were ancient coal fired steam engines only one generation removed from Stephenson's 'Puffing Billy'. They spewed out clouds of acrid effluent into the surrounding atmosphere which was ingested by man and beast alike, not to mention the incursions of smoke and gritty coal dust endured by passengers as these iron Trojans negotiated tunnels and cuttings along the way towards their final destination.

Sirens and Grey Balloons

When my mother and I reached Sunningdale Station we were collected by Mr Matthews who owned the local Windlesham Garage which, apart from having a petrol pump and general store, also boasted two hire cars, one of which was always driven by Mr Matthews himself.

Mr Matthews always seemed to me to have been very old, at least a contemporary of Methuselah or even older. His taxi was of a similar vintage and looking back I can imagine Mr. Matthews lining up to take delivery of the first Model T Ford and dispensing with it only when trading it for the vehicle in which he came to collect us.

The taxi was dark blue with wooden spoked wheels and a cabriolet body where on sunny days the rear passengers could draw back the canvas hood to enjoy the sunshine although I cannot recall the hood ever having been lowered. Conversation with the driver appears not to have been encouraged as the driver was divorced from his passengers by a glass partition although there was an inbuilt sliding window should communication be necessary. However our journey to Windlesham was enjoyed in mutual solitude.

The Matthews Garage also owned a beautiful black Wolseley saloon car which must have made it off the production line just prior to the outbreak of war in 1939. A young employee was fortunate enough to have had the pleasure of being appointed to drive this marvel of British engineering and in recognition of this privilege he used to spend hours looking after it although I cannot actually recall his ever taking to the road in it. He used to attack this Adonis of the highway with gallons of soap suds the like of which was never seen elsewhere except at the Lightwater Model Laundry. Having clothed it with a white jacket of suds, he would then swamp it with mega litres of water which flowed in cascades from his hose onto the car, into the gutter and thence along the road to Lightwater, Bagshot and beyond. He then used to caress its beautiful lines with a large chamois leather until he could see the reflection of his face in its sleek contours and well proportioned mudguards. I longed for a ride in the Wolseley but alas such a pleasure was ever denied me.

During the holidays I used to spend a lot of time amusing myself, the frequency of my trips to the laundry having diminished somewhat in the wake of my foray into the clutches of the laundry well. My Gran rigged up a garden swing suspended from a horizontal bough of an apple tree. I used to swing there for hours but always kept an eye open just in case my grandfather was required to deliver a telegram.

My mother's sister, May, who had been in service at Monty's home, lived in nearby Lightwater with her husband and their son John. I used to love their company and got on very well with my cousin. One day I decided to take a walk via a short cut to their home and wandered off past Matthews Garage, through some public nurseries and over a stream called The Bourne until I ended up at my aunt's home some two or three kilometres away. When my aunt saw that I was on my own she was mortified and rang my Gran at Windlesham. Needless Gran and Kath were rather upset and rang my grandfather at the laundry who instructed a Mr. Saunders, their delivery driver, to pick me up and take me back to Windlesham in his Morris delivery van. Needless to say I received a severe ticking off from my grandmother and was given firm instructions not to tell my mother about the incident on her next visit.

Each day I kept my eye open for signs of my new bike and one day as I sat on the garden swing I was summoned to the house where I saw a sheet, under which was secreted my new bike. I was not disappointed. Dad had assembled from odd spare parts, a 'Halford' machine painted black embellished with decorative green lines on the frame and mudguards. Its twenty inch wheels were clothed with pneumatic tyres. An orange reflector on the rear mudguard added a suitable element of luxury to my newly acquired machine. I felt as proud as an outhouse rodent with a gold tooth as I wheeled it out onto the quiet road and pedalled it up to the Windlesham Women's Institute and back, my first outing being about three hundred metres but still very memorable.

Occasionally I used to go out for rides with my Gran and Gramp along the quieter local roads and I recall that my grandmother's steed was a very old fashioned bike with a cradle frame equipped with thin strands of cord threaded through the edges of the rear mudguard down towards the spindle, designed to prevent a lady's dress getting caught in the spokes. Gramps' bike was a rather robust affair and even boasted a set of three Sturmey Archer gears in the rear wheel with the triangular gear shift on the crossbar.

Sirens and Grey Balloons

By the autumn of 1942 my health had recovered sufficiently to enable me to return to London and my mother duly arrived to collect me from Windlesham where Mr Matthews drove us to Sunningdale Railway Station en route for Waterloo and thence to Chingford.

Upon arrival I spent a couple of weeks at home during which time my parents had time to discuss what to do about my education, deciding that I should be given a fresh start at a new school, eventually selecting a state run Church of England day school. Thus, in the autumn of 1942 I was enrolled at the Lady Blade Church of England Primary School located at Kings Road, North Chingford.

I experienced some trepidation as I was placed into the care of Mrs Reader, the principal of the infants' school, who duly walked me along a corridor and into a classroom where I met my new teacher, Miss Seager.

Miss Seager was a very kindly person, probably in her early twenties and it fell to her lot to endeavour to help me catch up with the other students, starting with the rudiments of writing and the elements of simple arithmetic. I still remember the names of some of the children in my class but the biggest impression whilst attending the infants' school was meeting and being taught by my next teacher from the beginning of 1943 until July, 1945.

Mrs Holt was, or appeared to have been to my young eyes, somewhat older than other members of staff, probably in her mid fifties, slim of build with penetrating but not unkindly eyes and with greying hair swept back and gathered up in a bun. She possessed a great talent for imparting knowledge to young children which combined with the gift for infinite patience made her an outstanding teacher.

In those two years she managed to transform my rather stunted efforts at printing letters and words into more fluent 'running writing' which instilled in me an interest in reading, arithmetic, history, geography and general knowledge.

Although most classrooms were heated by radiators, Mrs. Holt's classroom was equipped with an open fire and, whilst being very strict she was also aware of our creature comforts. When the school milk was delivered to our classroom she used to place the bottles in front of the fire to enable us to have warm milk when playtime came around.

The school, like all others, was equipped with air raid shelters and on some occasions when the air raid sirens sounded, we would be marched across the playground in an orderly fashion and into the damp and rather unpleasant murky atmosphere of the shelter until the 'all clear' was sounded.

However, from 1942 to 1943, German bombing activity, whilst sometimes taking place in daylight hours, was more typically carried out at night when our slumbers were sometimes interrupted by sirens which compelled us to scuttle down into the next door garden to settle in the Anderson shelter for the night. One morning Jerry emerged from the shelter and went into our house and came back beaming with pride with the news that we no longer had any doors or windows on the ground floor as they had been blown out during that night's raid.

Shortly afterwards our younger brother Rob contracted scarlet fever, a highly contagious condition which necessitated a six week stay in an isolation hospital. Although my parents were able to call at the hospital in Waltham Abbey during visiting hours, they were not allowed to have any contact with him. In the meantime Jerry and I had to be withdrawn from school for a couple of weeks until it was established that we were free from infection.

After six weeks an ambulance arrived and deposited Rob at the end of our drive where Mum was awaiting him in great anticipation. I can remember that day so clearly as this emaciated lily white little chap dressed in a white woollen coat and beret, took some faltering steps up the drive and looked at Mum in bewilderment without any sign of recognition. Mum with tears in her eyes exclaimed "He doesn't even recognise me". Years later she often recalled that event.

It was about this time that a German incendiary bomb dropped in our garden. It was not unusual for some of them to detach from their flight cases and hit the ground without exploding. This must have occurred in this case. For some reason unbeknown to either Jerry or me, the bomb was never reported as a UXB (unexploded bomb) although I am sure that my father must have known about it. After the war we never saw it again and seemingly forgot all about it until it reared its ugly head nearly fifty years later.

Having migrated to Australia in 1964 I settled into a new home in Sydney. Being single I started to travel back to England every year to see my parents and relatives. Sadly my father died in 1991 but naturally I continued my annual trip to UK to take my mother on holiday. On my visit in 1992 my mother asked me to do a few maintenance jobs around the house including the removal of a tree in the back garden which was pushing over a fence. Having climbed the tree I looked down from my vantage point and to my utter amazement espied the bomb nestling in a corrugation on the garage roof. Age had certainly wearied the bomb but it had never been condemned either for instead of looking like a pristine 3 kilogram magnesium incendiary bomb it rather resembled a concrete core from a construction site.

Not wishing to alarm my mother I decided to walk the 2 kilometres to Chingford Police Station to report my find. As I approached the Station Sergeant's desk, I took my New South Wales drivers' licence from my wallet to prove that I wasn't a prankster and told the sergeant of my find, also enquiring whether they ever received reports of unexploded ordnance so long after the war. Surprisingly she told me that even now they received about three notifications per year in the borough. I explained that as my mother lived alone I wanted to return to her house so that I could be there when the police arrived requesting they delay a visit from the police for an hour or so.

Having walked briskly home I rounded the corner of Blackthorne Drive only to find a police car already parked outside the house which made me quite annoyed given the sergeant's previous undertaking. I was even more alarmed when I was apprised of the conversation which had followed the arrival of the two constables.

Policeman: "Mrs Hurdwell, do you have a son, Peter Hurdwell?"

My mother gave them a blank stare before answering in the affirmative.

Policeman: "Your son has advised that there is a foreign body on the roof of the garage".

At this point my mother thought they had informed her of a dead body on the garage roof to which she responded "He's such a logical boy, I don't know what's come over him". This last comment was particularly droll given that I was fifty-four years old at the time. They then asked permission to go upstairs and look out into the garden in order to view the garage roof. Having done so they decided that there was no bomb.

When I walked in, the police were not only sceptical they were totally disbelieving and willingly accompanied me up the garden where I stood on tip toes to lift the bomb from the roof. However they still refused to believe that it was a bomb and asked why I was so sure that it was the genuine article. I told them that my brother and I had found it the day after it had been dropped in 1943 following an air raid. I wisely omitted to tell them that we had sometimes tossed it to one another in the garden.

By this time my mother had simmered down somewhat and had started to prepare our evening meal so I left the police to contact headquarters to see what the next move should be. Word then came that they had to evacuate the area within a certain radius. Presumably headquarters had assumed that it was an IRA bomb. I opined that as it wasn't an IRA bomb but a bomb dropped in 1943, it was hardly likely to go off whilst I was having my dinner. They then contacted central control again who said that they would contact the army bomb squad in Woolwich some 20 kilometres away.

An army Land Rover duly arrived and a soldier in mufti reached onto the garage roof, inspected the bomb and said "Hmm, a 1943 3 kilogram German incendiary bomb". The news was greeted with some surprise by the young cops but they countered by saying "But it's not alive though, is it?" which evinced a grin from the soldier who said "Oh yes it is - catch!" an invitation to which both guardians of the law demurred.

In retrospect I am unable to fathom how the bomb found its way onto the roof or where it had been for almost fifty years and can only surmise that my father, knowing that his days on earth were numbered, in tidying up as best he could prior to his death, put it on the roof hoping I would see it on one of my visits.

Sirens and Grey Balloons

Rationing was an ever present thread running through our lives throughout the war years although we were more fortunate than most as we kept chickens which not only meant a reasonable supply of fresh eggs but also the bonus of a roast chicken at Christmas, very much a luxury to which few town dwellers had access. Clothing, footwear and even soap was rationed and people managed as best they could by the parsimonious usage of their meagre soap ration.

Mrs Knee, a neighbour in our street arrived on our doorstep one day triumphantly waving a shaving stick, doubtless purloined from her husband, joyfully proclaiming that she had just done the family washing with it. This discovery was quite a triumph as sticks of shaving soap were exempt from rationing.

As children we used to fantasise about many items we had heard about but had never seen such as ice cream and bananas and tried to imagine how a banana tasted. The arrival of oranges from South Africa was very much dependent upon the cargo ships successfully running the blockade of German U boats which skulked in the maritime shipping lanes. However, a couple of times a year our local green grocer would obtain a supply which was sold only to his regular customers. All the housewives endeavoured to keep on the right side of 'Old Greenie' as fruit and vegetables were not rationed. It was therefore up to him to apportion scarce items at his discretion. We used to line up for hours just to buy one orange per person per household.

Greenie, being a cockney, was a real character wearing scruffy mud smarmed trousers and boots, open necked shirt with a somewhat less than white scarf tied a couple of times around his neck. He had a pet monkey called 'Oscar' who roamed the shop, piddling on the merchandise and generally making a nuisance of himself. However nobody complained to Greenie about it as his displeasure might have manifested itself in the lack of oranges when the occasion arose.

Apparently Greenie used to frequent the nearby Prince of Wales pub at lunchtime and was known to spend extended lunch breaks talking with his friends and sinking the odd jar or two. One afternoon I came across Greenie lying prostrate in a field just over the way from his shop. Being only six years of age and correspondingly naive, I thought that he might have been dead so I decided to investigate further. As I drew near to his outstretched body I could see no signs of life so in order to confirm my fears I picked up half a house brick from a nearby abandoned building site and tossed it in his direction striking him in the solar plexus. I was startled to find that he was very much alive as I ran from the scene of his previously peaceful repose. When I told my mother of the incident she was very worried and repeatedly asked me whether I thought that Greenie had recognised the identity of his assailant.

By 1943 the daytime bombing by German aircraft had petered out to a large extent in our area but many years later my father was to tell of some of his experiences whilst a policeman during the war and one incident he related told me a lot about his sensitivity and humanity as well.

My trips back to U K from home in Australia were always a pleasure and I shall always cherish that 'quality time' I was able to share with my parents. So many people seem to take their parents for granted when they live close by and thus tend to be in contact by way of fleeting visits discussing mundane topics. However, I was fortunate enough to have been able to return every year and spend hours with my parents, talking, laughing and strolling down memory lane re- discovering them without the constraints busy lives place upon so many people.

I used to walk miles and miles with Dad over fields and through country lanes and every so often we would stumble upon a certain location which would ignite the flame of some long lost memory. One such memory came to light when we were in Epping Forest in the 1980's. We were walking along a country road when Dad said "Come with me Pete" and as we strolled into a little glade in the forest he started to recall the time during the war when he had been instructed to go to this location in the forest following the shooting down of a German bomber. At the time he had no trouble in finding the spot as the remains of the bomber were still smouldering, and sifting through the remains he chanced upon a leather glove and was horrified to find a hand inside the glove. It was shortly before Christmas and his thoughts inevitably turned to the family of this poor airman and how miserable and desolate their Christmas would be. He told me that it was at that moment the war struck him at the human level and that we were all human beings sharing the same cares, responsibilities, love, compassion and humanity.

On a similar occasion we were walking along a road not far from Waltham Abbey and adjacent to a pub called 'The Plough' when another memory came flooding back to my father. He pointed to a small block of terrace houses and told me how, as a policeman, he had been given the unenviable task of calling upon a woman to advise her that both her husband and her son had been killed in action during the war.

He told me how he had tried to rehearse how best to break the tragic news to her. He walked through the garden gate and just before he reached her door he saw the woman's next door neighbour. Dad asked the neighbour if she knew the unfortunate woman very well and the neighbour said that they were close friends. He then told her that he had some very bad news to impart whereupon the neighbour said that she would accompany Dad and stayed as the devastating tidings were imparted. The grieving woman didn't weep. She was stunned and stared blankly as if into the vacuum of her future. Shortly afterwards my father left as her neighbour tried to offer what comfort she could.

Gradually our lives started to take on a more settled aspect although, of course, the evidence of war was ever present. Many houses had been reduced to heaps of rubble although the stairways of many shattered homes were still intact pointing skyward in a last act of defiance towards the enemy.

Chingford Plains, the site of many a pre-war funfair, had long since succumbed to the government's bulldozers which had dug trenches across the ground to prevent the enemy landing troops from gliders.

Large concrete pillars were also scattered along some main arterial roads to impair the movement of enemy tanks in the event of a land invasion. We often heard the strains of Vera Lynn singing "The White Cliffs of Dover" on the radio and wondered what it would be like when 'Johnny could indeed sleep in his own little bed again'.

V1 FLYING BOMBS

However, the comparative serenity in the skies was about to be shattered by a product of the enemy's ingenuity in the form of the German VI Flying Bomb.

In the summer of 1944 I was riding my bike not far from our home when, without warning the anti aircraft guns opened up and shrapnel started to drop from the sky. I was quite frightened as we usually received some warning of air raids, particularly since the recently perfected radar systems were able to pick up the images of enemy aircraft long before they arrived over their targets.

Looking up and for just a brief moment I saw what I thought was an aircraft although it appeared to be flying much faster than others I had seen. I pedalled home as fast as I could and upon reaching our driveway, hopped off my bike and rushed indoors to find my parents standing in the garden near the chicken run, peering skywards trying to work out what was going on. After a short time the 'plane' disappeared from view.

A day or so later we found out that it was a pilot-less plane packed with high explosives and propelled by a pulse jet. Such missiles were launched from enemy territory with enough fuel calculated to run out upon reaching targets in Britain. They reached speeds of up to 400 miles per hour (640 kilometres per hour) but as they approached their target and the weight of the fuel having diminished, they reached almost 500 miles per hour (800 kilometres per hour). After the engines cut out they glided for a short distance until they crashed and exploded causing widespread devastation. In all, 10,000 of these missiles were fired at England killing 6,000 inhabitants and causing enormous damage.

The more frightening aspect of the missile was that its engine, a pulse jet, made a rather sinister humming noise which warned of its approach but if the engine cut out, it signified that it was about to dive steeply and explode on impact nearby.

Consequently it was quite demoralising and everyone was wary when hearing its approach, particularly when the engine cut out.

Sirens and Grey Balloons

Due to the humming noise emitted by the pulse jet engine it soon earned the name of 'Doodlebug' which was apparently based on the generic name given to certain types of Australian insects.

We experienced many doodlebug incidents in our borough but whilst only one person was killed and six residents in our borough were severely injured by them, they were responsible for a huge amount of damage to property.

Doodlebug attacks lasted for about six months but fortunately the British radar system was eventually able to give some warning of their approach, although once again we started to sleep in the Anderson shelter overnight. One such night has indelibly etched itself in my memory.

On that particular night there was quite a lot of aerial activity as the air raid sirens intermittently warned of the V I bombs and then sounded the 'all clear' only to be followed shortly afterwards by the 'warning' signal again when another doodlebug was caught on the radar. However, we felt safe inside the shelter but when one flying bomb's engine cut out not far away, Mum opened the shelter door a little just in time for us to hear and feel a massive explosion and see the sky illuminated by a huge pink flash, silhouetting the nearby trees against the night sky. Fortunately for us, it had crashed on the other side of a railway embankment, severely damaging houses on that side but leaving our home intact, the embankment having taken the full force of the blast. Fortunately nobody was badly injured although many houses on the other side were severely damaged. Our house had only a door and quite a few windows blown out and some cracks on the ceiling.

By the end of 1944 the VI menace was broken as the RAF aircraft located and bombed some of the launch sites. RAF fighters also perfected the art of descending from a high altitude, picking up speed in the process and then levelling out to the same speed as the flying bombs whose wings they then tipped, causing the offending missiles to spiral innocuously into a watery grave below.

Meanwhile, from the south of England in June 1944 Allied forces launched an attack in France in order to fight their way through Europe and extinguish the Nazi menace. There was great excitement when the news of the D Day invasion of 6th of June was beamed into homes throughout England.

In the meantime at Kings Road School I was making steady progress at my lessons. However, as the school was situated a little further from home than my previous school, I was unable to go home for lunch and was therefore sentenced for a while to the rigours of inedible school dinners. Each lunch time we left school and traipsed up the road to the local Catholic School in Station Road where for three pence each we undertook the challenge of endeavouring to consume a meal provided by the government.

The meals were ghastly. Vans used to arrive as we were assembled at trestle tables and the aluminium food containers were opened releasing the most awful smell of rotten cabbage and other indigestible fare. The potatoes, usually mashed, were watery and sloppy and could well have passed as a rather lumpy soup, in fact they were actually served up with the aid of a ladle instead of a serving spoon. The cabbage was so over cooked it had lost any of the colour it had been born with and the gravy resembled cold tea.

Sweets usually consisted of rice and custard although the rice looked more like mashed maggots and the custard resembled something that a diarrhoeic cat had left behind in a hurry. Sometimes the person dispensing the gruel would be smoking and I can still recall one helper, cigarette dangling from her lower lip, dropping ash into my rice.

Fortunately my mother heeded my protestations and I was eventually allowed to take a sandwich to school instead.

With the crushing of the VI menace people seemed to become a little more relaxed as the doodlebug bombing stopped and the war in Europe was progressing well for the Allies. Once again we eschewed the Anderson shelter and started to sleep in our beds. However, unbeknown to us, Hitler had another surprise up his sleeve. The V I doodlebug had been superseded by the V2 Rocket.

V2 LONG RANGE ROCKET

The V2 long range rocket was actually a much more sophisticated weapon than its predecessor. It was developed by the German Scientist

Sirens and Grey Balloons

Wernher Von Braun who, after the war was persuaded to live in the USA where his genius was channelled into the more peaceful applications in pioneering the space age.

The V 2 rocket could travel well beyond the speed of sound and could carry a heavier payload of high explosives and arrive at its final destination without detection or warning. In our borough this weapon was responsible for seventeen deaths and had a wider field of devastation than the doodlebug.

As mentioned before the doodlebug had eventually become detectable and air raid sirens could be activated giving most people time to find cover. In addition the doodlebug's engine was audible and if it cut out, most people had time to dive into an air raid shelter or seek some other sanctuary However, the long range rocket gave no prior warning and its arrival was only realised after it had exploded. Ironically its noise followed later as it had broken through the sound barrier thus leaving its sound trailing behind.

Quite a number of V 2 rockets devastated homes near our house, the nearest being less than 800 metres away. Although the first rocket arrived in January 1945 the duration of their attacks lasted for only four months as Allied intelligence managed to locate their launch sites in enemy occupied Europe and the RAF bombed them out of action.

One incident of a rocket attack stands out in my mind above all others. I was riding my bike one afternoon when I heard an almighty explosion as a rocket came down quite nearby, shaking the ground as though an earthquake had struck.

Later that day news came through that the rocket had come down about 100 metres from the Queen Elizabeth Hunting Lodge at North Chingford which was about eight hundred metres from where I had been cycling at the time of its impact. Although a woman had been standing near the hunting lodge at the time the rocket's arrival, it hit the soft ground with such force that it had partially buried itself before exploding, leaving the woman severely shaken but not physically injured. The crater later became a duck pond and is there to this day as a monument to the folly of war.

Conversely, a rocket exploded at nearby Waltham Abbey gaining a direct hit on a horse and cart. The explosion must have vaporised the horse, its driver and the whole cart and contents as no vestige of them was ever found.

By the time the last rocket had fallen on the British Isles Hitler's Germany had been remorselessly ground down and final victory was in sight. By the end of April 1945 the Russians were almost at the Brandenburg Gate in Berlin. It was with overwhelming joy that we heard that Hitler, the sub human monster of the twentieth century was dead. There was great rejoicing as we then knew that the war in Europe would soon be over and the lights would be turned on once again.

A few days later the war in Europe was finally over and the remnants of the Third Reich surrendered to the Allies on Luneburg Heath in May, 1945. Strangely enough, just ten years later I was to live in Luneburg as part of the British Army of the Rhine.

On almost the day of Hitler's suicide I ceased to be one of Mrs. Holt's students as I was to graduate from the Infants' Section of Kings Road School to the first form of the Juniors School. I still possess my Infants School final report written by hand by Mrs. Holt on very poor quality paper using a steel nib pen dipped in Indian ink. It proclaimed that I was very good at arithmetic and writing and good at English, geography and history but that my reading was only fair but that I was trying hard to improve it. Apparently my conduct was recorded as being good although I have a feeling that poor old Greenie might have averred sentiments to the contrary when reflecting upon his rude awakening from his alcoholic slumbers after being struck by the brick I had hurled at him some months before.

By May 1945 the war in the Far East had yet to be won, even though the Japanese were on their knees and the Americans were constantly bombing Japanese cities including massive raids on Tokyo itself. I have vivid memories of hearing the news of the Americans dropping the first atom bomb on Hiroshima and of the descriptions of the devastation which it caused. Naturally, few people could possibly have comprehended the destruction wreaked by this revolutionary weapon of mass destruction but it was only a short time later that another bomb was dropped on Nagasaki which brought the Second World War to an abrupt end. It was hard to believe that the war which had taken up over two thirds of my life had finally ended.

Within a very short time the celebrations began. The first party we attended was thrown by our school. Jellies and blancmange were served up from large basins and were a great treat for our sugar starved palates. Street parties were held in most neighbourhoods. Dog-eared bunting was excavated from cellars and attics and strewn about people's windows. Some residents even managed to unearth flood lights which had lain idly mouldering in drawers for years and it was not uncommon to see them dangling out of open windows in the shape of 'V' for victory. The streets were awash with happy and relieved party goers and people who hadn't seen each other for years and even total strangers greeted each other as though they had been bosom friends since childhood.

The local Council in Chingford put on a firework display in nearby Ridgeway Park which was duly thronged by hundreds of locals. In hindsight it does seem a little strange that having heard real explosions for so many years, celebrations included even more explosions, although we did enjoy these peace time explosions without being forced to take refuge in air raid shelters. Unfortunately the evening ended rather chaotically when one rogue rocket (firework that is) its touch paper having been lit, took off and flew into the tent where other fireworks were stored, igniting all the other fireworks which were awaiting their turn to perform. As the tent had been erected under a tree in the park, tongues of fire scorched the lower boughs of the tree, much to the discomfort of two boys who had climbed the tree for a better view.

An old lady who was standing near us started to have hysterics which shocked my brothers and me considerably but a neighbour of ours slapped her across the face which had the effect of stopping the old lady from yelling although it also had the effect of shocking us boys even more.

CHAPTER IV PEACE

To a child's simplistic and uncomplicated mind, now that the war was over we thought that the shops would open immediately and divulge their stores of bounteous goodies such as sweets, bananas and as much ice cream as our unaccustomed tummies would be able to accommodate. It came as quite a shock that rationing continued, in fact rationing did not end until the following decade.

However some signs that the war was finally over were in evidence immediately. At home the blackout curtains were dispensed with, the sticky tape was prised off the windows and one or two street lights came on again. But above all there was no chance of any bombing and for the first time in six years we felt safe.

HOLIDAYS

Shortly after hostilities had ceased Dad came home from police duty one summer's evening and told us that our family was going to join our Aunt, Uncle and cousins from Bagshot for a holiday by the sea at Rustington in Hampshire. This thrilled us no end, particularly as Rob and I had no recollection of seeing the ocean. We were ecstatic with joy at the prospect.

Our Uncle Sid who was a partner in a furniture removal and haulage company, arranged to send a lorry to pick up our family plus various chattels including our bikes and other paraphernalia required for our holiday at Rustington.

We were so excited and every hour prior to our holiday seemed to drag until finally the great day dawned. A lorry with a canvas canopy duly arrived at our door and the driver, Mr. Taylor, helped load our bikes and luggage into the back before resuming his place at the wheel, accompanied by our mother and Rob. Jerry and I settled down in the back of the truck amongst all the odds and ends required for a fortnight's holiday.

After a couple of hours we could tell that we were nearing our destination as we managed to get our first whiff of the sea, whetting our appetites for our first view of the beach and ocean.

Sirens and Grey Balloons

At last we arrived at our destination and were greeted by our father who had preceded us and within a short time we had placed all our belongings into the two bedroom bungalow which was to be home for the nine members of the two families. Nobody seemed to care about the cramped conditions – we were on holiday, we were safe and ready for any new experiences which might come our way.

We took little time to unload our bikes and were soon cycling along a narrow avenue of trees to the beach. I shall never forget the first time I saw the sea. Having left our bikes by the side of the track we walked across the sand dunes full of the visions our fertile imaginations had conjured up over the years;   flat blue water, and gently rolling waves as depicted in the children's books we had so avidly consumed. What a shock the reality was. On gaining the peak of the highest dune with the sound of the waves becoming ever closer I was amazed to behold the swirling white foam being stirred up in a sea of green.

Only a small section of the beach was open to holiday makers, which were few anyway, as structures like scaffolding had been erected a little way from the shoreline, apparently built to prevent mines from washing ashore.

Further up the beach rolls of barbed wire had been placed and signs were in evidence, warning people to proceed no further as mines might have been washed up and buried in the sand. However, we had enough sand to lie on and enough water in which to paddle. It certainly didn't inhibit our enjoyment of the beach particularly as the younger members of our families hadn't known what to expect anyway.

Within cycling distance of our little bungalow was a small boating lake. I found that I possessed more than a moderate ability in the art of rowing, encouraging me to cycle to the lake as often as I could and invest sixpence to hire a single scull rowing boat and propel myself along the lake and do circuits around the island in the middle.

The beach also held a fascination for all the members of both families. Mum and her sister were quite content to chat whilst comfortably ensconced in deck chairs with their thermos of tea whilst the male members of our party waded out amongst the waves making sure that we didn't encroach upon the mine trap scaffolding. This was easy for us boys as none of us at that time were able to swim very well and were not about to test our skills by straying out of our respective depths.

Looking back I can see my Dad now, wearing his black knitted swimming trunks with legs down to the upper part of the thighs and secured by a white cotton belt fastened by a chromium buckle. He must have borne a striking resemblance to the indomitable Captain Webb, the first person to swim the English Channel although my father's skills were not exactly in the same class as that of the long departed Captain.

Our Gran had given each of her grand children five shillings in pocket money for our holiday which, added to our somewhat meagre savings (scraped together out of our pocket money of sixpence a week) afforded all the boys the opportunity to purchase kites which, when the breeze was up, enabled us to print their outlines against the blue sky.

One of the many highlights of the holiday was a fishing expedition to nearby Worthing. Our Uncle Sid loaned Dad his 1934 Wolseley 9 car which, incidentally had a pneumatic back seat that at times required to be inflated by using a bicycle pump. We all piled in and after a short drive arrived at Worthing where Dad found an appropriate spot on the esplanade from which to demonstrate his angling skills.

In those days there were no nylon fishing lines although I must admit that we had progressed a little from the days when Izaak Walton had to find a suitable cart horse for the supply of his fishing lines. The sea fishing lines were made from cotton and dyed green presumably a colour which was difficult for unsuspecting fish to detect under water.

His hand line and ledgering equipment consisted of a round lead weight which nestled upon the sandy ocean floor with a hook baited with a rag worm secured further up the line so as to protrude a little way off the bottom.

It was with great anticipation that we witnessed him casting his line from the reel with the lead weight dragging the equipment into the water below. Within a few minutes Dad's spectators vastly outnumbered family members as we all waited in wrapt anticipation. We were not to be disappointed. After what appeared to have been an eternity there was a sudden jolt and he reeled in the line and swung it behind him and onto the promenade whacking a bearded old gentleman in the face with the flapping fish in the process, much to the mirth of the assembled multitude. He'd caught a beautiful bream.

Although that was the sum total of his catch for the day and of the holiday, we all returned to our tiny bungalow thrilled with the evening's endeavours and insisting that we eat the caught fish for lunch the next day.

Next day all nine of us consumed ample portions of the fish although in retrospect I suspect that either Dad had been inspired by divine guidance which enabled him to multiply the fish several times over or Mum had paid a call on the local fishmonger and purchased more fish with which to supplement the one Dad had so expertly snared. At any rate, the meal was delicious.

I hadn't been to see a movie since I was three years old and that had turned out to have been a traumatic experience, particularly when Bambi the little deer had been separated from its mother during a raging forest fire.

I really wanted to see the film 'Meet me in St. Louis' which was on at the local cinema in Worthing but only some of the grown-ups went to see it and for some reason I was not allowed to go. As I was really keen to see the film I was promised that when we returned home to Chingford I would be able to see it at our local cinema. The promise was duly kept but once again it became a circumstance I shall not forget.

When my paternal grandparents came to stay with us a few months later they took me to the local Doric cinema where we were able to enjoy Judy Garland in the principal role singing the 'Trolley Song'. Sadly, that was the last time I ever saw my Granny as she had a stroke a short time later and died on New Year's Day, 1946.

JUNIOR SCHOOL

Following the conclusion of my time in the Infants class at school, I was duly transferred to the Junior School situated in the adjoining building and it was there that I first came into contact with the Head Master, Mr William Swindell. He had been the headmaster of the school for many years and had risen to that position seven years after fighting in the First

World War and, as we were to find out later, it had made a deep impression on him as he had been injured by enemy fire in the trenches.

He was quite an unusual character, very much of the old school and was seldom seen without a cigarette in his mouth. On some occasions he would invite himself into a classroom dressed in his well worn tweed jacket, informing us that he was going to give us a test and then proceeding to throw up a whole pile of blank exercise papers which we would scramble to retrieve and upon which our answers were to be recorded.

Apparently he remained at the school until his retirement in 1955 and was credited with achieving excellent results from his pupils during his tenure as head master.

At the start of the school year in September 1945 my first teacher was Mrs Clayton who, whilst possessing a different style to Mrs Holt was, nevertheless a very able tutor and much respected by her pupils. She was slim of build, fairly tall with light coloured hair and possessed a very pleasant manner. I was beginning to relax and tolerate school quite well under her tutelage but sadly as winter set in I developed a bad bout of coughs, colds and influenza which compelled me to miss over three months of schooling.

When I returned to school in the early spring of 1946 after a long break though illness, I was so far behind in the teaching syllabus that I was demoted to the 'B' class where the somewhat less bright and less able students were taught at a slower pace. I was shattered, not because I was unable to understand the tasks we were given but because a Mr. Marr was my new teacher.

Mr Marr was an absolute brute of a man with humanity and compassion having been totally excluded from his nature, a sadistic streak having been implanted in his psyche in its stead. He possessed a voracious appetite for corporal punishment whether justified or not which manifested itself in the enjoyment of thrashing the children in his class, the eldest of which would have been no more than nine years of age. He stood a little short of six feet tall (180 centimetres) with dark hair and a lean face upon which always lurked a very pronounced five o'clock shadow even when school first assembled in the morning. His slim build belied what was probably a very strong body which had doubtless been enhanced over the years by the number of thrashings he had meted out upon his terrified students. The children in our class used to creep deferentially into the classroom when Mr. Marr was in charge, trying to appear as anonymous as possible in the presence of this latter day Maquis de Sad.

Generally speaking, the students in his class appeared to be slow on the uptake but looking back it is more than probable that some of them had by dint of wartime evacuation been starved of a coherent education and were endeavouring to catch up with their studies and to cobble together some sense of achievement. Mr. Marr was sure to have obliterated any such aspirations by his sadistic behaviour.

In our class of 2b was a little boy, one David Dingwall, whose intellectual development was quite retarded and as a consequence, he was hopelessly lost in the normal school environment. This singled him out as a rather sorry figure deserving of patient care and special consideration. That didn't worry Marr for he possessed not a single grain of kindness in any fibre of his being and if there was something he taught us which we were unable to comprehend, the children in his care were thrashed. He thrived on corporal punishment and used two long rulers with which to flay a child's backside. Presumably the noise of the two rulers flapping against each other engendered a vicarious thrill to his warped mind. On one occasion a gentle and quietly spoken girl named Maureen Hammond had committed some minor misdemeanour and was subsequently called out in front of the class whereupon he pulled up her dress exposing her thin knickers and thrashed her leaving her to return to her desk in tears.

Ironically Mr. Marr was also required to teach us religious instruction which upon reflection would have been akin to anointing Adolph Hitler as Pope. He chose to give us a lesson on lying, telling us of the biblical characters Ananias and his wife Sapphira. Having outlined their sinful habit of telling lies he then told us that on the following day he would test us on the previous day's lesson and any child who hadn't remembered the names would be punished. Poor little Dingwall had no chance of retaining two such unusual names let alone the context in which they were famous and next day he was blinking nervously when questioned by Marr. Needless to say he was made an example of and despite his tearful protestations was beaten in front of the class.

I must say that I was fortunate in that I received only one thrashing from this man and at the time was wearing rather old and well patched shorts handed down from my brother Jerry. The effect was that the rulers did little damage although Marr accused me of placing something in my pants to cushion the blows.

Each morning at school the partitions separating the classrooms were drawn back on their hinges to make one large assembly area where the whole of the Junior School united to sing hymns and have morning prayers. On one occasion when we were thus assembled, Mr. Swindell advised us that Mr. Marr was ill in hospital and proceeded to lead us in prayer, praying for Mr. Marr's speedy recovery and return to his school duties. I prayed that he would die but felt so guilty as I came out of assembly that I felt compelled to tell somebody. It's likely I may have thought that confiding in someone would in some way excoriate the sin from my soul whilst also hoping that my prayer for his early demise might be answered.

I chose to confide my sin to Kenny Mercer, a fellow student and told him that I had prayed that Marr would die, expecting a reproachful response. I was amazed and somewhat comforted when Kenny looked relieved and said "So did I!" Alas, Marr lived.

By July, 1946 it was with great relief that our class escaped the tyrannical reign of Mr. Marr as we commenced the six week school summer holidays. However it was during these holidays that I had a very frightening experience.

PEDOPHILE ATTACK

One warm summer day our part German shepherd part everything dog called Tess returned from the nearby Highams Park Lake stinking like a sewer and upon inspection was found to have been rolling in swan's poo. For some reason she loved this unique aroma and it was not the first time she had come home in this state. It would have taken a brave soul to wash the caked on excrement from her coat before giving her a bath but we found that the least offensive way of ameliorating the smell was to walk her back to the lake and give her a long swim as far away as possible from where the swans had made their home.

Accordingly I whispered "walkies" and she excitedly took off with me down to the woods and coming to the lake plunged in, emerging some minutes later hopefully having left some of the foul aroma to dissolve in the waters from which it had emanated. Walking home she came across some cows in the nearby woods and as was her wont decided to chase them.

Shortly afterwards a man approached me and asked if I knew where Chingford Lane was situated. He was probably in his mid thirties, tall and slim with dark receding hair but the feature which caught my attention most was his high cheek bones which gave him a somewhat cadaverous aspect. I told him that I didn't know where Chingford Lane was but he said that he would walk along with me until he got his bearings. I was very suspicious particularly as we had been instructed never to talk to strange men. However, I felt that it would be folly to make a run for it.

As we reached some bushes he started to say something but then hesitated for a moment before suddenly making a lunge at me, grabbing me across my chest with one arm and putting his free hand around my throat whilst trying to drag me into the bushes.

At that precise moment Tess returned from her diversion, took one look at the man and snarled in preparation for an attack whereupon he promptly let go and ran off.

When I returned home I was in two minds about telling my mother of the incident but as I looked quite shaken she asked what had happened.

As we didn't have a phone Mum went next door and telephoned Dad's police station and within minutes a squad car arrived and a plain clothes detective drove me to the perimeter of the woods where we wandered for an hour or so, the detective stopping anyone we found and asking if they had seen anything untoward happening in the vicinity. We found no sign of my assailant that day.

About a week later I saw the man again and a friend who was with me suggested that we ring the police emergency number 999 which we duly did. I explained over the phone who I was and what had happened and also that my father was stationed at Chingford Police Station. The receptionist told me to go home straight away and wait there which I duly did.

After reaching home I found to my surprise that my father had just arrived home on his red Triumph Speed Twin police motorbike. It transpired that Scotland Yard had found out that Dad was in a local court giving evidence and the magistrate upon hearing the news had adjourned the court sitting and Dad was given a motor bike and sent home.

I mounted the rear mudguard of the machine which possessed no pillion seat or footrests and we careered all over the forest looking for my assailant. I hung onto Dad for dear life as we thumped and bumped over corrugations, ditches and tree roots but to no avail. Returning home it felt as though my pelvis had become fused to my rib cage and I was very sore indeed.

A full year passed and whilst I certainly hadn't forgotten the attack in the forest I felt that I would never see the man again. However, I was wrong.

Walking along a road in North Chingford I happened to see a grey car driving by and to my surprise it was driven by my assailant. The car was a pre-war grey Standard 8 saloon with the number plate HLP 89.

Upon returning home I told my father the car's registration number and upon checking the police found that it was a hire car. This led to the man's arrest and although pleading insanity he was sent to prison for five years.

LONDON ZOO

During this holiday break our parents took us to the London Zoo. Naturally we were duly fascinated by the various animals, birds, reptiles and insects we encountered especially two quite different exhibits. One was a bird eating spider which was quite terrifying and the other was Rotor the Lion. An inscription on the cage denoted the fact that this very large lion was owned by no lesser personage than Mr Winston Churchill, Britain's wartime prime minister.

Sirens and Grey Balloons

Rotor looked distinctly unhappy as we gawped at him from the safety of the opposite side of the high railings separating us. We were filled with excitement as he sauntered to the front of his prison not far from where Jerry and I were standing.

We became even more excited when he faced us, sat down and unleashed a burst of urine through his front legs scoring a direct hit on the front of Jerry's shirt. The smell of his urine was quite overpowering and I was fortunate that he missed me and Jerry had received the lion's share.

GERMAN PRISONERS OF WAR

It was also during that school holiday that I experienced a chance meeting which had an effect on the lives of our family for many years to come. I was walking Tess, nicely groomed on this occasion, not far from our home when I came across some German prisoners of war digging the footings for some homes which were to become a post war housing estate. Thousands of German servicemen captured during the war were kept in Britain for several years after hostilities has ceased and were put to work in various ways including working on building sites.

As I walked past the trench in which they were working one of them asked the name of my dog and I told him that it was Tess. I also told him my name as well. Ironically where they were working was but a stone's throw from where a doodlebug had exploded near to the railway embankment. He introduced himself as Karl Phillip and that he came from Frankfurt. When I got home I told my parents what had happened and they said that as the war was over the German prisoners were allowed out at weekends although they had to wear their uniforms at all times. The uniforms were dark brown, the material being similar to British Army battledress but with a diamond shaped patch on the back upon which 'POW' was printed in white.

My parents asked if I would go back to see Karl and invite him and a friend home for tea on the following Sunday. I think we had to give written confirmation for Karl to pass on to the Camp Commandant in order to prove that an English family had issued an invitation. Thus, I saw Karl the next day and we arranged to meet him and a friend the following Sunday afternoon.

On that Sunday afternoon I decided to walk towards the camp in which they lived and about halfway there I saw Karl and his friend Heinrich coming towards me whereupon I ran to greet them. Upon reaching them they both gathered me up in their arms and gave a great hug. I was to learn later that both men had little girls at home in Germany whom they had never seen.

They both got on very well with our family and spoke quite good English as they had been stationed in the Channel Islands during their war service. Mum had prepared a nice tea for us and as we had kept chickens right through the war we had hard boiled eggs, much to the embarrassment of Heinrich who couldn't eat eggs.

When it came time to go back to camp a rather humorous incident occurred. Heinrich said that he was very worried about the 'Russians'. Mum and Dad couldn't understand why they should be concerned about the Russians as the war was over, although at the time of the Cold War nobody liked either Stalin or the Russians come to that. It transpired that they were actually worried about the rations, particularly as food was still rationed. However, as my mother used to make her own jams and preserves and my father worked his own allotment we were better off than many people.

By this time I was old enough to go to school on my bike and had even graduated from my little Halford bike to another larger machine which Dad had cobbled together from spare parts. Most lunch times I used to call in to where the prisoners were enjoying a lunch break. They always made me very welcome and I suppose I felt important mixing with adults, particularly as I was only nine years old.

Talking of school, during one morning assembly our Headmaster, Mr Swindell told us that it had come to his notice that a large number of children had parents who allowed German prisoners of war into their homes. He said that he had fought the Germans during the First World War and had bullet wounds on his back and was disgusted that we should be friendly with them. I went home and told my parents who assured me that this was a very ignorant thing to say and to ignore his comments. I'm sure all the kids at school did just that.

Sirens and Grey Balloons

Every three months the POWs were allowed to send a parcel weighing no more than seven pounds back to their loved ones in Germany and the two of them used to come to our house, which was really their second home, and meticulously weigh out the items they had purchased which mainly consisted of warm underwear (usually purchased from army surplus stores), coffee (which wasn't rationed) and sweets for the children (which were rationed).

At weekends I often used to walk up to a place near Epping Forest where the prisoners lived and was able to wander in to see them. They pointed out one prisoner who disliked the English and had declined any invitation into a local home. One day, we were told that this man's mother in Germany was very ill and that he was about to be repatriated to Germany as a result. Quite a few of the local residents made up a parcel for him to take back to Germany. He took the parcel but I don't know whether that softened his attitude toward the British. I would like to think that this might have done so but of course will never know.

Both Karl and Heinrich loved to go to the soccer and the local club was Tottenham Hotspur. Unfortunately the Tottenham ground was outside the territory in which they were allowed to travel and, of course they had to wear their POW uniform.

Dad made up a couple of bikes for them from old spare parts and loaned them some of his clothes which enabled them to cycle to soccer matches but with strict instructions not to talk to anyone.

They used to spend a lot of time with our family including Christmas Day at our home. Most of the German prisoners were very clever: Karl used to make some wonderful wood carvings of doves, eagles on mountain tops and also chickens pecking at grain. Heinrich, being a saddler by trade used to painstakingly unravel hessian sacks then hand spin the strands into rope which were then fashioned into beautiful carpet slippers.

They departed for home on 5th March, 1948 (the day I took my Eleven Plus Examination), and we were all very sorry to see them go as the German prisoners had been such great ambassadors for their country in helping to heal the scars of war.

Over twenty years later, Heinrich invited my parents over to his village in Germany and treated them to a wonderful holiday. My parents were amazed that everyone in the village had heard of 'the family Hurdwell' and the warmth of the locals was palpable. Now, in the twenty-first century I am still in correspondence with Arne, Heinrich's grandson.

GRUMPY

I suppose young boys will always be noisy and most grown-ups can quite happily accommodate an innocent commotion, putting it down to the exuberance of youth. Not so 'Grumpy'. Grumpy was a man probably in his seventies who lived in an adjoining street about a hundred metres from where we lived.

He was slim in stature, well dressed with well pressed trousers and smart jacket. He looked immaculate in any garb he chose to wear. Although he was always wore smart attire I never once saw him wear even the slightest hint of a smile.

He lived with his wife although we seldom set eyes on her. By all accounts she was extremely deaf as was evidenced by her use of an ear trumpet. An ear trumpet was probably the precursor of the modern hearing aid and was sometimes referred to as an amplifying cone. As its name implies, it looked like a straight trumpet about thirty centimetres long whereby the deaf person placed the slim end of the instrument into the ear leaving the bell end free for the person at the opposite end to speak. We felt sorry for his wife on the odd occasion we saw them together as he yelled down the cone until he saw a sign of recognition from his wife that she had comprehended his message.

Grumpy loathed children, in fact I think that he may have bypassed childhood altogether and had graduated into a grumpy old man during his teenage years. As children we would walk past his front garden only to be greeted by grumblings of his displeasure about the youth of today. Even if we were playing in the street on roller skates some distance from his home he would yell at us to keep quiet.

We told our mother about old Grumpy one day and she told us to ignore him because he was just a grumpy old man.

Sirens and Grey Balloons

One day he started to verbally abuse us which prompted me to tell him that our mother had told us to ignore him because he was just a grumpy old man. He later called on our mother who insulted him even further by admitting that she had in fact given her offspring that advice. Perhaps his wife's deafness was a defence mechanism to combat his miserable outpourings.

In September, 1946 I returned to school and relaxed somewhat as I regained my place in the 'A' class, knowing that I would only have ancillary contact with Mr. Marr, my new teacher being a Mr. Salter. Under him, progress was steady although I must observe that my new teacher had a mindset for a particular book called 'Chang' which described the life and times of a certain Siamese (Thai) white elephant and he read to us about this animal's adventures almost on a daily basis, sometimes to the exclusion of other more necessary lessons such as English and arithmetic.

However, the most enduring memory I have retained during that period related to the ghastly winter of 1946 – 1947.

WINTER 1946 - 1947

The winter really started in January 1947 and was the most severe winter I had ever experienced during my short life. Temperatures seemed to drop almost by the hour with each succeeding day appearing worse than the one before. The frost glistened on the bare branches of trees which could have reminded us of Christmas cards when viewed from the comfort of an armchair in front of a blazing fire. Unfortunately there was no blazing fire and we were mere mortals frozen to the marrow as the mercury continued to recede into negative territory. Winter steadily sank further into even deeper sub zero depths. Houses were not centrally heated in those days and their only source of warmth was usually an open coal fire in the main living room. We used to crouch around the glowing coals as the fire laboured to draw air from the cracks beneath the doors and gaps around the windows creating huge drafts and leaving us with semi warm fronts and frozen backs.

Bedrooms were bitterly cold and well below freezing as the condensation of our breath on the window panes transformed them into beautiful frosted patterns of mystic ferns of ice. In order to keep warm we used to wrap our pyjamas around stone hot water bottles and deposit them in the bed just prior to retiring and then, having stripped off our clothing, we would put on the warm garments with great celerity, snuggling up to the water bottle and gradually pushing it down the bed until the whole bed was warm.

In the morning we were in no mood to admire nature's handiwork scribed on the windows as we extricated ourselves from the blankets, donned dressing gowns and sped to the bathroom for a strip wash before eating our porridge and going off to school. Quite often the water pipes in the house would have frozen overnight, sometimes bursting, forming puddles, usually in the kitchen.

During the war we often used to ask grown-ups what it had been like before the war and the responses we received had given us the distinct impression that life in Merry England had been little short of a second Utopia. Thus, after the war we were unable to reconcile that vision with the current reality as, early in 1947 there was a crisis as the cold weather impeded the transportation of coal not only to our hearths but also to the electricity power stations as well.

Subsequently coal ceased to become available to the general population who had already suffered enough privations during the hostilities of the past six years.

As a back-up we did have a solitary electric heater whose element glowed red when switched on producing about as much warmth as a soldering iron in its death throes. Alas during the coal strike electricity generating power stations which relied on coal, developed the habit of cutting off power supplies, plunging homes into darkness and starving electric heaters of their means of employment.

I vividly recall a bitterly cold day when my mother threw open the french doors leading into the garden. On that day we had no coal for a fire and no electricity for the heater. I complained and asked her to close the doors only to be told that it was as cold inside as it was out of doors and that I should run around to get warm.

Our kitchen and bathroom were adjacent to each other and in the kitchen there was a 'Vivo' gas fired water heater which in theory provided hot water for both areas. Unfortunately it was never able to deliver hot water to the bathroom for although the water may have been hot when it left the kitchen heater it had, for some reason, to be piped from the kitchen, up though the kitchen ceiling and into the cold loft and then down again into the bathroom, fighting off multifarious sub zero gremlins along its circuitous route before limping into the bathroom basin, a mere tepid dribble of its former self.

By April, 1947 the British population had managed to survive the vicissitudes of a severe winter. The snow had thawed and we were able to greet a most welcome spring. The rest of my school year under Mr. Salter ended without incident or illness as we looked forward to the six weeks of school summer holidays.

CHAPTER V ELEVEN PLUS EXAMINATION

I was more fortunate than Jerry as we had returned from evacuation before I was due to commence my formal education. However, Jerry had attended a dozen schools during the war years. At this juncture of my life the newly introduced 'Eleven Plus' or 'Scholarship' examination was looming ever menacingly on the horizon and the coming year at Junior school was vital to my aspirations to earn a place at high school.

By 1944 when Britain felt confident enough to look towards peacetime governance the Churchill led coalition had formulated a new state education policy known as the Butler Education Act, developed by the then Minister for Education, Mr R A Butler.

He proposed that all school students should sit an examination around the age of eleven and that based on those results children would be streamed into three types of secondary school, namely grammar, technical and secondary moderns schools. Those attaining sufficient marks would be selected to go to a grammar or technical school whilst those who had failed to gain the necessary marks would go to secondary modern schools.

Although the Act specifically stated that there should be parity of esteem amongst all secondary schools, this was obviously anathema as it was more prestigious to win a place to a grammar or technical school than be drafted into a secondary modern school. Thus, much of a student's future relied on passing the eleven plus exam. The final year at junior school was therefore vital in providing the tools and guidance for 'winning a scholarship'.

Unfortunately, just as I was about to return to school in the autumn of 1947, I succumbed to another bout of chest infections, coughs, breathing problems and to cap it all, a large carbuncle on the back of my knee. As I was a likely candidate for tuberculosis I had also to attend a nearby clinic for X rays and tests but fortunately my lungs were clear.

I can remember lying in bed at home worrying about losing schooling that might result in having an adverse effect on my performance in the run up for the eleven plus examination which I was due to take in March of the following year.

Sirens and Grey Balloons

As a result of my illness I lost two months of schooling and it was not until the November that I set out on my bike and pedalled the two kilometres to school where I again resumed my studies in Form 4A. The critical task of steering us upon the road to passing the scholarship examination fell to our new teacher, Miss Theakston who was an extremely able teacher although it was only later that I had a chance to assess her true merits.

My first week in Form 4A was absolutely shattering for me as we were given long multiplication and long division sums to work out and other arithmetic conundrums which were quite foreign to me, having missed the previous two months of schooling. I hadn't a clue as to what the lessons were all about and sat there dumbstruck as the other children rattled off the answers to questions I couldn't even comprehend, let alone answer. I used to go home worried, low in self esteem and with a dread of what the next school day would have in store.

My father tried to give me tuition and whilst what he taught me was doubtless correct it only served to confuse me even more. The prospect of the forthcoming eleven plus examination seemed to be pressing ever closer redolent of the nightmares I used to have when suffering from pneumonia. Everything seemed to be closing in on me and in my own mind I felt that I had become the class dunce. The problem was doubtless exacerbated by the fact that in those days children did not have the confidence to ask many questions of their teachers but just muddled along hoping for the best. The weekly test we were given became a nightmare in its own right.

Although it took quite a while, the dust storms of confusion gradually abated. Slowly I found myself piecing together wisps of information which started to weave themselves into logical patterns. In this way I was able to make some progress in the classroom, becoming reasonably proficient at my school work although falling well short of claiming genius status.

One afternoon we heard on the grapevine that a confectionary shop in North Chingford was selling ice creams, a treat which both Rob and I had never encountered and of which Jerry had only a vague recollection. Jerry and I walked the two kilometres to the shop called 'The Top Hat' and joined the long queue. The pavement was thronged with excited school kids some of whom had made their purchase and were busy savouring this new experience. This gave those in the queue the opportunity to judge whether a cone or wafer configuration yielded the greater portion of ice cream, the price for either being the same. Jerry and I were apprehensive that the shop might run out of stock before our turn came but our fears were without foundation and we eagerly grabbed our wafers and joined our friends on the pavement where we licked them slowly into oblivion, commenting that they were somewhat better than Mum's war time efforts which had consisted of a cup of custard left out in the winter frost until gaining the consistency of ice cream.

We always enjoyed our home life and with the more relaxed atmosphere promoted by the absence of the bombing were able most nights to sit by the fire as Dad read us children's books. R.M Ballantyne's 'The Coral Island' stands out in my memory and I cried when the cat was grabbed by its tail and hurled into the sea.

Each year our father used to read us Charles Dickens' 'A Christmas Carol'. It must have been an abridged version as he was always able to finish the last chapter on Christmas Eve itself and with Tiny Tim having uttered the final words "God bless us every one" we were sent to bed with the prospect of a wondrous day ahead.

My father was quite handy at carpentry and although at that time there were very few toys to be purchased in the shops, he used to make presents for us including 'Beau Jest' forts, wooden tommy guns which rattled away when the trigger was pressed and one year he even found a couple of old cycle dynamo lights which he painted and fixed to our bikes.

Most of the students in Form 4A came from what would in those days have been referred to 'lower middle class' homes where the families, whilst not being anywhere near well off, nevertheless managed to just about balance their budgets. However, there were some exceptions, one being in the form of a lad named Ronnie Wiggins. On the coldest of days he would come to school wearing shoes but no socks and a thin shirt with only a lightweight grey jumper. His nose was usually running and his legs were quite blue with cold but he never seemed to complain about anything, not even the cold.

One winter's afternoon I returned home and told my mother about this unfortunate little chap and a couple of days later Mum gave me a parcel of clothes Jerry had grown out of and told me to give it to Ronnie. I duly took the package to school and tried to find a quiet place in which to hand it over to him but Miss Theakston saw what was happening and took the package from me and put it away so that she could give it to him privately at the conclusion of school.

He didn't seem to have been embarrassed as he brought a note from his mother to school the next day thanking Mum for the parcel and asking if she had a shirt to match the trousers she had received. I'm not sure whether my mother was able to oblige or not.

As a child it always appeared to me that when looking forward with anticipation to a great event like Christmas or school holidays, time always seemed to be mired in a despond of lethargy. However, when a dreaded event was looming on the horizon precious time tended to speed up like a condemned man's appointment with the gallows.

So it was that after years of apprehensive anticipation the eleven plus scholarship examination was almost upon us. By the February, 1948 I had managed to climb up to somewhere near the middle of the class if our weekly tests were any guide. Miss Theakston implemented 'mock examinations' based on what questions the scholarship examinations would be likely to contain. Mr Swindell used to exhibit an extravagant interest in Form 4A particularly as his reputation to a large degree was judged on the number of students graduating from his junior school into grammar of technical schools.

By the beginning of March our nerves were on edge as the date of the scholarship examination was only a few days away. Some students in the class had been promised bikes or wrist watches by their parents if they passed the exam and my efforts to pass had also been stimulated by the prospect of a new bike.

On the day preceding the examination we did not undertake any lessons as it was felt that we should relax and do some physical activity to help us sleep in readiness for the events of the following day. Thus, we assembled in the school playground and with packed lunches in our haversacks undertook a day long walk through Epping Forest under the guidance of Miss Theakston who on this occasion was accompanied by her mother.

In spite of the importance of the following day I slept well that night but upon waking up and greeting the new day which had been haunting me for so long, I felt a melange of emotions. The day was, scholastically speaking, the most important day of my life up to that point, but within twelve hours the burden which I had carried in my mind for several years would have been lifted. But where would I go from here? I was at a crossroads but the next part of the journey was to be navigated in yet still uncharted waters.

As I walked the two kilometres to Chingford County High School where the eleven plus examinations were to be held, I lost the feelings of trepidation and decided that I could do nothing more than to just do my best.

It took a couple of months for the results of the exam to come through but at last a rather official looking envelope dropped through our letterbox. It was opened in some trepidation and I was informed that my marks were sufficient for me to be interviewed with the prospect of gaining a place as a student at the William Morris County Technical School in nearby Walthamstow.

There was quite a pool of would be aspirants for a place at the school but only a limited number of places available, the final decision as to the choice of successful students resting on an interview at the school to be conducted by two senior teachers.

I had hoped that my educational fate would have already been sealed without the necessity of jumping through another set of educational hoops, but at least I was still hopeful of gaining a place at the school.

Knowing that a senior male and female teacher would be taking the interview, my parents tried to give me some useful hints on how to conduct myself and suggested that I refer to the male interviewer as 'sir' and the female as 'madam'. Whilst I felt comfortable with the nomenclature of 'sir' for the master, 'madam' didn't sit well with me, even though at the time I was ignorant of the fact that 'madam' was also the title given to a woman who ran a high class brothel. I decided to call her 'miss' as I had always addressed female teachers thus.

At the age of eleven I was very small by comparison to my contemporaries, standing only 4 feet seven inches (140 cms), slim to the point of being skinny with blue eyes and blond hair with a parting steadfastly kept in place with the aid of Brylcreem.

On the day of my interview I arrived well before the appointed time and sat in a small waiting room until I was called. Although there were two interviewers I can only recall the name of the female teacher which was Miss Herring who was at great pains to put me at my ease. She asked me about my family and how I liked school (I lied and told her how much I enjoyed it) and also whether I belonged to any organisations. I told her that I was a member of the local Lifeboys Team and that next year I would be able to graduate to become a member of the Boys Brigade Company.

The master asked me what I wanted to do when I grew up and as I had aspirations to join the Royal Navy I told him so, deviously avoiding advising my interlocutor that only a few months before I had become seasick whilst riding in a ferry on the tranquil waters of the River Thames.

It must have been my angelic appearance that managed to get me over the line as a week or so later I was advised that I had passed the interview and on the 7th September, 1948 would become a student at the William Morris County Technical School.

True to their word Mum and Dad put a deposit down on a new 'Norman' bike with straight handlebars, blue frame and no gears. I felt very proud especially when I rode it to school and showed my friends, many of whom had also become the proud owners of similar machines.

During the school summer holidays I spent many hours cycling with Brian Sargent, a friend from school who had also passed the examination and had become the owner of a black New Hudson bike with drop handlebars. We regularly cycled to High Beech, Waltham Abbey and even to Broxbourne where we used to park our bikes and watch the enormous Clydesdale horses pulling barges up the River Lea and adjacent canals. In those days the roads were quite safe for cyclists as few families owned motor cars and the roads were not laden with heavy traffic.

CAMPING HOLIDAY

Following the war there sprang up a number of shops selling ex-army equipment and as the option of a camping holiday offered a cheap means of getting away and staying at the seaside, Mum and Dad purchased an ex-army tent and various items of camping equipment in preparation of a holiday in the August. However, before the family holiday I again travelled down to my maternal grandmother's home which was now in nearby Lightwater, having sold the Windlesham Post Office.

She and my grandfather had both retired shortly before but Gramp had recently been diagnosed with Parkinson's disease. During my stay my Gramp's health deteriorated steadily and it hurt me to see how my Gran suffered during that time. She used to return from the Brookwood Hospital looking drawn and sad. Sometimes I would walk into the dining room and see her weeping. I had never seen her weep before and had not the wherewithal to offer her any comfort at the time. As I was her closest grandchild, maybe that was some sort of comfort in itself.

One afternoon we walked to a little spot down by a stream near Bagshot called 'The Bourne' and as I went for a paddle in the water I could see her surveying the ground close where our picnic had been laid out. She had chanced upon a four-leafed clover and told me that it signified good luck and that maybe Gramp would get better. Alas it was not to be.

She used to live near Windsor as a little girl and related how, when she was playing in the street with some friends not far from Windsor Castle, Queen Victoria drove past in her carriage whereupon the girls curtsied to Her Majesty who acknowledged their curtsies.

After a couple of weeks stay with Gran I returned to London and joined the family for a camping holiday at Shoeburyness, on the Essex coast.

Sirens and Grey Balloons

During the camping holiday my father used to ring Gran on a daily basis to enquire about Gramp's condition, knowing that he would never recover from his illness. On the 17th August, 1948 he returned from the public phone box and told us that Gramp had died that day. We were all very sad and it seemed so unfair that we had lost two caring grandparents within the space of less than two years. I found out many years later that not long before he died he had asked to see me but apparently the family felt that it would have placed too much of an emotional strain on such a young person.

A few days later my parents drove down to Windlesham for the funeral in Dad's ancient Singer Eight car, leaving Jerry in charge of Rob and myself. Reliability wasn't one of the car's strong points as every journey we had undertaken up to that time had been invariably punctuated by breakdowns. It was therefore with some surprise that they actually returned to Shoeburyness on the same day having attained the incredible feat of motoring over one hundred miles in the one day without breaking down. It was certainly a record for the old jalopy, but sadly, it was never able to perform an encore.

Upon returning home following our holiday, Jerry and I were looking forward to joining our respective schools. Jerry had attended twelve different schools during the war years which had included a short time of home tuition after his last school had been severely damaged by German bombing. Although he attended a secondary modern school for the next four years, such a fragmented education had left him ill equipped for the permanent workforce. At the age of fifteen he started work as an office junior at a large printing company but for several years thereafter he attended night school in order to complete the education he had been sadly denied during the war years.

Being a most tenacious boy he managed to pass his General Certificate of Education examinations before taking on other tertiary subjects connected with his work.

Peter Hurdwell

CHAPTER VI WILLIAM MORRIS SCHOOL

On the 7th September, 1948 I woke up and after my ablutions donned my new school uniform which comprised short grey trousers, grey shirt, blue blazer, blue, silver and maroon striped tie, grey socks with red piping at the top and a blue peaked cap with a maroon ring embossed on the crown. Both the blazer and cap were emblazoned with the school shield upon which was arranged a pair of crossed scimitars under which was woven the school Latin motto 'Respice Finem' which literally translated means 'Look to the end'. Although the motto seemed to be somewhat ambiguous it could have meant 'keep the end result in view' or possibly 'prepare to die' or even an invocation for certain students to select the stream of technical education which would result in their becoming undertakers. I never did quite work out what the school's founding fathers had in mind.

The name of the school derived from William Morris who had lived in the Walthamstow area from the time of his birth in 1834 until his death in 1896. During his short but busy life he became a leading light in the sphere of home furnishings, art, poetry, philosophy and socialism with his most famous quotation being 'Fellowship is Life and the Lack of Fellowship is Death' still to be found etched into the masonry of the Walthamstow Assembly Hall.

The school that bore his name was built in 1902 and was typical of the schools of that period. It was built in the midst of row upon row of slate roofed terrace houses of 1880's vintage whose serried ranks were lined up like battalions of soldiers ready for battle. Thus, the school possessed no adjacent playing fields although it was supplied with two large playgrounds. Prior to 1948 most British senior schools segregated boys from girls and required separate playing areas. However, following the war, more and more senior schools were becoming co-educational.

The building consisted of three storeys with an assembly hall on the ground and top floors and a large gymnasium occupying the middle floor.

It was almost with a sense of destiny that I walked through the school gate in my newly acquired finery, only to be confronted by a group of older boys from more senior classes who grabbed the new students' caps and proceeded to stamp on them and twist ties into distorted shapes before grudgingly returning them in a less than pristine state. Having undergone the traditional 'roughing up' routine we walked into our first school assembly hall looking like street urchins straight from the pages of 'Oliver Twist'.

Our first assembly consisted of a lecture from Mr. Herbert Williamson MSc who was the newly appointed Head Master and Miss Murdie, the School's Head Mistress. We were then split up into temporary classes for the first term which would enable the teachers to assess the strengths and weaknesses of each student before assigning them to more permanent classes based on the teachers' assessments. Students perceived to be the most able were assigned to W Class, the next were M and the final Class was T. (These followed the initials of William Morris Technical.)

The idea of the technical school system was founded on the principle that the first two years of high school would give an all round general education involving such subjects as English language, English literature, arithmetic, mathematics which included algebra, geometry and trigonometry, history, geography, science, music, art and physical training. After two years it was then assumed that students would have a fair idea of which career paths they were likely to follow and were then streamed into such courses as were likely to match their aspirations for future career paths. These courses included commercial subjects such as commerce, shorthand, typing and accountancy or physics and chemistry which would match their plans for scientific, medical or veterinary careers.

After the first term I was drafted into the M class which meant that I was considered around medium ability but not bright enough to claim a place in the more prestigious W class.

Like all young boys I fancied myself as having the potential of being a great sportsman and I loved the physical training classes conducted in the commodious, well equipped gymnasium. Due to my slight stature I found that I could shin up ropes and bars with alacrity and took delight in the gymnastic routines such as forward rolls, somersaults over the wooden horse as well as mat work. However when it came to the athletics aspect of the curriculum held on a sports field some distance from the school, I was found sadly wanting.

In order to assess our athletic abilities the Physical Training Instructor, Mr. Acres had devised what he called the 'Standard Tests' consisting of 100 yard sprints, hurdles, long jump and high jump. The benchmark time for the 100 yard sprint was to complete the run in 15 seconds, the long jump required a minimum distance of 12 feet and for the high jump a leap of at least three feet six inches was deemed necessary. Unfortunately, due to my diminutive stature I failed all four tests which saddened me considerably and it was over three years later that I was able to retrieve the situation when we were taken on a seven mile run. I then found that I was able to keep up with the leaders and eventually represented my school house in the one mile and two mile events. It did seem to bear testament to the adage that 'a good big'un will always beat a good little'un' except in the longer distance events where the longer the playing fields the more level they tended to become.

It was at my first term at William Morris that I met a boy who was destined to become a lifelong friend and confidant. John Humphrey became a true friend in every sense of the word and we remained in constant touch until his untimely death from leukaemia over fifty years later.

John and I had shared some similar experiences during the war although tragically his father had been killed whilst serving in the British army in Italy in 1944. He told me that his solitary recollection of his father was of waving goodbye to him at Waterloo Railway Station as he boarded a train to rejoin his unit.

Whilst John lived only about a kilometre from me, the terrace home which his mother rented was severely damaged by a VI flying bomb in 1944. Apparently John and his mother had no time to get into their air raid shelter and when the rescuers arrived they found them sheltering under the dining room table beneath the building rubble.

We had been friends for only a few months when we decided that it would be convenient to ride our bikes to school, weather permitting, and on one occasion when on our way home he asked if I would like to call in and meet his mother.

She struck me as a rather careworn person as she looked up from her sewing machine and greeted me. She was sewing together shirts for a company called Hookways, a local clothing manufacturer. As work was difficult to find at the time she was employed as an outworker presumably being paid a certain amount for each garment she produced. It must have been boring, repetitive work day in day out without any social access to any other fellow employees. Years after her death I was to find out from other members of her family that before the war she and her husband (John's father) had been a vivacious and happy couple, accomplished dancers and the life and soul of every party they attended. She was, alas, like so many others, the victim of the cruelty of war.

On this first visit John showed me a typewritten condolence card signed by King George VI received shortly after their tragic loss.

As the school was a technical school and streaming into likely professions was two years hence, our curriculum also included some unusual subjects, woodwork and metalwork being two of such subjects. I loved woodwork and enjoyed drawing project plans of items to be made and gained even more enjoyment from fashioning pieces of timber into basic items of furniture. This love of timber has lasted to this day.

As a child I had received very little exposure to classical music but our music teacher, Miss Lowe, introduced us to more serious music. After the playing of each 78 RPM vinyl disc, she would describe the life and times of the composer and explain the context in which the composition had been crafted.

Miss Lowe made a great impression on the students in our class, particularly the male members whose admiration of the female form was rapidly awakening from the hibernation of boyhood. She was quite tall with a lithe and beautifully upholstered figure, delicate hands and long auburn hair which trailed down her back in bouncing ringlets. Her smile was so captivating that it tended to light up her whole face with a youthful exuberance. She was gorgeous.

The first recording she played on a small portable record player was 'Schubert's Unfinished Symphony' followed by 'Mendelssohn's Fingals Cave'. I was captivated almost as much by the music as by Miss Lowe herself. In a later lesson on music appreciation she introduced us to Beethoven's Fifth Symphony and described the composer's life and times including his suffering from progressive deafness. Other works from different composers followed and her endeavours to sow an eclectic appreciation of music in our otherwise unmusical minds was, for me an experience for which I am eternally indebted to this charming teacher.

I have to say that although I never really enjoyed my school life I think that my first year at my new high school was a welcome experience, even though it was interrupted to a certain degree by time off due to coughs and colds, something I had long since accepted as part of life.

By July 1949, having broken up for the six weeks school summer holidays I could look back with some satisfaction on my first year at William Morris and was looking forward to the break.

As John lived only ten minutes cycling distance away from my home, he called round one morning and asked if I would be interested in a game of tennis at the nearby hard courts. It surprised me that John was a tennis player for, although he was quite tall, his figure did seem to suggest to the casual observer that any athletic prowess appeared to have been somewhat well camouflaged. However, having located my Dad's old pre-war tennis racquet (strung to the specifications of an old string shopping bag), I rode down to the courts for my first tennis lesson from John.

That summer, John and I must have played two or three times a week and usually we returned to my home for a cup of tea, in fact he soon became a virtual sixth member of the family as my parents and brothers enjoyed his company so much. This closeness to our family endured until the day he died in December, 1999.

END OF SWEET RATIONING

As the summer of 1949 came to a close it was time to return to school but not with any feelings of nervousness as had been the case one year earlier when facing the first day of high school. But one monumental political event took place shortly after resuming school. Chocolates and sweets were no longer subject to rationing. It had been ten years since people in Britain had been able to enter a confectioners shop and not be limited in their consumption of sweets but now the current Labour Government had felt that sufficient stocks had been accumulated to take off all restrictions.

Children and adults alike were wild with excitement on the day that sweet rationing ended. Corner shops were crowded with potential diabetic patients eager to grab whatever confections were available and queues redolent of the war years swarmed the pavements outside confectioners' shops like mosquitoes in a nudist colony. Kids triumphantly returned home, with mouths crammed full of chocolates, lollies, boiled sweets, gob stoppers, humbugs and just about anything that was sweet and for which their bodies had craved for years. Alas, the government had made a serious misjudgement and within a couple of days the shops were as bare as Mother Hubbard's cupboard and rationing was reintroduced, not to be lifted for another four years.

Our attendance at William Morris School was on a two years probationary footing. All students had to give of their best to enable them to remain at the school particularly as there were, as we were often reminded, many children at secondary modern schools who would have been only too willing to be given the opportunity to take our places.

I loved the physical training sessions in the school gymnasium and gained some degree of proficiency at mat work and gymnastics, leaping over the gymnasium's wooden horse. One of the reasons for this ability was due to my having progressed from the Lifeboys and into the ranks of the Boys Brigade Company at our local Methodist Church where gymnastics, arts and crafts, and the playing of a musical instrument in the company's band were encouraged.

The Boys Brigade was established by William Alexander Smith twenty-five years before Baden-Powell wrote the bestselling book 'Scouting for Boys' that sowed the seed for the establishment of the Boy Scouts Movement.

However, whilst the Scouts pursued the outdoor life and self reliance in the field, the Boys' Brigade was a Christian organisation anchored on the twin foundations of discipline and Christian values.

Each Tuesday evening, my brother Jerry and I would cycle (weather permitting) to the local church hall a kilometre or so from our home for Company Drill Practice. By the time I had joined the ranks of the Boys' Brigade, Jerry had progressed through the ranks to become a sergeant and by dint of hard work and immaculate turnout had become one of the few young men to win 'The King's Badge' which was the highest and most prestigious award in the Movement, similar to being a 'Kings Scout' in the Boy Scouts' Movement.

In 1951 he was selected out of all the boys in Britain to become a member of the Boys' Brigade Guard of Honour at Buckingham Palace in the presence of King George VI in recognition of the start of the Festival of Britain. Sadly the King died in February the following year.

My very first drill night happened to coincide with the retirement of the lady who for many years had attended Drill Parade to make tea and coffee for the officers and boys. There was to be a presentation of a bouquet of flowers in recognition of her many years of service. Two Boys' Brigade officers approached me and asked if I would present the bouquet on behalf of the assembled Company. As I had never met the lady concerned, a Mrs Twyman, let alone had an opportunity to sample the quality of her beverages, I declined. The officers were quite upset with me and I can only imagine that I had been selected only because I had blond hair, blue eyes and was so small that I bore a striking resemblance to a page boy. Fortunately the officers never showed any ill will towards me in the years that followed.

Within a few months I had enrolled in the Morse code and Semaphore course and had also been inducted into the Company's band, playing the b flat trumpet alongside my brother. The Brigade gave everyone the opportunity to make new friends and I was lucky enough to renew my friendship with Alex, the boy who had tied me to the school railings eight years before.

By July 1950, after two years at William Morris my probationary period was at an end and parents were invited to the school one evening to discuss with the teaching staff whether their children had satisfied the requirements of their probation and also what technical stream would best be suited to their capabilities and career aspirations.

My parents duly attended the meeting and came home to tell me that I had been accepted to continue at the school for another three years and that we needed to discuss what career path I had in mind.

Most parents whose children were teenagers in the 1950's were no strangers to financial hardship having indelible memories of the depression following the First World War and then the long years of the great depression following the bursting of the American financial bubble of 1929.

It was therefore no surprise that many parents' aspirations for their children was to have a reliable and secure career path which as far as possible could be insulated from the ebb and flow of supply and demand and other global factors.

Britain in the 1950's was far from being an egalitarian society even though some class structures had been diluted to some degree by the common cause engendered by fighting a war. However, the class structure in British society was still alive and well, not necessarily created wittingly by the so called 'upper classes' but to some degree as much by the acceptance of class consciousness by the so called 'lower classes' at the other end of the spectrum.

There was, therefore, another aspect which could be introduced into the equation. It appeared to many people in the lower middle classes that to don a suit, collar, tie and other necessary accoutrements and to travel to the city to a white collar occupation had a lot to commend it, even though senior management of those companies hailed mainly from the top public schools such as Eaton, Harrow, Dulwich and Haileybury etc. Such occupations were regarded by many people as being 'respectable' when compared with working in a trade.

I thought long and hard about what direction I would take, particularly as I very much enjoyed working with my hands and generally pottering around with tools. I considered training to become a plumber which would certainly have meant that I would always have enough work given the severe British winters. However my interest was quickly extinguished as I imagined repairing water pipes in cold, damp attics in mid winter, particularly as I possessed a well established aversion to the cold.

During the first two years at William Morris some of our teachers, knowing that we would eventually be streamed into different classes, had from time to time given us information about the history of certain occupations and I had become interested in the story of how Lloyds of London came about. In fact it held a certain fascination for me.

Edward Lloyd opened a coffee shop in Lombard Street, London, in the seventeenth century to which merchants and shipowners were attracted. The main topic of conversation and worry always centred on the crippling loss a merchant or shipowner would sustain if a ship foundered. After discussions at the coffee shop some merchants got together and decided that they would enter into agreements to spread the risk of loss among several of their number and this eventually led to the establishment of Lloyds of London.

However, I satisfied myself with the notion that as I had a full three years before I would need to worry about looking for my first job, I would be able to whittle down my choices to a career in commerce during that time particularly as the City of London was but a short train journey from my home.

John Humphrey came to the same conclusion and it was decided that we would opt for the Commercial stream, enrolling into Form 3C (commercial) for the coming three years.

September, 1950

In the September of 1950 the Commercial students assembled in the classroom of our new Form Mistress, Miss Ryder the thirty students consisting of an unusual mix of twenty-five girls and only five boys.

Apart from the staple subjects of English language and literature, mathematics, art and physical training we were also introduced to the new subjects into which we had been streamed, namely Pittman's shorthand, typing, commercial practice and book keeping..

It was fascinating to take our first steps in writing shorthand and to observe that we were using exactly the same outlines that Charles

Dickens had been using when he was a parliamentary reporter for a London newspaper in the 1830's.

Typing became quite a challenge for John and myself as inherently the girls possessed fingers which were more dextrous than those possessed by we mere males and when we became proficient enough to 'touch type' without looking at the keyboard, we were given two kinds of test per week. The speed test consisted of rattling away on the ivories for ten minutes at the conclusion of which we totalled up the exact number of words attained. The accuracy test was an exercise where the student typed until a set piece of copy was completed.

Initially John and I were the last to finish the test which enabled those who had completed their work to stare at those poor unfortunates who were still pounding away. It was terribly embarrassing having twenty-eight pairs of eyes boring into the male duet of key thumpers and as such I resolved to do something about it.

I started to arrive at the school an hour earlier each day and sitting at my ancient Remington typewriter, managed to coax a little more speed out of its tired old levers in an endeavour to sharpen my brain and fingers into a more speedy combination. The medicine seemed to have worked as from then on I managed to finish the weekly accuracy test in sublime anonymity whilst John languished, giving a solo performance to the assembled company, repeatedly jamming the levers together whilst thumping away on a dreadful 'Barlock' machine.

Book keeping always seemed to me to have been a mystery enshrouded in an enigma and although I mastered the idea of 'debit the door and credit the window', the finer points of double entry were lost on me. I could never grasp the idea of converting a set of jumbled figures they called a 'trial balance' into a Trading, Profit & Loss and Balance Sheet. To me the word 'trial' possessed a totally different connotation. Nevertheless I persevered and applied the exercises I had learnt by rote and eventually scraped through my final examinations a few years later.

Looking back on the days of those old Remington, Olivetti, Royal and Barlock typewriters it seems almost bizarre that such machines were in use in my lifetime and even more strange when I remember that each desk at school was fitted with an ink well which was refilled on a weekly basis and steel nibbed pens which were supplied by the school.

Fountain pens were allowed to be used but when I came to school with a 'new fangled' Biro ball point pen, the English teacher, Miss Cornu refused to allow me to use it. How times have changed, as I sit here at my computer able to access almost any information with a touch of the keyboard.

Miss Ryder, our Form Mistress was also our Commercial Practice and Typing teacher. She was a woman probably in her early thirties of medium height and slim build. She dressed rather conservatively but not to the point of frumpiness and in my mind's eye I can see her now with her dark hair swept back and kept in place by a rounded comb. She often wore a cream blouse with a pink and white plaid woollen skirt fastened at the waist by a black leather belt.

Although she laughed very little she was endowed with a serene smile which gave an overall impression that the wellbeing of her students was her *raison d'etre*.

Miss Ryder was certainly not the sort of person who would necessarily have stood out in a crowded room but nevertheless in such a situation a person to whom one would be drawn by her winsome smile.

She tried to instil in her pupils the more subtle aspects of good manners and acceptable behaviour which she insisted were of vital importance if we were to succeed in our adult lives, and one incident bears credence to the importance she placed on such precepts.

About a year before our time at William Morris was due to come to an end she asked the five boys in the class to leave the room as she had something very personal she wished to convey to the female members of the class. Accordingly the boys left the room, assuming that Miss Ryder wished to speak to the girls about 'secret women's business'.

When we had the chance to question the girls afterwards they told us that Miss Ryder had been troubled by the fact that some of the girls had allowed their slips to protrude below the hemline of their skirts and that such situations were unseemly given that there were male students in the class.

Sirens and Grey Balloons

Poor Miss Ryder would have been mortified had she known that those supposedly easily shocked male members of her class were not spectators at the girls' netball games merely for the love of the sport. In fact we stood on the sidelines to watch those comely nubile women dressed in skimpy gym knickers and tight blouses dashing around for half an hour or so hoping that their voluptuous breasts would somehow escape the sanctuary of their voluminous bras as they leapt for the high balls. Sadly we were always disappointed although the adage of 'hope springs eternal' was ever fertile in the mind of every fifteen year old male. Such was the innocence of our salad days.

As our Commercial Practice teacher Miss Ryder was also very innovative and in an endeavour to give us a more practical idea of how businesses were run, she split the class into five groups, each group being a business enterprise with a trading name and a trade occupation. It could be for example, a manufacturing company, branch of a bank or an insurance company. Each company had to appoint a manager and company secretary and each company was periodically given details of their expenses, turnover and staff levels etc to enable them to check staff levels against turnover and expenses and to budget for the future.

Every month or so all companies would get together in a sort of forum and give an account of their activities and be questioned by the other companies similar to an Annual General Meeting of shareholders. It was a very useful and practical experience and did much credit to our commercial practice tutor, particularly as our burgeoning shorthand, typing and book keeping skills were able to be utilised.

OUTDOOR LIFE

I also had become very friendly with a really interesting boy at school called Brian Gilbey and loved the fact that he was very much an outdoor type and didn't mind roughing it. He enjoyed cycling long distances and also had a yen for camping.

Unfortunately neither of us possessed a tent or stove and had no pannier bags on our bikes for transporting such equipment, even had we possessed any camping gear. However, my parents gave me a kerosene primus stove for Christmas and my Dad made me a small box trailer which I could tow on the back of my bike. Thus, by March, 1951 we had managed to scrape together a few pieces of camping equipment for our first trip but with the exception of a tent.

In the post war years many goods which we now take for granted were not available in the shops and a lightweight tent was one such item. However, Brian saw in a local ex army shop, a wartime parachute and thought it would make a good tent. He purchased some thick wire which he fashioned into tent pegs and found a washing line which he cut up for guy ropes.

Armed with these accoutrements and a supply of tinned food etc we piled them into my box trailer and started out for a two day camping holiday on the banks of the River Lea at Broxbourne.

Brian had taken the precaution of waterproofing the parachute but we nevertheless hoped that it wouldn't rain. March can be quite cold in England but by the time we arrived at our destination we were quite warm, especially me, as I had been towing the trailer with most of the equipment and when we arrived I was a lather of sweat.

Erecting the tent was quite interesting as the parachute seemed to be intent on resuming its previous occupation as it found itself in all kinds of difficulties adapting to its new role. Also, having pitched the tent, apart from billowing out at even the slightest suggestion of a breeze, there was no opening by which to gain access.

However, we did manage to crawl inside having removed one of the tent pegs and proceeded to place the groundsheet on the floor of the tent. Brian had brought a couple of blankets but I had packed my rather bulky sleeping bag. I am not sure how my parents had come by it but they had given me a training mat made of shiny black rayon with panels filled with kapok which had once been owned by Jose Collins, the famous English singer and star of early British films who had been best known for her starring role in 'Maid of the Mountains'. I managed to sew up the quilt at the bottom and side thus ending up with a rather bulky but very warm sleeping bag.

Life certainly contains many ironies as, in 1967, I escorted an attractive young lady in Sydney, Australia to a ball and she told me that she was to be wearing a very special ball gown made out of material from a dress that her aunt had worn whilst starring in a very popular Australian production of 'Maid of the Mountains.' Furthermore her aunt asked if we would call on her in her Sydney home before the ball so that she could see her niece wearing the dress. Her aunt was none other than Gladys Moncrieff, the famous Australian singer of light opera who was once auditioned by Dame Nellie Melba and had become a household name in Australian entertainment. We spent a couple of hours with Gladys whom I found to be an absolutely charming and gracious lady.

Back at Broxbourne, having completed our chores and taken a walk along the banks of the River Lea we returned to camp and cooked ourselves a sumptuous meal of beans on toast before turning in for the night.

Brian fashioned himself a bed out of his blankets as I snuggled into my sleeping bag and started to doze off to the strains of Brian scratching around trying to find extra items of warm clothing from his limited wardrobe. The mercury dropped lower and lower with each epithet emitted from his side of the tent. The more Brian shivered the more fortunate I was feeling as I luxuriated in my sleeping bag blessing dear Jose Collins as my slumbers beckoned.

Alas, my feeling of wellbeing was abruptly terminated when Brian said "Luddy" (this was my school nick name) "I'm bloody freezing; move over, I'm getting into your bag". Thus he puffed and grunted until we were both sharing the same sleeping bag. It was dreadfully cramped and we joked that it might facilitate matters if one of us breathed in whilst the other breathed out but we gave up the idea as synchronisation was impossible.

The parachute threatened to take off during the night and it even rained a little but by far the worst hazard actually emanated from the copious amount of baked beans we had consumed. Both of us were given to billows of flatulence and sharing the same sleeping bag didn't help matters as we farted the night away like a couple of old dray horses en route to their next delivery. I am sure that the parachute hadn't encompassed such turbulence since the last time it had been airborne during active service.

Peter Hurdwell

ERRAND BOY

My mother had always purchased her groceries from a retail store a couple of kilometres from our home. The company of A.J.Gibson & Co. had been established for many years and when my parents settled in Chingford in 1935, Gibsons was the nearest grocery shop to their home.

Mum had always used their services during the war and had become a loyal customer, a loyalty somewhat reinforced by the fact that if a certain grocery item was difficult to obtain or was in limited supply, loyal customers received preferential consideration.

It was always quite a chore for my mother to make the trip to Gibsons particularly when her only means of making the journey was by walking the two kilometres which in itself was not a difficulty, but the walk home laden with the family's weekly supplies of food and household items was another matter.

I am not sure whether my father's creation of a box trailer for my bike had originated with any sinister intentions in mind but it did appear more than just a coincidence that having been given the trailer Mum conceived the brilliant idea that, armed with the shopping list I should ride down to Gibsons, pile the groceries into the trailer and deliver them home each week. I acceded to her request although with a very ill grace which did me no credit. Thus I was made responsible for the family's shopping.

As a result I came to know the shop's manager very well and after a few months Mr. Baker offered me the job as errand boy, even though I was still very small for my age.

I took the job which involved delivering groceries and other provisions on a heavy errand bike which must have been yearning for retirement even before the First World War let alone after the Second. The bike was built with a large metal carrier on the front where boxes of groceries could be packed. For two hours on a Friday evening and nine hours on a Saturday I received the princely sum of eight shillings and sixpence per week which in today's British currency was forty-five pence. However with tips from customers it could total about seventy-five pence on average. Obviously the buying power of those seventy-five pence cannot be compared with today's inflated prices.

Sirens and Grey Balloons

Although it was quite an impost on my time, particularly being at work all day each Saturday, it did give me welcome financial independence even though I gave my mother five shillings a week towards my keep, part of which she put by for a new suit when it eventually came time for me to commence full time employment.

I enjoyed working for Gibsons for I was out in the fresh air most of the time and Mr Baker was a very fair person to work for. I initially had problems with the errand bike as I wasn't quite tall enough to fully sit in the saddle and was forced to waggle my bum from side to side as my undersized legs pumped the pedals.

There was one occasion early in my employment, which must have encouraged my legs to hurry up and grow. I was instructed to deliver a quarter of a hundredweight (17 kilograms) of seed potatoes to an address in Woodford, quite some distance from the shop. I had almost finished piling the potatoes into the front carrier when the weight of the load started to lift the rear wheel off the ground. I somehow managed to stabilise the load and hastily mounted the bike and set off on my journey but in order to keep the load stable I had to keep my weight on the saddle.

I was progressing quite well until I took a short cut up a bridle path through a wood, but as I approached a short but steep hillock I accelerated to keep up my momentum. Nearing the pinnacle I needed to make one final thrust which necessitated lifting my bum from the saddle. Unfortunately this made the front of the bike heavier than its rear, bucking me off my steed and sending me crashing to the ground where I rolled backwards down the hill with a posse of frantic seed potatoes in hot pursuit.

BOYS BRIGADE CAMP

With each Saturday being committed to my errand boy's job it meant that I had to organise my time to enable me to attend Boys Brigade activities during the week plus attend to my school homework which was now starting to intensify. Nevertheless by the middle of July 1951 our school broke up for the summer holidays and we were able to attend the Boys Brigade annual summer camp on the Isle of Wight.

Peter Hurdwell

I had not visited the Isle of Wight before and it was quite an adventure to board the train at London's Waterloo Station with the other boys, decked out in our Boys Brigade uniforms bound for Portsmouth where we boarded the 'Ryde Queen' ferry. The ferry chugged its ponderous progress across The Solent to Ryde where we took an ancient steam train which meandered its way to Bembridge via Shanklin and thence to St Helens.

Our first port of call after arriving at the camp site at Guildford Park, St Helens was to a large hut used for the storage of bedding which we were to use during our two weeks stay. We were each issued with a palliasse made from thick cotton duck material into which we stuffed copious amounts of straw that transformed them into mattresses on which we were expected to sleep for the duration of the holiday. It struck me at the time that had I been able, I would love to have taken Jose Collins sleeping bag with me for this holiday. However, armed with our mattresses and blankets we were marched to our tents that were lined up on the perimeter of the field in which the camp had been set up.

The bell tents in which we slept were spacious enough for six persons and instead of a groundsheet, wooden duck boards had been fastened into place which kept the inside of the tent dry during wet weather.

Each night we attended an evening service in the marquee which had been erected as a dining area and other indoor activities. Following the service the duty bugler sounded the Last Post as the sun slipped over the horizon. I enjoyed that part of the day and took some delight in playing the last post when called upon to do so.

And then as twilight faded into darkness we nestled down under canvas as the aromas of the meadow and canvas competed with the smell of the straw now seeping from the palliasses beneath us.

Being an organisation where discipline was an essential element, we had to undergo a kit inspection every morning and evening which I found rather irksome, particularly as we were on holiday and not on drill parade.

Another aspect which rather rankled was that our Company's Captain, Mr Twyman, appeared to feel that the boys were there for his convenience and insisted that he be waited upon with the other officers at mealtimes.

However, notwithstanding these minor annoyances we had a great time and enjoyed the camaraderie, visits to the tuck shop and the daily swimming parades on St Helens Beach not far from the stone fort situated a few hundred metres out to sea. It was close to this fort that Nelson's flagship HMS Victory lay at anchor having returned from Trafalgar with Nelson's body prior to his being transported to the mainland for a state funeral in London.

Looking out to sea up the Solent we sometimes saw ships of gargantuan proportions compared with HMS Victory as they steamed into Southampton from New York, the most spectacular being the three funnelled Queen Mary and the two funnelled Queen Elisabeth and Mauretania. These ships made the ground beneath our feet shudder as they blew their foghorns whilst a couple of kilometres off the coast.

CLASS VISIT TO THE CITY

The school summer holidays were over all too soon, particularly as prior to resuming school, members of our Class would have been scrambling to finish their school break homework bequeathed to them by some of the teachers prior to the vacation. The motive might have been to ensure that their minds didn't rust during the vacation or to teach them a valuable lesson in the evils of procrastination.

We returned to school invigorated and ready to strike off another year from the calendar which separated us from the restrictions of school life to the perceived freedom and sunlit uplands of the workforce.

During the holidays Miss Ryder must have donned her thinking cap in an endeavour to infuse some further interest into her lessons and, as always she managed to succeed.

In quite a democratic manner unusual for those times, she floated the idea of making a trip to the City of London to visit some historic places of interest in order to give us a feel of the central business district of the great metropolis. She assumed, quite correctly, that most of the students in her class would gravitate towards working in the City and her suggestion was very well received.

Prior to her taking up a career in teaching she had worked at an old and well established insurance broking house in London which meant that she obviously possessed a good feel for the practical side of how commerce was run in the great City.

It was on a cold November day that almost every member of the class assembled at the main Walthamstow Railway Station in Hoe Street and caught the steam train to London's Liverpool Street Station.

We visited a number of interesting places that day starting with the Billingsgate Fish Market which was the hub of London's wholesale fish distribution system and at one time used to be the largest fish market in the world. It was extremely cold on the market floor and deep freeze areas and we were more than happy to quit the location and take the short walk to 'The Monument' nearby.

The Monument was built by Christopher Wren in the 1670's to commemorate the great fire of London of 1666. It was two hundred and two feet tall, being the exact distance from where the great fire had started in nearby Pudding Lane. We all dutifully climbed up the three hundred or so steps to the top of the edifice where I recall meeting a middle aged American tourist and his wife. His name was Helmut Land and hailed from Lanioni, Iowa. We chatted for a while and he wrote his name and address on a piece of paper and told me that I would be very welcome to stay with his family if ever I went to the States. I never took him up on his offer as I might just as well have been invited to the moon, so geographically circumscribed were our lives at that time.

Our next place of interest was to St Andrews Undershaft Church off Cheapside where we saw a statue immortalising John Stow, the historian and chronicler very famous in the sixteenth century for his writings about the City of London. By tradition, the quill pen held in the statue's hand is renewed at regular intervals to encourage him to continue his writings.

As Miss Ryder had previously worked for a Lloyds Broking house, we were bound to visit Lombard Street where Edward Lloyd's coffee house had originally been situated. I was surprised to note that at the time of our visit the street was actually paved with rubber tiles. We admired the blue historical plaque on the wall denoting where he had carried out his business in the seventeenth century before walking the short distance to what was then the current Lloyd's of London Building.

The building which we visited and where "The Room" was situated was in Leadenhall Street and had been opened by George V and Queen Mary in 1928. It was interesting to see the brokers and underwriters at their underwriting boxes, all in clerical grey business suits and, of course the employees who ran the organisation. They were dressed in bright red cloaks and were called 'waiters' just as they would have been in Edward Lloyd's day when he ran a coffee house just around the corner.

Since then the building has been replaced by the newer Lloyds building nearby which was opened by the Queen Mother in 1957. Whilst this gracious building is still used by Lloyds as an office centre, yet another building is situated about fifty metres away. The latest Lloyds building was designed by Richard Rogers and was opened in 1986. This is where business in 'The Room' is still transacted today. Underwriters and brokers alike now refer to this building as 'the gasworks', an apt nick name as it bears a startling resemblance to a gas works and is surely the most ghastly monstrosity ever to visually pollute the city skyline. It is significant that this building was the one Lloyds building which royalty didn't feel inclined to open.

A short walk took us from Lloyds down to Fleet Street and up an alleyway which led to the home of Dr Samuel Johnson, the great English essayist and compiler of the first English Dictionary. As there was quite a crowd of us we didn't go in for the tour although we did retreat from the small square in which the great man's house was situated and back along the alley to 'Ye Olde Cheshire Cheese' pub where he used to fraternise with his friends.

On the way back to Liverpool Street Station we took a look at the Old Bailey, another iconic building mentioned in historical and fictional books for centuries. As we looked up at the statue of a woman holding the scales of justice atop the building I had at that time no idea that in 1827 two of my ancestors had been summoned to the Old Bailey and been condemned to death by hanging for sheep stealing. Fortunately for them their sentences were commuted to transportation to Sydney Cove where presumably labourers were needed for work in the newly established colony of New South Wales. Having served their time they eventually settled in Bathurst, a country town some two hundred and fifty kilometres west of Sydney.

The day out in London was a great success and Miss Ryder's attempt to lay the foundation of an interest in English commercial history was not wasted. For me I can only say that it whetted my appetite for further discoveries especially when years later I was to make my annual pilgrimages back to Britain from my new home in Australia.

Author's maternal grandparents

Author's Mother outside Percy Gorton's shop in 1913

Peter Hurdwell

Maternal grandparents grave: Windlesham Church

Author's Mother aged 17

Peter Hurdwell

20 Monkswood Avenue, Waltham Abbey

Private Hurdwell at Brigade HQ

Author's Mother with son Jerry outside 7 Blackthorne Drive in 1936

Peter Hurdwell

The author and Johnny Norris outside Brigade HQ offices

Mr Davis with his wife and son

The Austin three tonner in Denmark

NATO Exercise 1957

Peter Hurdwell

The Little Mermaid - Copenhagan

Sirens and Grey Balloons

Chingford Bomb Damage – 1940 - 1945

Peter Hurdwell

Chingford Bomb Damage – 1940 - 1945

Sirens and Grey Balloons

Chingford Bomb Damage – 1940 - 1945

Peter Hurdwell

Reg Hurdwell's birthplace

Sirens and Grey Balloons

1910 Rover Motorbike

Our family in 1948

Peter Hurdwell

Police Constable Reg Hurdwell

One of the world's first Speed Cops

Peter Hurdwell

Granny and Grandad Hurdwell in 1941

Sirens and Grey Balloons

The author aged two years in 1939

Peter Hurdwell

Kath from Windlesham Post Office taken in 1976

Sirens and Grey Balloons

> **Chingford (C.E.) Infts' School**
>
> Report   Date April 1945
>
> Name Peter Hurdwell
>
> Read.   Fair
> Arith   V Good
> Writing   V Good
> English   Good
> Geography   Good
> History   Good
> General Knowledge. Good
>
> Progress   Peter is intelligent and if his Reading was better, could do more than he does. He tries very hard and improvement is steady
>
> Conduct   Good.
>
> signed Class Teacher
>   E. M. Holt
> Hd Mistress,
>   L. Reader

School Report 1945

CHAPTER VII DEATH OF THE KING

In England in 1952 the vast majority of people were staunch monarchists not necessarily because of the traditional principle of the monarchical system but more for an admiration of the incumbent king and queen whom they held in very high regard. King George VI and Queen Elizabeth seemed to have typified the British tradition of 'stiff upper lip' during the war years, particularly during the dark days of the German blitz on London. During that time the King and Queen steadfastly refused to leave London's Buckingham Palace for a safer haven in the country, preferring to stay with their subjects and face the onslaught of the Nazi attack. When a wall of the palace had been demolished by Luftwaffe bombs, the Queen merely noted that she had a better view of London now that the wall was out of the way. She and the King travelled from bomb site to bomb site and maintained constant touch with those whose homes had been destroyed.

Also, many people admired the king immensely as he was a reluctant monarch having acceded to the throne following the abdication of his brother Edward VIII. He also suffered from a stammer which became a constant worry as he became a figure more in the public eye than ever before.

Each Christmas Day the King gave the traditional speech at 3pm from Sandringham. When he delivered his speech 'live' on radio, people's hearts went out to him as they willed him not to stumble over the text. Ironically his speech therapist was Lionel Logue, an Australian who appears to have done a great job although never once did we hear the king refer to anyone as "cobber" or "mate".

In late 1951 the King underwent surgery for the removal of a lung following his contracting cancer and appeared to have recovered quite well, much to the relief of the general community. However, sadly a few months later having farewelled his eldest daughter Elizabeth at London Airport en route for her tour of the African Continent, he returned to Sandringham where he died on 6th February, 1952.

The mood in Britain was sombre following his death at the early age of fifty-six. People turned out in their thousands to walk past his coffin as it lay in state on a catafalque in the Great Hall Westminster prior being transported by rail to Windsor's St Georges Chapel where the funeral service took place.

At school we sat in our classrooms and listened to the funeral service on the radio. There were outpourings of genuine grief for a much loved and very decent human being who had borne a cross with distinction; a burden which he could never have envisaged prior to his brother's abdication.

Although traditionally new monarchs in the United Kingdom are not crowned until a considerable time after their accession to the throne, it didn't take long for people to wish to see the new queen as they flocked to functions where the Queen and Prince Phillip were scheduled to attend. However it would be another sixteen months before the Queen would be crowned in Westminster Abbey and it was not until the beginning of 1953 that the first coins bearing her image were minted.

The advent of the Second Elizabethan Era was rather special for me as a member of the Boys' Brigade. Over the previous three years I had attended and passed quite a number of courses including Morse code, semaphore, trumpet playing and conducting company drill. As a result I became one of the first boys in the Boys' Brigade organisation to be awarded the Queens Badge. I was very proud to be following in my Brother Jerry's footsteps.

It is a truism that the older we become time seems to speed up and whilst it hadn't reached the break-neck speed people experience in later years, nevertheless even as a teenager I found that my fourth year at high school was suddenly coming to an end.

As I looked back on the school year which had just passed I felt quite happy with the results. Although I had not attained star status by any means in the class, I felt comfortable with the end of term examination results although book keeping and certain algebraic equations seemed to still transgress my own ideas of logic. As this had only been the penultimate year of my formal education it meant that the next and final year would by crucial.

Peter Hurdwell

The annual Boys' Brigade camp on the Isle of Wight had been arranged as usual. Alex and I were very much looking forward to seeing the Island again together with boys from our company and towards the end of July 1952 we arrived at the same camp site and prepared for two weeks fun. Although Jerry was awaiting his call up papers for his stint in the Army, he had not yet been summoned to army barracks and so he joined us, arriving late in the evening on his 125 cc Francis Barnett motor bike.

After a few days it became abundantly clear to a few of us at least that our Company Captain's delusions of grandeur so annoyingly displayed during the previous year's camp, had taken an even firmer grip on his psyche to the point where his didactic comments and sarcastic remarks were seldom warranted and always unwelcome. He was given to making disparaging remarks about members of the company in front of other boys which, whilst possibly being acceptable within the confines of a school classroom, were totally unacceptable at a holiday camp where boys were there to enjoy themselves.

The daily kit inspections continued unabated and after a few days there were rumblings of discontent within the ranks as the boys felt that they had saved up their pocket money to attend a camp to enjoy a holiday and not put up with a leader who was captivated by his own importance and intoxicated by his own rhetoric.

By now I was a senior NCO and was unable to indicate to the boys what I felt but Alex and I together with another senior boy decided that this would be the last Boys' Brigade Camp we would attend if Mr Twyman was going to attend the camp next year. We had no plans to undermine his captaincy but took the more pragmatic view that in a year's time we would be in the permanent workforce with only two weeks holiday per year. We did not want to squander two precious weeks undertaking a holiday we could not enjoy.

THE DEFINING YEAR

September dawned and once back at school we all knew that this would be a defining year in our lives as we undertook the transition from school to becoming members of the permanent workforce. However we had a further ten months before the final examinations in the June, of 1953.

Sirens and Grey Balloons

As we were students at a technical school, the newly introduced General Certificate of Education, whilst applying to the general subjects such as English, mathematics, geography, history and science etc did not encompass the needs of students who had undertaken more specific technical subjects like shorthand, typing, book keeping and commerce. Thus, the students in our class were engaged in subjects which were outside the G C E parameters. Accordingly we were advised that our skills in all subjects would best be reflected by sitting the Royal Society of Arts examinations and our studies in the fifth year were targeted towards that end.

One bright aspect of my last year of school was that I had appeared to have outgrown my weakness for coughs, colds and general chest infections, in fact I counted myself as being no longer a 'chesty boy'. In later years I have enjoyed very robust health and I can look back with gratitude to the earlier poor health in my life. Since then I have never taken good health for granted and have gone to considerable lengths to maintain fitness by strenuous regular exercise and a healthy diet.

One period in 1952 was to test just how well people could cope with the English climate. That was the great London smog.

THE GREAT LONDON SMOG

We were in a shorthand class taking down dictation from our teacher, Mr. O'Hea when the school bell rang and we were advised that the atmosphere outside, having been decidedly murky in the early morning had deteriorated. We were told that the fog was expected to become even thicker and that school lunch would be served early to enable students to make their own way home afterwards whilst conditions still allowed.

As we left the classroom and walked through the playground to the refectory we noticed how heavy the fog had become. Within an hour it had advanced in intensity to have become a real 'pea souper' with visibility down to about three metres.

Having resided in London for the whole of our lives we were quite used to fogs but this struck us as being quite out of the ordinary as we started to wend our way homewards.

Peter Hurdwell

I lost John after a few minutes but as all motor traffic had ground to a standstill I decided to find the main road towards Chingford and by the process of walking with one foot on the kerb and one in the gutter was able to make quite good headway until the challenge of a road intersection had to be negotiated. By now visibility was so restricted that one could be standing under a street light but the light could not be seen although one could touch its outline to identify its shape.

Intersections were very difficult to negotiate. It might sound simple to maintain a straight line from one side of the road to the other but at the time when nothing at all was visible, all sense of direction seemed to disappear into the murkiness.

After wandering along in this fashion, sometimes bumping into other pedestrians and occasionally tripping up kerbs, I noticed that my mouth seemed to feel 'gritty' and a slight taste of rotten eggs seemed to pervade the atmosphere.

An eerie silence had taken hold as cars, buses and even ambulances ground to a halt giving way to an unusual air of hollowness, punctuated by the occasional oath as some poor soul tripped down a gutter or collided with a careless tree which had impeded his homeward progress.

About halfway home my face appeared quite moist and my eyes, battling the mixture of sulphur dioxide, nitrogen dioxide and soot plus the freezing temperature, formed tears which dripped in small rivulets down my face leaving a black tidemark on either bank. By this time I was looking forward to getting home and sitting in front of a welcoming fire in the hearth.

Arriving home was somewhat of an anticlimactic experience because there was no fire. The heavy fog had descended to chimney pot level, stifling the escape of our fire's smoke into the outside atmosphere. Added to this was a damp and clammy feeling in the house and even indoors the visibility had been restricted to a few murky metres. I looked at myself in the mirror and was shocked at what I saw. I could at that moment have successfully auditioned for the then famous 'Black and White Minstrel Show'. Having washed my face I observed that the flannelette face washer was as black as pitch.

Sirens and Grey Balloons

The fog lifted after a few days but it left in its wake a trail of human devastation and sadness. Four thousand people in London had died as a result of the smog but later it was estimated that overall, twelve thousand Londoners has lost their lives through smog related illnesses.

Naturally we were unable to attend school for the duration of the fog but being cold and dank indoors and hardly any visibility outside, we were not able to enjoy our enforced holiday.

The aftermath of 'the great London smog' as it came to be known, gave rise to many personal accounts of people's humorous experiences during those five days.

One told of a lorry driver and his mate driving near the London Docks when their truck was suddenly blanketed by fog. As it thickened the driver became apprehensive about driving into a canal or ditch in the dock area. Having stopped the vehicle he asked his mate to find out where they were. His mate duly opened the passenger door and hopped onto the running board and into some water which prompted them to abandon the lorry and make their way home on foot.

When they returned to the truck a few days later they found that they had parked the truck next to a horse trough.

Three years later Britain passed the Clean Air Act which amongst other precautions forbade the use of domestic coal fires.

FINAL MONTHS AT SCHOOL

When 1953 arrived I knew that this was to be the year in which my formal education was to end and everyone in our class supercharged their efforts for the next seven months. Greater attention was shown during lessons and the volume of homework increased considerably.

The first priority for students was to hone their skills not only by increasing their shorthand speeds but also the accuracy of their shorthand outlines. Mr. O'Shea, a very inclusive and somewhat laid back teacher took great pains to impress upon us that we would be marked in the final examinations not only on the transcription of our notes but also on the accuracy of our shorthand outlines.

Miss Ryder gave us more and more speed and accuracy typing tests which enhanced our speeds to the point where each person in the class could maintain a speed of at least thirty words per minute. She also gave us practical advice when testing our business acumen during the discussion sessions involving the 'companies' we were running in the Commerce class.

I was always interested in English literature and for some years had kept a notebook of words I came across in my reading, jotting down any unfamiliar word to enable me to bolster my vocabulary. For the coming Royal Society of Arts examinations we were required to study one play and one novel. The novel was Robert Louis Stevenson's 'Kidnapped' an interesting book presenting few pitfalls when being analysed for the examination.

Shakespeare's 'Julius Caesar' was the play selected and it proved more complex but probably more enthralling, particularly as our English master, Mr. Westlake engaged the class in an analysis not only of the plot but also the nobility of Brutus. He also encouraged us to discuss the political landscape of the times in which the events were enacted. We learned great chunks of the play and speeches of the main characters and most of us were suitably rewarded when we took our first glance at the examination paper.

Algebra was always a problem for me with simultaneous and quadratic equations becoming the enemy from the first time I was introduced to their vagaries. I could never comprehend why, when working out these sums, one had to introduce letters from the English alphabet, imprison them within the confines of two brackets only to repatriate them at the end of the exercise where they joined another jumble of letters and numbers.

Algebra graphs were equally troublesome and reminded me very much of childhood birthday party games. We used to play 'pinning the donkey's tail' which involved a board being set up on which there was the outline of a donkey minus a tail. The participant was blindfolded and handed a piece of cardboard in the shape of a donkey's tail. The idea was to pin the cardboard tail as near to its rightful position as possible, the winner being the one whose effort was closest.

Sirens and Grey Balloons

Try as I might, my attempts at algebra graphs met with far less success than my blindfold efforts at children's parties.

THE CORONATION

At the beginning of June the much awaited coronation of Queen Elizabeth II took place and the high spirits of her subjects were palpable almost rivalling the end of war celebrations eight years before. People flocked to London to gain a vantage point from which to view the new queen as she passed by in her Coronation Coach which had been ridden in by her ancestors since the first time it was used to crown King George IV in 1820.

As she stepped into the coach, used only five times since its first official outing, her mind must surely have looked back to the last time it was used sixteen years before when her father and mother rode in it at their coronation. Now her father's reign was being consigned into the pages of history as a new Elizabethan era was being heralded.

With the exception of my father, the family was glued to our nine inch (22cm) black and white television set as we viewed the procession making its progress in the pouring rain to Westminster Abbey where the crowning ceremony took place.

The reason for our father's absence was that all police were called up to London to supervise the crowds. We were all very amused when next day there appeared a photograph in one of the daily newspapers depicting a little boy sheltering from the rain under Dad's police cape, his head protruding between the buttons.

Naturally the evening television coverage was full to overflowing with the day's events but by then I had withdrawn to my room with my nose buried in my studies in readiness for the forthcoming examinations.

It was at this time that arrangements were being made for the next Boys Brigade Camp on the Isle of Wight and it was assumed by the officers that the senior NCO's would again participate. However three of us advised the officers that we had made alternative arrangements for our summer holidays that year and would not be available. Pressed for our reasons we reluctantly told them that we would no longer go to the camp if Mr Twyman, our captain, was to attend.

The officers then asked us why we resented the captain and each of us when questioned separately gave similar answers.

Unbeknown to us, three of the officers approached the Captain and broached our concerns but apparently he was obdurate that he would not alter the way he conducted himself.

Subsequently at a meeting of all the boys in our Company everyone was sounded out about their feelings and it was almost unanimously agreed that as far as the camp was concerned, very few boys wished to attend.

A few days later at the next evening Drill Parade we were told that our Captain had been dismissed by his fellow officers and a new captain had been appointed.

As our holiday had been booked already we were unable to attend the camp but advised that in future years we would be more than happy to attend.

The week of our final examinations arrived and for three hours morning and afternoon for the whole week we sat the exams.

John had given me some tuition in algebra and book keeping in exchange for my helping him along with his French. For me the tuition paid off quite well as I gained a pass in both papers.

In algebra, having learned some of the equations by rote, I went through the required motions and made as good a try as possible but when it came to the algebra graph I hadn't a clue as to what was required so decided to plot a conventional and not an algebraic graph instead. I was later to learn that this had been a trick question and that a conventional graph was what had been required.

Regarding book keeping, I tackled the trial balance and for the very first time in three years, managed to balance my Trading, Profit and Loss and Balance Sheets. I couldn't believe my great good fortune and felt as excited as Archimedes after his discovery of the theory of water displacement. However I refrained from ripping off my school uniform and running naked through the streets of Walthamstow.

During the next week I travelled up to London for an interview at a large insurance broking house, having been introduced by Miss Ryder. The interview seemed to go well and I was later offered a position with that company. However, after discussions with my parents I decided to join a smaller insurance broking company which promised a wider sphere of experience.

On 17th July, 1953 I left school for the last time with a feeling of sadness that I had never previously contemplated.

C.A Mace, the teaching guru of the twentieth century once said "education is that which we retain when we have forgotten all we learned".

Looking back on William Morris Technical School, apart from forging lifelong friendships, I feel that I had benefitted greatly from the experience as it had provided me with some direction and skills sufficient to enable me to navigate the future uncharted waters which life was yet to reveal.

Peter Hurdwell

CHAPTER VIII FIRST JOB

Before starting my first job I was able to enjoy a wonderful camping holiday with Alex and another friend from the Boys Brigade, at Whitecliff Bay on the Isle of Wight. It was the first time any of us had been away on our own for any length of time and it seemed fitting that we should be away from home on the eve of taking our place in the permanent workforce.

Having returned home we all went our separate ways in terms of our careers, Alex joining a printing company in Fleet Street whilst the other friend and I joined insurance broking companies in the City.

On the 10th of August, 1953 I donned my new blue pin striped suit, a recent acquisition from Burtons, the local gentlemen's outfitters, and felt very smart in the accompanying white shirt with stiff starched detachable collar.

Boarding the train at the local Higham's Park Railway Station I felt quite nervous and even more so as I walked in some trepidation from Liverpool Street Station, along Houndsditch and into Fenchurch Street.

The offices of S H Cannon & Company were opposite Fenchurch Street Railway Station and appeared very dark and dingy as they were situated on what was euphemistically described as the Lower Ground Floor. It appeared to become even gloomier as I descended the steps and I thought that 'dungeon' would have been a more appropriate description.

However, having gained the main entrance to the offices I found the area to be well illuminated, partly due to the high wattage light globes but also the glass tiles in the ceiling which were also the paving tiles for the footpath above. The atmosphere was one of a well lit subterranean toilet, particularly as the noise of the typewriters had to compete with the footfall of the thousands of pedestrians who traversed the pavement above. Quite possibly Tolkien may have had such a place in mind when he wrote 'The Hobbit'.

There were only ten members of staff, comprising Mr Cannon, the Managing Director and whose name the company bore, two directors, the broking manager, company secretary and myself, being the office

143

junior, the term 'office boy' no longer being in vogue. The female staff comprised two secretaries, the company secretary's assistant and a female office junior. A strict protocol of formality in offices was normal for this era and managers were always referred to as 'Mister' and the female staff, however junior, as 'Miss' although younger male staff were referred to merely by their surname. Thus I was addressed by the male managerial staff as just 'Hurdwell' although the girls called me 'Pete'.

Having been introduced to members of staff my duties were outlined, and whilst not promising to be overburdened with opportunities for technical tutelage in the sphere of insurance, they did afford some latitude for learning some insurance terminologies. Most of my time, however, was spent filing, going to the local post office to purchase postage stamps for which the office had an insatiable appetite, and posting the daily correspondence which had been churned out by the secretaries.

The first day seemed an eternity and I felt a little downcast as I returned home. On the homeward train journey I had time to mull over the day and restore the hope that hum drum office work would give way eventually to more interesting and technical tasks.

Having commenced work on the 10th of August, I was very much looking forward to the coming Friday, the 14th for two reasons. My first pay day fell on my sixteenth birthday and upon that very day, having obtained my learner drivers' licence, I was about to drive a motor bike for the first time. On my birthday I received my first pay packet of three pounds twelve and sixpence and hurried home to mount my brother's motor bike.

By now, my brother Jerry had been called up for service in the British Army and had been posted to the Suez Canal Zone area in Egypt. He was generous enough to let me drive his motor bike in his absence and after a hurried meal I threw my leg over the saddle, and kick started the Francis Barnett. I was overwhelmed by an ethereal feeling of freedom as the wind ruffled my hair and I experienced the thrill of twisting the throttle to gain more speed.

Looking back, although the machine was only four years old, its technology really belonged to a bygone age. There was no suspension over the rear wheel and the girder front forks would have been more at home in a motor cycle museum as would the hand change gear lever and the 125 cc Villiers engine whose spark plug whiskered up on a seemingly regular basis.

However, I was very grateful indeed as the machine gave me the opportunity to travel over a much wider area. It enabled me to visit towns and villages in the surrounding countryside well beyond the limits previously attained on my push bike. Nevertheless for the first few months I rode the motor bike unaccompanied until I passed my driving test which then enabled me to take a pillion passenger.

After a few days the broking manager asked me if I wished to accompany him to the 'holy of holies' namely the Underwriting Room at Lloyds. Although I had been there before whilst in Miss Ryder's class, the impact on that occasion had been somewhat diluted by the size of our group. However, on this day I was to be given a personal tour.

I was enthralled to witness the activity in 'The Room' as brokers sat next to underwriters at their ancient looking underwriting boxes and for the first time I was able to look up at the rostrum in the middle of 'The Room' and see the 'Lutine Bell'. The 80 pound bell had been salvaged from a French vessel 'La Lutine' finding its way into Lloyds some time later. Traditionally the bell is struck once to herald bad news and twice to announce good news.

The waiters looked resplendent in their scarlet robes and I was schooled by the broking manager on how to contact him whilst he was in the confines of 'The Room' bearing in mind that strangers were not allowed to stray past the entrance to the inner sanctum unless authorised.

If wishing to make contact with our broking representative I had to pass on the request to a waiter who in turn wrote the name and company to which that person belonged, on an electronic pad, whereupon the name was announced on a loud speaker and the handwritten image appeared on a central notice board in 'The Room'. It was undoubtedly the pinnacle of high technology for the 1950's.

I had only been with the company for a short time when I struck up a conversation with a petite cockney girl called Moira Aldridge. Her long dark hair and twinkling eyes matched her vivacious, bubbling sense of humour and we soon became good friends. American servicemen were still stationed in the United Kingdom at the time and she had met several American Servicemen and as a consequence, had developed a yen to migrate to The States which she did a few years later.

Mr Cannon made only a few appearances at the office each week. Unfortunately he had a predilection for hard liquor which was not necessarily confined to the odd whisky after lunch in fact he sometimes looked somewhat the worse for wear even when he first arrived at the office during his spasmodic attendances.

On some occasions I was called upon to look after the ancient 'eyeball' switchboard and normally coped quite well. However, if I was on duty when Mr Cannon arrived I sat in fear and trepidation of his picking up his phone and telling me to get a certain client or friend on the phone. Often his words were so slurred I had to ask him several times to repeat the name in question. Alas, he was not a happy inebriate and used to bellow rather unflattering remarks down the line, such remarks striking me like a dagger.

Not long after joining the company we received word that the office was to move from Fenchurch Street to more commodious accommodation nearby on the 4th Floor at 6/8 Crutched Friars.

The new offices were a vast improvement on the previous dungeon. Not only did the sunshine and natural daylight give it a more uplifting air but we could also look out over the rooftops and see other buildings near the River Thames, in fact the Tower of London was but a few hundred metres distant. Moira and I used to sometimes take our sandwiches and have lunch sitting on park benches overlooking the Tower Moat.

At the outset, I set a goal of eventually becoming an ACII (Associate of the Chartered Insurance Institute) and accordingly made enquiries about evening classes. As John Humphrey and I were of the same mind, we approached the Institute and after giving it our particulars were advised that they did not recognise the Royal Society of Arts examinations we had spent so many years to pass. We were therefore obliged to go to evening classes at the institute in Aldermanbury, quite near St Pauls Cathedral.

On our first visit to the Institute we were amazed to see bomb sites and evidence of the devastation of German bombing during the wartime blitz, even though the war had been over for eight years. It was quite strange to see such massive damage all around the area and to witness the great dome of St Pauls standing as if in defiance of all that the Luftwaffe could throw at it.

After a few months we sat the compulsory preliminary examination and felt quite insulted that our RSA examination certificates had not been recognised. The standard required of the RSA far exceeded the Insurance Institute preliminary examinations and we passed easily, albeit having lost a whole year from the opportunity of working for the 'real' insurance examinations.

After about eight months I started to realise that although working for a small insurance broking company offered a wider exposure to different types of insurance, such experience was limited to smaller insurance accounts with no opportunity in the area of national and multinational programmes. I therefore decided to look for another position with a larger broker recognised in the national and international market.

The building in Crutched Friars, whilst being salubrious by comparison to the previous office in Fenchurch Street, was still quite quaint in other ways and the ancient elevator system was one such contraption in question. Although it was automatic in terms of not requiring a lift attendant, it was a tedious task to gain access as one was required to slide open two sets of grilles and to close them when leaving the lift. Thus it was my habit to walk or run down or up the spiral staircase which wound its way around the lift shaft.

For several months I had noticed that under the floor at the front of the lift itself was situated a red button which kept me constantly wondering what would happen if the button were pressed as the lift was engaged in its ponderous journey.

One afternoon I was told to deliver a message to our broking manager at Lloyds and, having returned to our building walked, up the winding stairway. Upon reaching the third floor, what should I see but the lift on its journey transporting Mr Cannon down to street level. I was able to

Sirens and Grey Balloons

tell the identity of the passenger by the black shoes, grey trousers and the lower portion of his bespoke tailored beige Crombie overcoat.

I struck! Thrusting my hand through the steel latticework I pushed the red button whereupon the lift juddered to its untimely halt leaving a doubtless inebriated Mr Cannon marooned betwixt the fourth and third floors.

Knowing that he could not possibly have worked out what had occurred let alone who was responsible, I scurried down the stairs as quietly as I could and killed time on Fenchurch Street Station until I deemed it safe to return.

Upon my return I tried to assume the guise of one who had been studiously about the company's business although I was immediately called into the General Manager's office. He questioned whether I knew anything about Mr Cannon's recent incarceration in the lift and told me how they had summoned the elevator company and how upset (I thought 'befuddled' would have been more accurate) Mr Cannon had been at the incident.

I feigned complete surprise peppered with a degree of concern for Mr Cannon's wellbeing whilst also suppressing the urge to laugh at the mental picture of an inebriated Mr Cannon being dragged feet first like a sack of potatoes from the lift which had held him captive for the best part of an hour.

The next day when Moira and I were clear of the office I told her what had happened and she laughed so much I thought she was about to pee her knickers, but nothing about the event was ever mentioned again in the office.

However, the guile involved in the imprisonment of poor Mr Cannon pales into insignificance compared with the experience of a friend who had been employed in the office of another small insurance broking company in London.

The head of that company was a rather remote character, very much of the old school, staid in his habits and totally without humour. He apparently ruled his underlings with uncompromising negativity and was never seen with even the faintest hint of a smile upon his countenance.

Upon his arrival at the office, a dark, sombre atmosphere used to descend upon their place of employment only to be lifted upon his departure for lunch or at the day's end.

Being very much of the old school it was his habit to wear a black bowler hat, a fairly usual garb for senior office workers in London in the 1950's.

Unfortunately for him, his junior staff possessed a particular brand of collective ingenuity which they used to good effect and in the pub one night they concocted a fiendish plot.

One day, during the manager's absence in the toilet, one brave member of staff stole into his office and opened the cupboard in which his hat was stowed. She took a note of his outfitter's business name and address together with the maker's brand and hat size.

After clubbing together for the money, a male staff member called at the shop and purchased the same brand of hat but one size larger. After a couple of days another male staff member went to the same shop and purchased another identical hat but one size smaller than the manager's hat.

The scene was set and the plot was hatched. When the boss went to the toilet for his pre lunch visit, they took his hat and substituted the larger hat in its place. Thus, the old misery went to lunch with his hat slung a little lower than usual.

The same procedure was adopted in the afternoon as the poor fellow returned home with the smaller hat worn well above his ears.

This lasted for several days until one morning his wife rang the office to say that he would be in late that day as he had arranged a morning appointment with his doctor. One can only imagine the speculation in the office as his employees discussed the nature of his malady.

Having made up my mind that I wanted to move to another company I kept my eyes open, scanning the insurance journals in case a position became vacant that would be likely to suit my plans.

After several months I came across an advertisement for a young clerk required to work for a motor underwriter in 'The Room' at Lloyds.

Sirens and Grey Balloons

Although the work would have given me experience in only one specific class of business, I was nevertheless attracted by the prospect of gaining access to permanent employment in the Holy Grail of the world of insurance.

I therefore rang them and gained an interview with a Mr. Shrapnel, the chief underwriter.

Mr Shrapnel was very friendly and quite informal as he asked me the usual questions about myself including my reason for wanting to leave my current employer. He told me that he would be happy to offer me a position but said that it would not provide me with the exposure to the range of insurance classes I was seeking. However, a large broking company with whom he had an excellent relationship was looking for persons who had recently left school and would I be interested if he could arrange an interview with them. Naturally I was very grateful for his thoughtfulness and he rang that company's staff manager straight away, and within the hour I had made contact with a Mr Raymond of L Hammond & Company, a large international broking company for an interview.

As the offices of L Hammond & Company were situated at Portsoken House in The Minories, just around the corner from S H Cannon's in Crutched Friars it enabled me to call and be interviewed by Mr Raymond. I was offered the job straight away and we agreed that I should commence employment in a couple of week's time on the 16th of August, 1954.

I duly gave notice to my boss at S H Cannon and pointed out that as I had been at the company for exactly a year and had only taken a week's holiday, I should be entitled to a week's outstanding holiday pay.

This raised my manager's eyebrows and he told me that I would need to speak to the Company Secretary. He too raised his eyebrows and referred me to Mr Cannon.

As I had now secured another position I had nothing to lose and my previous fear of Mr Cannon had dissipated with the knowledge that he no longer had a lien over me.

Next morning I knocked on his office door and found him in a reasonable mood until I suggested I was entitled to a week's pay for holidays not taken.

His mood changed immediately as he told me that he had started work at the age of thirteen, life had been difficult in those days and that he wouldn't have had the bloody audacity to ask for such a thing. I knew there was no point in arguing so I just told him, very politely, that I would leave without the four pounds but would think the lesser of him for it. He always had a strawberry coloured nose but at this his whole face changed to match it.

Just as I was leaving his office he said "Hurdwell, come back here". I walked back to his desk and he looked me straight in the eye and said "I don't agree with you but I admire your courage. You shall have the money!" I felt I didn't deserve the compliment of being courageous as, under the circumstances, this had not been an act of bravura on my part.

Four pounds was a lot of money to me and I almost felt like apologising for the lift episode. I think we left on good terms but I'm not too sure. However, I left the company with no regrets.

L HAMMOND & COMPANY

L Hammond & Company was a very large international insurance broking house which, whilst having a substantial department devoted to domestic types of business, nevertheless specialised in multi million pound international accounts.

The offices themselves were quite different from S H Cannon & Co. The company occupied several floors in The Minories where it had operated since well before the Second World War, in fact one or two of the older staff members actually remembered the building being evacuated when it was badly damaged in a German bombing raid during the London blitz. They joked that as they left the office during the raid they jettisoned the files of the more troublesome clients as the ensuing fire engulfed the building. I am sure that these stories were somewhat apocryphal and had been well burnished over the intervening years.

My job was to work in the Foreign Department on the 4th Floor and it took little time to observe how different things were from my previous employment. The staff, whilst appearing to put in a solid day's work, always seemed to have time for some fun and the age of employees, of whom there were many, would have spanned from sixteen years to retirement age or even beyond.

However what struck me most forcibly was the number of senior staff members, many of whom were young in years, who had been educated at British Public Schools such as Eton, Harrow, Westminster and Charterhouse etc. Their accents were quite different from most other members of staff, most of whom had attended state run high schools situated in the London suburbs or Home Counties.

The term 'Public School' can be quite confusing to persons living outside the British Isles. Elsewhere the term itself would imply an education paid for by the state but in Britain the opposite was the case. Originally the public schools were set up for the education of poor children but by the late 18th century they had evolved into prestigious private schools where the rich gentry and well off upper classes paid expensive fees for the education of their children who usually boarded at the schools.

It soon became apparent that the career paths of the ex public school employees were such that a large proportion would eventually climb to the upper echelons of the company structure whereas the management ceiling for ex high school employees was usually somewhat lower. Looking back it seems to me that the ex public school employees accepted that they would go further up the managerial ladder as much as we lower mortals were prepared to accept the status quo and not to question why.

However, although this observation, whilst being a criticism of the class system prevailing at the time, it is by no means a criticism of the public school employees themselves. I found almost all of them to be friendly and kind and imbued with a great sense of humour and a pleasure to work with. They did not affect any airs or graces as far as I was aware and were only too happy to share a joke with those around them. Nevertheless their different English accents marked them apart.

One such fellow employee who was in his early twenties, had been a junior officer in the British Army and had only recently been demobilised after serving his two years national service. He had served as a lieutenant in the Cavalry but was still in the army reserve force.

Martin came into the office one Monday morning and related how he had been away at an army training camp for the weekend during which time he had been obliged to attend a church parade in his formal 'blues uniform' complete with boots and spurs. As he knelt down to take communion at the Anglican Church, the rowels in his spurs ran up his buttocks whereupon he shot up with an exclamation, much to the surprise of the vicar administering the sacraments, not to mention his fellow communicants. It was a delight to hear him tell the tale with his very pukka English accent.

My departmental boss, not the product of a public school, was a man in his forties who had been engaged in British Intelligence during the war. He was a fairly thick set man, immaculately dressed with receding hair atop a large head which was literally packed with brains. I was summoned to his office where he instructed me on how to calculate premium appropriations to various Lloyds underwriters. I sat in awe as he multiplied six and seven digit figures by four or five digit figures, filling in the answers from left to right. Having completed the calculation with great celerity he said "Do you agree with that, Hurdwell?" Needless to say, Hurdwell always agreed. It struck me at the time that he would have been working out simultaneous and quadratic equations whilst still in rompers.

In the 1950's the delineation of tasks between male and female staff members was usually well defined, having become almost a class structure in its own right. I am unable to recall seeing a female broker in 'The Room' at Lloyds and almost all the women in the office were either secretaries or comptometer operators, comptometers being 'Burroughs' calculators. Furthermore, secretarial staff, having taken their Dictaphone recorded notes, would return to the typing pool where dozens of ladies sat typing correspondence each day. Upon walking into the typing pool normal conversation was drowned out by the sound of manual typewriters clanging away like the fettling shop at an engineering works.

Likewise, the 'comp girls' were situated upstairs in a similar set-up. It was always a thrill visiting the 'comp room' especially if Fay, the girl assigned to my work, asked if I wished to wait whilst she completed my calculations. The room was a veritable smorgasbord of talent and she was absolutely stunning. She had long black hair, a pretty face and a meticulously crafted figure which I would secretly admire as her delicate fingers equipped with long red varnished nails, lured the required calculations from her machine. The fragrances of a dozen competing perfumes in the room used to send shivers down my spine.

In our department was a bachelor called Jack Warner who was the person described in a previous chapter as having served in the Fleet Air Arm on HMS Victorious during the Second World War. He used to recall some of his experiences whilst on the aircraft carrier which, amongst other assignments was ordered to attack the German pocket battle ship 'Tirpitz'. Apparently, before going to action stations the captain used to issue his instructions for the battle and always ended up by saying "Finally, men, don't panic, just remember you're British". "Trust in the Lord and keep your bowels open". The final invocation was, by all accounts by far the easiest to obey.

Several years later when my brothers and I decided to take the overland trip to Australia, Jack decided to come with us and he settled in Sydney until his untimely death at the age of seventy. He was greatly missed by our family.

Not long after I had joined Hammond's my brother Jerry returned from his army service in the Suez Canal Zone in Egypt and was demobilised after serving two years in the Royal Army Pay Corps.

One would imagine that returning to the comparative freedom of civilian life would have been an easy transition but in most cases the adjustment to the routine of civilian life proved anything but that.

As with most national service personnel, Jerry returned to his original job on the clerical staff of a large printing company but found that his career path seemed to be leading nowhere.

At a tea break one morning I mentioned this to Jack who asked whether my brother had ever considered a career in insurance. That evening I mentioned the conversation to Jerry and after a few days he expressed some interest in the idea.

Jack was pleased that Jerry was considering a change in his career and he mentioned the matter to our manager, Jim Steward who indicated that he would be very keen to speak to Jerry.

The interview went very well and Jerry was offered a job on the spot, not in the Foreign Department but in the adjoining Home Department whose clients were usually large British industrial and commercial enterprises.

It seemed strange to see my brother at a desk in the same building for although we were employed in different departments, we were both situated on the same floor.

Jerry enjoyed his time at Hammond's and before long Jack, Jerry and I were having an occasional lunch together, using luncheon vouchers issued to company staff. We also had a few day trips to Brighton in Jack's 1939 Vauxhall 10 car, a luxurious limousine compared to Dad's ancient Singer 8.

It felt great to be part of a team in the Foreign Department as all the staff were great fun. I recall one day Jack coming over to my desk and showing me a file which had just been returned from the typing pool. The subject of his mirth was a long schedule of items on a Jewellery and Furs All Risks Policy. One item appearing on the schedule was a hand muff made out of four mole skins. Unfortunately the typist had abbreviated the item to 'one four skin muff'. We could only conjecture that the owner could not have been Jewish and if in need of such a muff must have been a well endowed Eskimo.

As I approached my eighteenth birthday I knew it would be only a short time before I would be called up for my two years national service. Several of my friends had already joined the armed forces including Alex who had already served three months and John who had just received word that he was shortly to join the RAF.

In September, 1955 I decided to request an early call-up, the logic being that if I joined the military in early autumn, I would undertake my basic training before the severest winter weather set in.

Sirens and Grey Balloons

To my surprise, two weeks later I received a communication advising me that I should attend a clinic in Ilford, Essex for my army medical examination.

CHAPTER IX ARMY MEDICAL

The clinic which potential soldiers were required to attend was situated adjacent to a large park in Ilford in Essex where mothers pushed their children in prams or just idly chatted to friends along the way. It so happened that many of the footpaths passed very close to the clinic whose windows were not only wide but very low to the ground as well. However, the proximity of the clinic to the thoroughfares didn't strike us as being particularly unusual until a little later on.

Having been marshalled into a large locker room we were instructed to undress. Naturally the assembled company of about fifty youths of all shapes and sizes, stripped down until their only item of clothing was their underpants. However, the sergeant in charge, having scant regard for an individual's comfort, instructed us to remove every stitch of clothing.

Most of us felt it was a little unusual and assumed that after a doctor had inspected our box of tricks for sexually transmitted diseases or hernias, we would be allowed to return our underpants to their accustomed position and our modesty would be restored.

How wrong we were. For the whole medical examination we were as naked as the day we were born. We walked from room to room where specific tests were conducted. Still naked we underwent eye tests, hearing assessments and having hopped onto a bench a doctor tapped each knee with a small mallet to test our reflexes.

It was a beautiful, warm autumn day and the low windows of the clinic had been thrown wide open allowing us to view the adjacent footpath and the women taking their morning stroll. However, being naked we sprinted past open windows and into the sanctuary of the next room whenever the necessity arose.

Finally, after three hours of piddling, listening, peering at eye charts, coughing and groping hands, the medical was concluded except for the final interview. They had made sure that the most bizarre experience was left until last.

Sirens and Grey Balloons

We were not allowed, as yet, to replace our clothing but, still without a stitch on were ushered one by one into a rather well appointed office, complete with a view of the park, where an army major sat behind his imposingly large wooden desk. Soon it was my turn to go in.

He looked up as I walked through the door and I handed him a folder containing my particulars. He seemed to be quite a reasonable sort of person, probably in his mid thirties with plenty of hair and a fresh complexion. He sat there in his khaki officers' uniform wearing a highly polished Sam Browne belt, his officers' cap resting on his desk next to a filing tray.

He beckoned me to sit on the opposite side of the desk on a bentwood chair which instead of having a wicker base was equipped with a thin plywood bottom punctuated with a hundred or so small holes.

I obeyed his bidding and placed my nether regions on the chair. It occurred to me at the time that thousands of bare unwashed bums had graced this very chair before and perhaps quite a number would have been in varying conditions of cleanliness.

I felt decidedly awkward sitting naked in front of a man who was not only fully clothed but immaculately dressed in his khaki serge uniform which displayed great credit to his batman. Feeling uncomfortable I decided to cross my legs but this made matters even worse as my penis and both testicles decided to assume a higher profile. I therefore uncrossed my legs in an endeavour to reclaim what modicum of equilibrium remained.

He asked me questions about myself, pointed out the financial advantages of signing on for a three year term but when I indicated that the compulsory two years would be ample he smiled, rose from his chair and, leaning over his desk, held out his hand for me to shake as he wished me luck in the army. I also rose, but as I extended my hand found that the base of the chair had annealed itself to my bum.

I attempted to look intelligent and unabashed and, staring the major straight in the eye as if such an experience was part of everyday life, I shook his hand whilst at the same time peeling the chair from my sweating buttocks with the other hand. This must have been a crude introduction to my first challenge at multi tasking.

In another two weeks I had received my call-up papers and travel pass to report to the Royal Army Ordnance Corps Barracks at Hilsea, not far from Portsmouth.

CHAPTER X THE ARMY

At the outset I would make the observation that whilst my accounts are critical of the British Army during the two years of my national service, these events, whilst being mainly humorous, occurred over fifty years ago and thus bear little resemblance to the British Army of the twenty-first century.

Since my service in the forces in the mid 1950's, the British Army has become one of the finest fighting forces in the world having served with distinction in the Falklands, two wars in Iraq and also in Afghanistan.

My tenure in the army began when the Second World War had ended only a decade before. Many of the officers I served under had gained promotion through normal attrition during that war, often having taken the place of officers who had perished in combat.

Hopefully, my observations will be viewed in the light of the experiences of a civilian conscripted to serve as a soldier in a bygone era.

The 27th October, 1955 was a bright sunny day with just a hint of autumn freshness in the air as I hopped out of the bath and dressed, ready for my train journey to join the army.

Although it was well over half a century ago I can still remember it as though it was yesterday and I am still able to recapture the sad look on my mother's face as I prepared to leave the house.

She was doing her housework as I walked into the dining room, suitcase in hand and ready to say 'goodbye'. She had been through the same experience when Jerry had been called up three years before, but he had only been restored to the family fold for less than a year and now it was my turn to go.

As I stood before her she switched off the noisy cylindrical 'Goblin' vacuum cleaner she was using and looked at me with a faraway look of sadness in her eyes. In those days, maybe because we were British or possibly a reflection of the times in which we lived, but youths didn't tell their mothers that they loved them. Possibly it was an unexpressed emotion which was taken as a given but seldom if ever expressed. I wanted to tell her but sadly I did not. I gave her a hug, told her I would see her in three weeks time and left the house.

I boarded the local number 35 bus which took me to Dalston Junction where I changed to a number 76 bus which conveyed me to London's Waterloo Railway Station.

I felt sure I would come across other youths in a similar situation to my own on the train but as there were no such persons fitting that description I settled down in silence as the electric train conveyed me through the peace and tranquillity of the picturesque English countryside. I knew that it wouldn't be long before such peace and tranquillity would give way to the yelling of sergeants and drill instructors as they tried to knock the edges off us raw recruits.

Eventually, as the train neared Portsmouth it slowed down and came to a stop at Hilsea Station. Clutching my suitcase and looking for all the world like a prospective national serviceman, I emerged from my carriage. After a few seconds a tall, well dressed corporal asked me if I had come to join the Royal Army Ordnance Corps. He seemed quite friendly as he motioned me towards the platform exit where I was immediately confronted by another corporal who, whilst being well turned out, had a roughened and truculent look about him. He too asked in a quiet voice if I had come to join the army and when I replied in the affirmative he stepped towards me, placed his face right up against my ear and bellowed "Well, get on that fuckin' lorry". I can't even remember climbing onto the back of the army one tonner as I was so startled, but having done so I found myself amongst several other recruits who had undergone a similar welcome.

The journey from the railway station still remains a blur as my mind began to grapple with the prospect that I wouldn't be free of the army for another two years, one of which was a leap year as well.

We soon arrived at Hilsea Army Barracks and coming to a halt at a large number of old timber huts, the truck disgorged its cargo of unwilling and apprehensive raw recruits. The process was accompanied by the mindless hectoring of the cockney corporal who was as dim as a 'Toc H' lamp and was soon joined by a sergeant of similar disposition. The sergeant bore a striking resemblance to Doris Day, the popular American film star and vocalist of the day. From then on he was unaffectionately known as 'Doris'.

After a while we were each assigned to barrack rooms which were required to accommodate the new recruits of 'C Company'. Each barrack room had enough space to sleep eighteen men. The rooms did not stand alone but were connected by narrow covered corridors which led to the ablutions huts and also other barrack rooms. As four barrack rooms either side were connected by a central corridor, each complex was referred to as a 'spider'.

We quickly deposited our belongings next to the beds to which we had been allotted and were told to line up outside. The corporal then lined us up in two ranks one behind the other facing him and then instructed us to turn to the left, thus forming a line two abreast. In this manner we were marched to the quartermasters store to be greeted by a sign displayed on the wall which read 'SHOULD ANYTHING FIT, BRING IT BACK AND WE WILL CHANGE IT'.

The corporal in charge of the store gave each one of us a perfunctory look as he issued us with shirts, battledress trousers and tunics, socks, vests, great coats and khaki underpants described as 'green drawers cellular'. We were also issued with our canvas webbing equipment consisting of a belt, large pack, small pack, and ammunition pouches.

When it came to the issue of boots he displayed a little more care. Unfortunately I was one of the last recruits to receive my boots and was asked my size of shoe. I told him that I took a broad fitting 9 and to my surprise he produced boots of that very size. Miraculously they fitted. As we were required to own two pairs of boots he went away, rummaged around a pile of footwear and advised that they were out of size nines and he only had a size 8 or 11.

I tried on the size 11 but it was like stepping onto the deck of a rowing boat which thus limited me to the size 8. He told me not to worry as the second pair was only for show at kit inspections. They were actually officers' boots of superior quality and it turned out that they responded well when it came to spit and polishing them for inspections.

By this time it was early afternoon as we were marched back to our barrack room where we sorted out our gear and climbed into our newly acquired army uniforms including our thin green drawers cellular which were designed to stop the chaffing of the rough battledress on our thighs. It was a pity they weren't ' long johns' as the battledress material was very rough to the point where they rubbed off the hair on our calves.

Most of us looked like sacks of potatoes but as an electric iron and barrack room table were on hand, we queued up to iron our battledresses with varying degrees of success. Although we had only been in the army a couple of hours, the oppression of authority had started to make us aware of each other's needs and group morale had started to manifest itself.

The cookhouse was nearby and having been marched there clutching our steel cutlery and one pint china mugs, we gobbled down our stew, heavily laden with potatoes and returned to our barrack room.

There we were greeted by a particularly nasty little corporal who was as thick as two planks and revelled in his role as an instructor, obviously deriving a vicarious thrill at our discomfiture. His first task was to instruct us how to spit and polish our boots and 'Brasso' our belt buckles and belt fasteners. As highly polished boots constituted the main centre of a soldier's turnout, it took us several days to polish them to a satisfactory standard.

Firstly we were marched to the NAAFI where we could purchase black 'Kiwi' boot polish and a supply of candles before work on our boots could commence. The boots we had been supplied were made of thick chrome leather characterised by small regular bumps on their surface. We were required to remove those bumps on both the toes and heels so that the surface of the leather became perfectly smooth.

We then had to heat the handle of our spoon over the candle and when hot, wipe boot polish onto the leather and then run the hot spoon over the polished leather. After a few applications the bumps disappeared and the spit and polish could commence.

Sirens and Grey Balloons

The process of spit and polish involved the smearing a thin layer of polish onto the boot and when the polish had adhered to the boot and assumed a glutinous consistency, spit on the surface and rub in the polish with a duster until a sheen started to appear. After the process had been carried out many times the desired effect would manifest itself. Eventually the boot toe caps would be so highly polished that a well turned out soldier would, upon looking down at his boots be able to see his face reflected in the mirror-like toe caps.

Similarly, our canvas webbing belts and gaiters had to be covered with a similar compound to boot polish in the form of 'Pickerings Blanco'. This paste was khaki in colour and was also purchased from the NAAFI. The same process was adopted for our small packs, large packs and ammunition pouches which were attached to various parts of our bodies with the use of webbing straps. One can imagine that during a war, soldiers wearing these accoutrements into battle would have looked more like tailor's dummies than soldiers.

After such an initiation into the army's ranks we were happy to crawl into our iron beds and sleep soundly until 5 am, knowing that we only had another seven hundred and thirty days to serve before we were demobbed.

Next morning just before 5 am we heard the sound of heavy army boots pounding along the corridor of our spider followed by our door being flung open by a corporal and sergeant who yelled "Get out of bed, move, move, move, I'll charge the last man out, you 'orrible lot of bastards!" They quite obviously relished seeing the stunned reaction of the latest crop of raw recruits as we clutched our shaving gear and toiletries and rushed across to the ablutions block dressed only in our 'green drawers cellular'.

Having dressed in our denims we arrived at the cookhouse for breakfast at 5.30 where we were served a large dollop of porridge and a glutinous serving of what must have passed as scrambled eggs. The eggs had probably been concocted from packets of dried eggs as the portions had a greenish tinge about them. It didn't really worry us as we gobbled them down with copious 'doorsteps' of bread.

By 6.30 we had tidied up our bed spaces and were lined up outside our barrack room as the autumn sun began to peep over the eastern horizon. Having been sorted out into ranks, the tallest at one end and the shortest at the other, we were taught to march, turn to the left and right, halt, about turn and such other manoeuvres as were necessary for a platoon of men to be mobilised and controlled.

Later in the morning sergeant 'Doris Day' appeared, accompanied by our platoon officer, Lieutenant Cooper. Lt. Cooper had a certain presence about him as he walked up and down our ranks asking questions of the men and looking genuinely interested in us as Doris looked on.

Lieutenant Cooper was apparently a regular soldier, about twenty-five years of age, quite tall and lean looking with an intelligent light in his eyes. After questioning several of the men he outlined what was expected of us including the necessity to be proud of being British soldiers, even though we were national servicemen. He also told us that we could expect to be seeing him almost every day during our six weeks of basic training. He was true to his word.

In the meantime Doris stood to attention in the background glowering at his new recruits and the mean look in his eyes did not augur well for our wellbeing for the next six weeks.

At the conclusion of our platoon commander's talk, Lt. Cooper handed us over to Doris who then drilled us for the whole morning. He ranted and raved, bellowed and screamed at us as he issued his commands. One recruit stood out from the rest of us and was quickly recognised as being different. Pte Jenks was a tall and skinny lad from Wolverhampton who wore a curiously vacant gaze from behind his steel rimmed spectacles. He seemed to be continuously surprised at the events surrounding him as his lower lip drooped and never seemed to adequately cover his teeth and seldom had much to do with his upper lip. He often dribbled saliva down the front of his shirt or denim top.

As Doris marched us all over the barrack square, poor Jenks couldn't keep in step and annoyed those around him as he continually skipped in trying to keep in step with the rest of the platoon. Being the tallest recruit he was situated at one end of the double file of men and on one occasion when Doris gave the order "about turn!" Jenks, being oblivious of the command, continued straight on towards a nearby field.

Doris turned almost purple as he pursued the hapless lad and escorted him back into the ranks, ranting and raving in the process.

Later that day a corporal, having taken over from the sergeant, lined us up, drew us to attention and made us stand rigidly in that position for a few minutes. It was at this point that the corporal saw Jenks staring at him with a faraway look, not unlike a doting Labrador eager to please his master.

The corporal, seeing the look on Jenks' face yelled out "Jenks, do you love me?" to which Jenks replied "Yes Corporal". We didn't dare laugh but the corporal's expression was a mixture of fury mingled with despair. At least Jenks made the rest of us look quite good by comparison.

After a morning's drill we were marched down to the company barber for our first military haircut. By now we had been able to observe that all army personnel had very short hair, doubtless emanating from the scourge of lice the First World War soldiers had to contend with in the trenches. However, we drew some comfort from the assurance that what hair there was under our berets was ours to keep. This was not true.

We emerged from the shearing shed more than keen to put on our berets as we possessed very little hair with which to combat the chill autumn air. Since my days in the forces I have never sported short hair.

Our barrack rooms were supposed to be maintained in a clean and tidy manner and this is where the lunacy of the army of the 1950's came into its own.

Each morning (and some evenings) we had to 'bull up' our barrack room. 'Bull' was the term used for cleaning and polishing, in fact the motto was 'if it moves, salute it, and if it doesn't, polish it' tended to apply nowhere more than in the barrack room.

Thus, each day we had a kit inspection. Our beds had to be stripped and bed covers were meticulously stretched over the mattresses where envelope ends were folded at each corner. The blankets had to be 'boxed'. This involved obtaining cardboard and cutting several pieces into 30cm x 5cm so that sheets, blankets and gym T shirts could be stretched over them in symmetrical layers around which a folded blanket was wrapped. The result was a mound of sheets, blankets and gym T shirts stiffened by cardboard and resembling a rather large layer cake. This edifice was placed at the head of the bed for inspection.

Other polished and spotless equipment was then laid out on the bed. These items included highly polished best boots, greatcoat 'dollied' or folded in a special manner, razor, soap dish, china mug webbing equipment and kit bag.

The pine barrack room table had to be scrubbed and when it had dried, a film of Brasso metal polish was applied to make it look lighter in colour. The galvanised barrack room bucket did not escape attention and also had to be polished with Brasso.

It took several days to acquire the art of 'bulling up' the room and most of us purchased an extra razor, soap dish and china mug to be used solely for the purpose of kit inspections.

After a week our barrack room became reasonably presentable and when the thick little corporal announced that the next evening there would be a full scale room inspection we felt quite confident.

At about 9.30 the next evening the order 'stand by your beds' was received and the thick corporal entered our barrack room with fire in his nostrils.

He strutted in and stopped at the third bed from the door, inspected the 'boxed' blankets on the bed and threw them into the middle of the room saying that they were a disgrace. A little further down the room he picked up a gleaming, unused newly purchased china mug and advising the owner that it was so full of shit that he could plant potatoes in it, hurled it at a steel radiator causing it to break into several shattered pieces and then, adding insult to injury, announced that it would cost the owner one and sixpence (ten pence) to replace. As we only received one pound forty pence per week, it was quite an expense.

Progressing down the room he was almost foaming at the mouth as he threw several razors on the floor, overturned the table from its trestles scattered webbing everywhere and as a final act of lunacy, overturned a recruit's bed, together with the kit which had been placed upon it.

Sirens and Grey Balloons

We stood there in disbelief after his departure as we surveyed the devastation wreaked by this latter day Goebbels.

As we struggled to identify our own kit, the time for 'lights out' was rapidly approaching but by 10.00 pm we still had not been able to restore any semblance of order. Thus, at the appointed time we had no option but to turn off the barrack room light and try to work by the light of several candles. However it was impossible to identify our army numbers stencilled onto the various pieces of webbing so decided, against company orders, that we would switch the lights back on again for a short time.

Within a few minutes we heard a loud voice outside shout "put that light out!" whereupon a loud chorus of "Fuck off!" was heard to resonate from our quarters and into the still night air outside.

Seconds later the duty officer dressed in his ceremonial blues accompanied by a sergeant stormed into our room but was taken aback by the mangled mass of equipment on the floor. After enquiring what had happened the officer regained his composure and told us that we could retain the lights for another fifteen minutes.

The next evening Lt Cooper visited our barrack room which gave us an opportunity to relate the previous evening's events. Naturally he was non committal although he was obviously aware of such goings on. However, such occurrences did not happen again although a certain pattern of behaviour relating to the training of recruits was starting to emerge.

The training NCO's were trying their best to reduce us to the status of non thinking robots who would automatically obey any command regardless of its logic, similar to that which obtained in the First World War. The army was endeavouring to turn us into unthinking drones. However, to ensure that the troops' morale was not entirely shattered, the platoon officers kept in close touch with the men under their command. It was a cumbersome strategy which would surely lead to obedient soldiers entirely bereft of initiative which only officers were supposed to possess.

One evening we were told that nurses from the local Red Cross were to visit the camp the next day to take blood from donors in our unit. We were assured that it was entirely voluntary but those men who did not wish to donate would be required to spend an afternoon in the cookhouse peeling potatoes. Given the subtle choice, few men demurred.

A few days later we were told that on the following day we would be marched to the Medical Officer's block to receive our T A B injections. Accordingly we were woken up at 4.30am and marched over to the cookhouse for an early breakfast.

By 6.00 am we were standing 'at ease' outside the M O's quarters on a crisp morning with frost on the ground. It was most uncomfortable as our only clothing consisted of boots, socks, gym shorts and T shirts. The order to remove our T shirts was then given which exposed us to the breeze which had sprung up. We became colder and colder but could not run around to get warm as the increased breeze on our bodies accentuated the cold on our already frozen torsos.

Finally the M O arrived at 11 am and we were admitted for the jabs. The old army adage "hurry up and wait" struck again.

I was still quite a skinny youth at the time and as I braced my arm to the needle, the sergeant administering the serum forced the needle in but it pinched the flesh and came out the other side of my arm, causing him to swear at me as he reloaded the weapon and tried again.

The effect of the injection was not immediate but having returned to our barrack room the thick corporal decided to give us saluting practice. By then our right arms were beginning to become stiff and sore and he revelled in our discomfort shouting at us to keep our arms up higher when saluting. After a raving spree on his part we hadn't the energy to care.

By the evening most of us felt really ill and were allowed to go to bed. I recall waking up during the night, my bed sheets completely sodden with perspiration, stripping the sheets off the bed and draping them over the warm radiators until they were dry.

Mercifully, the next day we were allowed to recover without any contact with our NCO instructors. As usual, Lt Cooper visited us that evening.

Sirens and Grey Balloons

I am sure that nobody in our intake had ever used a firearm and most of us were looking forward to our first instruction on the firing of a rifle.

It was felt by the military authorities that to introduce newly enlisted recruits to the British Lee Enfield .303 calibre rifle too early in their training might be unwise. Although this rifle had been in use since 1895 and had undergone improvements during two world wars, it still possessed no mechanism for reducing the severe recoil action when the weapon was fired. Thus, our first initiation into using a firearm was undertaken with the lower calibre .22 weapon.

We were marched to a large hall where we were given details of the mechanism of the rifle and how to use it during combat. It was when we were observing the weapon and listening intently to the sergeant instructor, that we noticed that one recruit was not present. Pte Jenks had not been included and we surmised, probably correctly, that the army had considered it unwise to give him instruction on the use of such a lethal item of equipment.

Having witnessed the sergeant firing the .22 rifle, we were each given a few rounds of ammunition to fire at a small cardboard 'bullseye' target at the other end of the hall.

Next day we were marched down to the outdoor firing range where each of us was issued the larger and more powerful Lee Enfield .303 calibre rifle.

It was a relatively simple weapon to use and consisted of a wooden stock attached to a steel body which contained the breach, barrel, firing bolt and magazine beneath the breach. When the trigger was squeezed and the rifle had been fired, the bolt was pulled back by the marksman allowing the spent cartridge to be jettisoned and the new round of ammunition to slip into the breach ready for the next shot.

It was a very cold, bleak morning as we listened to the sergeant's instructions. He emphasised that the first round of ammunition produced the heaviest recoil kick in the shoulder, particularly in cold conditions when the bore of the barrel had contracted due to the low temperature.

One by one we lay on the ground, took aim at a large 'bullseye' target two hundred yards away, pressed the rifle butt into our shoulders and gently squeezing the trigger fired the first round. The rifle possessed the kick of a mule and emitted such a loud bang that it left the marksman with ringing in the ears which lasted for some time afterwards. During my time in the army I never saw an earplug with which to protect the eardrum.

One recruit in our platoon was a diminutive little 'Geordie' from Newcastle who weighed less than fifty kilograms. I watched him as he lay down, clutched the rifle and, pushing it into his shoulder, fired. The kick of the recoil pushed his whole body a couple of centimetres backwards like a miniature cannon.

Upon our return from the firing range we were shown how to clean our rifles by pouring boiling water down the barrel several times and then with a piece of cotton gauze measuring four inches by two inches (known as 4 by 2) attached to a length of cord, pulled it through the barrel several times. By then the barrel was quite clean and the remaining task was to soak another piece of 4 by 2 in oil and pull that through the barrel as well.

The rifles we used were manufactured in Enfield, England in the 1940's and had been used in World War II although when I was first posted to Germany I was issued with a 1917 Lee Enfield. One can only conjecture as to where that rifle had been and who had been assigned to use it in the trenches of France.

A few days later we were introduced to a light machine gun called the Bren gun. This weapon used the standard British .303 cartridge and was capable of firing over five hundred rounds per minute. In reality of course, as the magazine only held thirty rounds of ammunition, this restricted the rate of firing as a full magazine had to be attached every time the previous one had run out of ammunition.

We were taught how to assemble and dismantle the Bren and to enable us to remember the correct sequence we had to learn a little phrase, pertinent to that exercise. 'The dog pissed on the barrel but not on the body'. Thus, when dismantling the weapon we took out the piston followed by barrel, then butt and finally the body was left.

Sirens and Grey Balloons

The Bren was quite a heavy weapon and it amazed me to learn that when the Australian army fought the Japanese on the Kokoda Track in the Owen Stanley Mountain ranges of New Guinea, many soldiers fired this machine gun from the hip to devastating effect.

After three weeks intensive basic training we were issued with our 48 hour leave passes and travel vouchers and were allowed to go home for the weekend.

The train back to Waterloo Station filled me with excitement, especially as the whole journey home took less than three hours in all. Unfortunately some recruits came from further afield with one or two having to catch another train to Scotland, thus depriving them of some quality time with their loved ones.

What an experience it was to be home with the family and to savour the luxury of climbing into bed at night, safe in the knowledge that in the morning I could turn over and doze again, free from the offensive racket of corporals and sergeants yelling their lungs out.

One positive aspect of national service lay in the fact that it drew a line between being a youth and becoming a man. When I lived at home I was expected to be home and in bed by a reasonable hour but after my first weekend leave I was able to return home at any hour, the logic being that if I was old enough to fight in a war I would certainly be old enough to choose the time of my comings and goings.

The two days at home passed all too quickly and in no time at all it was time to don my battle dress again and make my way to Waterloo Station with my leave pass safely stowed within the pages of my army pay book.

Soldiers were always a little apprehensive when within the precincts of London's major railway stations and we were always on the look-out for the 'red caps'. The duties of the Royal Military Police (known as Red Caps) were ostensibly to check soldiers to see whether they had leave passes and if not, the hapless soldier would be taken into custody and be charged as being absent without leave (AWOL) However, some Military Police Personnel were very officious and could well cause the unsuspecting soldier a lot of trouble without any apparent reason.

Fortunately I was never apprehended by a 'red cap' whilst travelling and felt that it was always prudent to avoid eye contact with them.

As we became more accustomed to the routine of army life we were able to relax a little. By now, Pte Jenks had been assessed by the army authorities as being unfit for military service and had been told that he would be discharged within the coming week.

Having received the good news his behaviour in private underwent a dramatic change. He still tended to dribble on occasions, particularly when trying to secure the top button of his denim jacket but the rest of the barrack room started to suspect that he had masterminded the difficult task of 'working his ticket' back to the freedom of civilian life. By the time we eventually said 'goodbye' to him we had started to hold him in quite high regard as having beaten the army at its own game.

Another person in our barrack room was also discharged at the same time. Mike was a very sincere and genuine person whose vision was seriously impaired to the point where, when endeavouring to fire a rifle, he was unable to see the target even when wearing his thick lens spectacles. He was very hopeful of being discharged but we joked that with such impairment he would doubtless be transferred to the Royal Army Observer Corps. However, eventually sanity prevailed and we farewelled him shortly after Jenks' departure.

The last two weeks of training were quite frenetic as we prepared for the final 'Passing out Parade'.

By now our boots would have put a mirror to shame, our webbing buckles glistened in the winter sunlight and the creases in our battle dress trousers were razor sharp.

We were drilled each morning and afternoon which left little time in the evenings for us to maintain our barrack room in a spotless condition.

After breakfast each morning we would prepare for the daily kit inspection having boxed our blankets, put out our dummy razors and mugs for inspection and 'dollied' our greatcoats which hung beneath our steel helmets behind our bed heads like oversized chocolate soldiers.

The Passing out Parade went off without a hitch and it was with a sense of great relief that we farewelled Hilsea Barracks and, clutching our leave passes, took the train home for the weekend prior to reporting to the Royal Army Ordnance Corps barracks at Blackdown where we would undergo a two month clerical trade training course.

BLACKDOWN

My journey from home in Chingford to Blackdown in Surrey was a rather difficult undertaking as I was required to carry all my army equipment together with what few personal items I deemed necessary for the next two months in the armed forces.

I clipped on my webbing belt to which two ammunition pouches had been affixed at the front and then hoisted my small pack and large pack onto my back. My steel helmet had already been strapped to the back of the large pack, giving my whole being the profile of a latter day Quasimodo, the celebrated Hunchback of Notre Dame. With the kitbag hoisted onto my shoulder and a small suitcase in the other hand, I left the house.

I was not sorry to be stationed at Blackdown as the army camp situated near the village of Deepcut was only eight kilometres from where my Gran was living in Lightwater and also close to the home of my aunt, uncle and two cousins for whom I had a great affection.

For some reason it was necessary for me to travel to Waterloo Railway Station on the London Underground system which gave me a few logistical problems. I found that each underground carriage was packed with commuters and it was difficult to shove my way into a carriage with my burden strapped to various parts of my body. As fellow commuters joined and alighted from the carriage they brushed past me, coming into contact with my steel helmet and spinning me first one way and then the other. I started to feel a great sympathy for poor Quasimodo as I was buffeted by my fellow travellers for half an hour or so.

The surface train from Waterloo to Brookwood Station took barely an hour and as there were a number of other servicemen destined for the barracks at Blackdown a lorry had been dispatched to convey us to Alma Barracks for the next stage of our army careers.

Arriving at Brookwood awakened a not too distant memory for me as it was at Brookwood Hospital where my Gramp had died eight years before, his death probably being related to his being gassed during World War I.

As we had by now completed our basic training we expected that our trade training would prove to be a little less arduous and to a degree this turned out to be true. Although the timber barrack rooms were similar to those at Hilsea and also accommodated eighteen soldiers, the instructors appeared to be considerably more intelligent to those under whom we had laboured during our basic training. Mind you, that would not have been very difficult. Also the food at Blackdown was of a very high order although I recall that we were obliged to contribute a small amount out of our pay for certain extra luxuries.

As long term professional soldiers were stationed at Blackdown there were situated some distance from the main parade ground, a number of old terrace houses occupied as married quarters.

Within the army compound there was even a small picture theatre and when I attended a screening of 'The Student Prince' starring Ann Blyth and Edmund Purdom I was amazed to note that no smoking was permitted in the cinema. In those days in Britain smoking was allowed in cinemas and a majority of cinema goers sat amidst the fug of stale tobacco smoke.

Just across the road from the cinema was Keys Cafe where we used to purchase such luxuries as chocolate and potato crisps to the accompaniment on the juke box playing the current hit tune of the era 'Davy Crocket'.

The aim of the trade training course was to teach us the structure of the supply chain required to look after the needs of the British Army with a heavy emphasis on the supply of ordnance such as arms and ammunition, however it was drummed into us that we were soldiers first and foremost and discipline remained strict but not peppered with mindless lunacy as had been the case a Hilsea.

After a couple of weeks we were allowed to leave the camp in the evenings and I took these opportunities to walk the eight kilometres to see Gran, my maternal grandmother of whom I was very fond. Sometimes I would be able to hitch a lift from a passing motorist which allowed me more time with my Gran and cousins, one of whom always drove me back to barracks afterwards.

There were few cars on this road and occasionally there would be either heavy cloud cover or no moon to guide me along the way to Lightwater and on one occasion I came to a crossroads where there was a signpost. However, I was unable to read the directions on it due to the darkness and was therefore compelled to wait for it to be illuminated by the light of a passing car. The experience could not help but remind me of the London fogs except that the Surrey country air was fresh and sweet by comparison.

Having been issued leave passes to spend Christmas with our families we again returned to Blackdown as the chill of winter set in.

Every ten days or so we were required to undertake guard duty where the period of duty varied, the shortest period being 12 hours up to the longest stint of 48 hours.

One such duty stood out from the others as it entailed 48 hours of sleep deprivation spanning two days from Friday night until the following Monday morning. After inspection, each pair of soldiers was required to patrol an allotted area of the barracks for two hours after which there was a four hour rest period in the guard room before the next two hour duty. Being winter, we had to keep our greatcoats on even when resting in the guard room.

The weather was bitterly cold and my fellow guard, Jerry Harris and I wandered around the barrack square with our heads tucked as far down into our upturned greatcoat collars as possible and our berets fastened over our ears in an attempt to stave off the cold night air. As it was during a period of renewed I.R.A. activity we were supposed to be vigilant and keep quiet but such instructions were impossible to carry out as the noise from our army boots rang out when they struck the frost covered parade ground beneath our feet.

As the hours ticked by, the only picture in our minds was of a luxurious warm bed and a deep, restful sleep.

On the Monday morning we were dismissed from guard duty by the orderly officer (who had been snuggled up at home for the duration), but after a shower and breakfast we were obliged to attend trade training until 5 pm.

We filed into the training room like zombies and tried valiantly to stave off sleep but with ever diminishing success. Unfortunately I dozed off only to be awoken by our instructor, Corporal Monks who banged on my desk and shouted "Hurdwell, you were asleep!" I responded that I was only thinking at the time to which he rejoined "Do you always snore when you think?"

To digress, I met Brian Monks many years later who by then had become a very religious person engaged in helping old and needy members of society.

In the midst of this very cold spell disaster struck. The central heating to the 'other ranks' barrack rooms was no longer in service due to a lack of coal. Fortunately for the officers, they had enough coal and were not inconvenienced at all.

Nevertheless our hot water system was still working but the barrack rooms were bitterly cold and cheerless. Our routines changed a little to accommodate the arctic conditions. Before going to bed, each soldier filled a glass lemonade bottle with hot water, piled as much clothing on the bed as possible and enjoyed a hot shower before enveloping himself under the mound of clothing and bedclothes. Some men even wrapped scarves around their necks as well.

One Saturday afternoon I was so cold and miserable I was given to thinking how I could get warm and had a brainwave. I walked over to the boiler house where the hot water was generated, climbed on top of a ledge overlooking the stored coal and managed several hours of uninterrupted slumber.

After two weeks we were told that there had been a delivery of coal and that the heating was about to be restored. This intelligence coincided with a decree that there was shortly to be a greatcoat inspection. Accordingly we were instructed to put on our greatcoats and stand by our beds until a senior officer had inspected each one.

Thus, with the barrack room windows closed and dressed in our greatcoats we waited for several hours, by which time the radiators filled up with hot water. Within the space of three hours we had graduated from sub zero Arctic temperatures to a tropical heatwave, still wearing our thick army greatcoats. It was a wonder that nobody was taken to the sick bay with heatstroke as the sweat poured down our necks and backs washing away our resident goose bumps.

It was about this time that one of the senior staff, Warrant Officer Johnson, came into our classroom and asked if anyone could write shorthand. By this time I had learned never to volunteer for anything in the army. I knew that had I put my hand up I would have been told that they were short handed in the kitchen and I would have been delegated to do a stint of 'spud bashing" (potato peeling) in the cookhouse. I decided to hide my talent under a bushel so to speak, but not through any modesty on my part.

A week or so later the same senior NCO again came into the classroom and asked if Private Hurdwell was present. When I stood up he told me that he wanted to see me in his office.

Once in his office he asked me to take a seat which was very comforting as this time I was fully clothed. He told me that he had been looking through my records and that not only was I able to write shorthand but that I had a reasonable typing speed as well. Apparently the RAOC needed stenographers and as it was an 'A' Class trade, I would be paid an extra pound a week after a year in the army. Also, because of the 'A' classification of the trade, promotion to corporal was not uncommon. The extra pay for that rank was also considerable.

I therefore told him that I would like to take the shorthand and typing examination and it was arranged that after completing my current course of trade training I would be transferred to Willems Barracks in Aldershot for a shorthand course.

After subsequently passing my trade training examination, I left Blackdown Barracks for what would normally have been a five months shorthand typing course with the Royal Army Service Corps at Aldershot. Aldershot is usually considered as being the epicentre of the British Army particularly as it is only a few kilometres from the Royal Staff College in Camberley.

Peter Hurdwell

When I arrived at Willems Barracks I was struck by how old the barracks were, with no central heating and rather decrepit food halls and assembly areas. The heating in the area in which I was housed was by way of a coal fired cast iron stove probably dating back to the days of the Crimean War. As it was in the centre of the room we used to crouch around it each evening before 'lights out'.

The two storey brick building had wooden floors and as we sat around the stove we were able to observe shafts of light from the office below as they peeped through the cracks between the floor boards. Each morning we were required to clean out our fireplace so that it was free from coaldust or dirt of any description.

One morning we were about to vacate our barrack room to attend muster when a sergeant burst into our barrack room and yelled at us to 'put that fire out'. It transpired that he had seen smoke coming from our room and had assumed that a fire was still burning in our stove. Upon inspection he found that the smoke had actually risen up from the office below through the cracks between the floorboards.

As I was already able to write shorthand and type at an acceptable speed, the corporal in charge of the classes, Cpl Graver, allowed me to skip the lessons although I was able to attend classes and take down dictation, transcribing my notes on an ancient Remington typewriter. By this means I was able to spend an easy month, by the end of which I took the eighty words per minute shorthand test and duly passed.

Typical of the army at the time, that was the very last time I wrote shorthand except for my own private purposes. From that day onwards I never wrote another stroke of shorthand during my entire army career although I had become an 'A' Class tradesman and was paid accordingly.

After about six weeks it was then back to Blackdown where I was stationed in limbo pending my final posting.

By now it was late April, 1956 and I still had no idea where I would be sent to carry out the rest of my national service. At the time the British Army had bases in Hong Kong, Singapore, Suez Canal, Cyprus, Germany and Malaya as well as countless bases in Britain.

Sirens and Grey Balloons

As this presented a golden opportunity to see the world I put my name down for an overseas posting and waited at Blackdown Barracks to learn my fate.

In the meantime I was able to travel home at weekends arriving back at barracks quite late at night.

On one occasion quite a number of soldiers alighted from the train at Brookwood Station to be confronted by total darkness with no moon to light the way back to barracks. As nobody had a torch we formed ourselves up into a very non military formation and followed the person in front and for several kilometres struck the ground with the heels of our boots, the sparks from the steel studs guiding those behind. On the way the only light we saw was as we passed the Guards Depot at Pirbright, halfway to Blackdown.

By the beginning of May the Company Adjutant summoned me to his office where he advised me that I was to be posted to the British Army of the Rhine in Luneburg, Northern Germany.

Peter Hurdwell

CHAPTER XI GERMANY

It was two weeks before I was due to travel to Germany which therefore made me eligible for a week's embarkation leave. My week at home saw me looking at maps of Germany in an effort to determine the exact whereabouts of Luneburg.

From what I was able to ascertain at the time, Luneburg was a very old town situated in northern Germany in the state of Lower Saxony. Unlike Hamburg to its north, Luneburg had been spared the horrors of allied bombing during the Second World War even though several German Army barracks had been situated on the perimeter of the town.

Located about 40 kilometres south west of Luneburg was the infamous Belsen concentration camp and it was at a local school in Luneburg that the SS men and women guards were tried for their war crimes leading to the execution of a number of them.

With Luneburg being quite close to Hamburg I had assumed that I would be travelling by sea via Hamburg. However I was wrong in that assumption. Instead we travelled by train through Holland and were able to enjoy some wonderful scenery in that country.

Thus, in the middle of May, 1956 I boarded a train for Harwich, a British North Sea port, where a British troopship, the 'Empire Wansbeck' was waiting to convey a large contingent of soldiers across the North Sea to the Hook of Holland on their way to the British Army of the Rhine.

The 'Empire Wansbeck' although built by Germany during the Second World War, became a war prize after the Allied victory and traversed the route from Harwich to the Hook of Holland on a nightly basis.

I was quite excited as I walked up the gangplank at Parkeston Quay carrying my kit and was soon directed to the bunk where I would spend the night together with hundreds of other soldiers. The sleeping quarters consisted of a set of steel uprights to which five tiers of canvas bunks had been secured. There was row upon row of identical bunks stretching from one end of the hold to the other.

In the aisles several galvanized iron dustbins were scattered about just in case any of the troops became seasick. I found out later that the

181

Sirens and Grey Balloons

Wansbeck's nickname was the 'Sick Tub' as it apparently bobbed around like a cork in heavy seas. Fortunately the emergency bins were not needed on this crossing.

Having stowed my luggage on the deck I was directed to a bunk where I would spend the night. Sadly for me it was in the middle of the tier of five bunks which presented quite a problem when it came to gaining access to my sleeping quarters. I was required to climb about three metres past two other bunks and then slither horizontally into the narrow bed space allotted to me. Having managed to lie on my back I was very much aware of the profile of the person above as the canvas base of his bed was only a few centimetres from my hips, making it impossible to turn over during the night.

The whole atmosphere was extremely claustrophobic and as the journey progressed overnight, the hold became more and more uncomfortable and clammy. Sleep became quite elusive as we chugged our way to the Hook of Holland. It was a great relief for me to lower myself over the side of my bunk, passing two other prostrate soldiers on the way down to the deck in the morning.

Looking out of the porthole I could see the docks on the Hook of Holland and I experienced a moment of anticipation as I realised that I would soon step onto foreign soil for the very first time in my life.

Many countries are famous for their unique beauty and I had the good fortune to witness Holland in the spring. As our train sped through the Dutch countryside I gazed in wonder on acre upon acre of tulips of every colour imaginable. Sometimes the spring breeze would catch the blooms unawares making them sway, forcing them to display a more delicate hue as the sun touched them for a moment.

I could hardly believe that I was now in another country and that I was destined to live abroad for the next seventeen months.

Travelling through the Dutch countryside local people paused from their work in the fields to wave to us, probably recalling that it was the Allies who had released them from the heavy yoke of the Nazi occupation only a decade before.

Eventually we reached the Dutch German border and I knew that my final destination was only a few hours away.

Several hours later the train ground to a halt. I looked out of the window and saw a sign above the next platform – LUNEBURG. My journey from England was finally at an end but a journey of new experiences was about to begin.

Waiting at the station was a driver from the Royal Army Service Corps who, having identified me, told me to accompany him to his khaki Volkswagen Kombi bus.

It was a beautiful spring afternoon as we sped along quiet, tree lined streets and being my first introduction to driving on the 'wrong' side of the road I felt a little unnerved, particularly as we were travelling at a fair speed. However, within a few minutes we approached the gates of the barracks where the driver identified himself and his passenger. The guard then raised the boom and we drove in giving me my first opportunity to observe my new surroundings.

Home for the next seventeen months was to be spent at Brigade Headquarters of the 7th Armoured Division whose insignia was a Desert Rat. By comparison to the barracks in which I had served in England, my new accommodation could only be described as Five Star. The barracks had originally been built during Hitler's time in the 1930's and had been laid out with typical Teutonic thoroughness and attention to detail.

As the RASC driver led me up the concrete stairway to my barrack room I expected to be confronted by sleeping accommodation for about eighteen men but to my surprise I was ushered into an airy room which housed only six men.

Pointing to an empty bedspace near the window, the driver told me that it must be mine and left me with my luggage as he abruptly quit the room leaving five other men staring at their new arrival.

Having introduced myself to my barrack room companions, we chatted about how each one of us fitted into the scheme of things at Brigade headquarters. Being a headquarters company, soldiers were drawn from many different regiments and in our room there were two national service infantrymen from the East Lancashire Regiment, one of whom came from Liverpool and the other from Newcastle. Both were batmen for officers who occupied senior positions in the main Headquarters Office. There were also two other conscripts from the Devon Regiment who in their civilian life had been farmers and as a consequence looked after the pigs and rabbits which were housed within the confines of the barracks.

Thus our barrack room was home to a polyglot company of men and initially I had to strain my ears in order to make sense of their different accents although in other rooms there was a fair sprinkling of men whose accents I had little chance of deciphering.

After showering I started to relax although I did feel somewhat in limbo as I still had no idea what my job was to be, whether I was to be employed as a stenographer, who I would be accountable to or whether I would be working on my own or with another soldier.

Concluding that my barrack room companions seemed to be an agreeable lot, a very kindly looking corporal from the Royal Army Service Corps walked into the room and introduced himself as Garth Grinham who was known to everyone as 'Clewey'. He was the Commanding Officer's clerk. After chatting for a while he advised me that I was to appear 'on orders' to be interviewed by the Commanding Officer himself in the morning.

At eight o'clock the next morning I stood at the C.O.'s door in the company of a sergeant who ordered me to come to attention and marched me into the C.O.'s office where the major from a tank regiment was sitting at his desk. As was the normal drill, I took a check pace and saluted him whereupon he ordered me to stand at ease.

He proceeded to give me a brief outline of how the Brigade Headquarters fitted into the structure of the 7th Armoured Division adding that more specific details would be explained when I met the brigade's chief NCO of the RAOC.

Having dispensed with these details he then endeavoured to give me some fatherly advice (extremely rare in the army) regarding my tenure at Brigade HQ and also outside the barracks in the town of Luneburg itself.

He said that there were many difficulties and temptations facing a young soldier away from his home environment and that I should never lose sight of the standards my parents had set. He also reminded me of the hazards associated with liquor and appeared pleased when I told him that I did not drink alcohol.

Following his homily he told me to dismiss whereupon I came to attention, saluted and was marched out of his presence feeling somewhat mystified as to exactly what types of hidden hazards were waiting to inveigle me into a life of debauchery and sin. However, I was grateful that this senior officer had taken the time to show his concern for such a junior soldier in the brigade.

There were only three RAOC personnel at Brigade HQ and immediately following my interview with the C.O. I met Pte. Ricky Giltname who boasted that he was 'the man with the golden name'.

Ricky was the person in charge of the company's store and was a dyed in the wool cockney with all the cockney slang and wit. He didn't stop talking all the way to the main Brigade HQ office block where the very senior officers of the brigade worked including the Brigadier in command of our brigade.

The person for whom I was to work for the rest of my army career had been in the RAOC for many years and had worked his way up to become the highest non commissioned rank in the British army. His title was the Brigade Ordnance Warrant Officer and was referred to as the BOWO. Although he was a WO1 (warrant officer 1st class) he actually held the rank of 'Conductor' which was peculiar only to the RAOC but was higher that a regimental sergeant major in an infantry regiment.

Ricky and I walked into his offices and the first person I was to meet was a German civilian clerk called Friedl Berg. She was slim, attractive lady of about thirty-eight years of age with dark hair, olive complexion and a most engaging smile. We shook hands very formally and she told me that she hoped we would get on well together as she walked me into the BOWO's office.

As Friedl and I walked into his vast office overlooking the well kept gardens, Conductor Davis was sitting behind his large desk. As he stood up it revealed him as being short in stature, the large office and huge desk appearing to accentuate his diminutive figure even further. He was probably in his early forties with dark hair and a sallow complexion.

Although I stood to attention he waved me to a seat in front of his desk and shook hands warmly and I immediately felt at home in his company. He started chatting about his work, the duties which I was expected to perform and also showed a keen interest in my family background. With the memories of basic training still fresh in my mind I felt as though I was in a dream, particularly as Conductor Davis was of a higher rank than a Regimental Sergeant Major, such men normally striking terror into just about every soldier beneath them.

The next few days I was engaged in settling into my new environment and to my great relief I found that my optimistic predictions about my boss, the BOWO and Friedl, his civilian clerk were well founded.

Mr Davis was at pains to explain how the area under his command operated and gave some indication that we could eventually work as a team together. I found it hard to reconcile his modus operandi with the treatment to which I had been subjected during my training in England where respect and common decency were a rare commodity.

I found Friedl to be a most delightful lady and as we started to get to know each other she felt comfortable enough to speak of matters about the recent war which to some was still a chapter in history to be avoided at all cost.

Before the war she had lived in Stettin in eastern Germany and, as with almost all young Germans of the time, had joined the Hitler Youth. She enjoyed the camaraderie of the organisation and, of course, when the Second World War had commenced was optimistic that it would soon be over and Germany's self esteem would be restored to the prestige it had enjoyed prior to the First World War.

However, as the war progressed, Hitler's oppression started to impinge on the German population and people became frightened to speak out. Fear became so entrenched that survival depended on anonymity and avoidance of Hitler's local Gauleiters. Whilst she observed many trains carrying 'refugees' and prisoners of war, it was only later that the

German population started to ponder the sinister nature of the Nazi's treatment of forced labourers and the Jews.

As the allied bombing intensified she recalled that many parts of her home town of Stettin were decimated. Towards the end of the war the skies were saturated by the silver outlines of American bombers by day as they dropped their lethal cargoes upon the citizens below. As daylight gave way to darkness the drone of a thousand British bombers could be heard as they replicated the terror of their allied partners, day after day; night after night.

One day she returned home from work to find her parents home reduced to a heap of rubble with, ironically, a flower from their garden lying atop the debris.

As it became ever apparent that the war was lost for Germany, those living in eastern Germany began to speculate as to where the armies of Russia and The Allies would meet at the conclusion of hostilities, leading to the surrender of the armed forces of the Third Reich.

Friedl was fluent in English and when sheltering in a neighbours cellar, she used to tune the radio into the BBC world news to ascertain the progress of the war, particularly the location of the Russian Army now on German soil. It soon became apparent that the Russian advance was very rapid and would extend further west than Berlin.

As the German population had a deeply entrenched dread of Communist Russia under Stalin, thousands of German civilians became refugees and moved west to avoid falling under communist rule. Fortunately Friedl ended up in Luneburg, finding safety in what was to become the post war British Zone protected by the British Army of The Rhine, or BOAR. It was indeed a matter of good fortune as Luneburg was nevertheless only fifteen kilometres from the Russian Zone to the east.

Clandestine listening in to the BBC broadcasts had paid off although had a local German been caught listening to the BBC they would have been summarily executed by the Gestapo.

Sadly, for Friedl, Stettin became annexed from Germany and is now part of Poland.

Sirens and Grey Balloons

After the war, she and her husband were divorced and at the time of our first meeting she was living in Luneburg with her son Georg.

She asked whether I would like to learn German and having told her that I thought it would be a good idea, I found the name of a German tutor who gave lessons every week in downtown Luneburg. Thus, after a week I had enrolled in his evening class after first having purchased a text book called 'Heute Abend'.

After a while I tried out my first faltering phrases on Friedl and within a few months we were speaking mainly German in the office.

After I had started to accustom myself to the language, I was walking along a street opposite the Rathaus (Town Hall) on a very hot summer's day when I espied a gentleman to whom I had been introduced recently. He gave me the usual greeting of "Wie Gehts, Ihnen?" to which I replied "Guten tag, Ich bin heiss." I noticed that he gave me a rather quizzical smile as he went on his way.

When I next saw Friedl, I mentioned the conversation and she frowned. I explained that I had said "Good day" and then said that I was hot. " Peter", she said, never say "Ich bin heiss". Upon further enquiry she told me that what I had said was what a dog would have said if he had been hot after a female dog. I am sure that the gentleman in question didn't for one moment think that I had 'the hots' for him but in future I always remembered to say "Mihre ist heiss".

I was looking forward to my first weekend in my newly adopted environment as I was anxious to see the sights of Luneburg. By this time I had struck up a friendship with Pte Jimmy Kelly, my barrack room companion who was a batman from the East Lancashire Regiment. He was eager to show me around the local town.

Although there was a bus service outside the barracks to the town centre, at Jimmy's suggestion we decided to walk the two or three kilometres into town. Having crossed the main road we made our way to the local park where its different areas were criss-crossed by wide paths upon which the locals could either walk or cycle.

One area was of special interest to me as it consisted of a high wall where a thick quilt of green ivy clung to the brickwork above beneath which was a series of water sprays emitting a fine mist. The mist percolated through the foliage and down to a gutter where presumably the water was again recycled.

On many future occasions I would sit on a bench near the wall and enjoy the misty spray on my face which gave the impression of being on a beach with the sound of the sea in the background.

Luneburg's main square struck me as being typically European with its cobbled paving and a large fountain in the centre. The Rathaus or town hall dominated one side of the square with its terra cotta tiled roof situated beneath a beautifully crafted wrought iron clock tower.

The town was situated on the Ilmenau River and boasted many old picturesque buildings on its banks including the beautiful church of St Nicolas.

Our afternoon of sightseeing was restricted to the more respectable locations the town offered although Jimmy did point out that there was a very thriving nightlife to be had as well. The red light area had sprung up with the town becoming a garrison for several British regiments stationed there as occupation forces within the NATO Alliance.

Although I had been at my newly appointed posting for little over a week, I had an experience which started to shed some light on my C.O's fatherly advice upon my first arriving in Germany.

One Saturday afternoon I was in the barrack room with another young soldier when we heard shouting and a scuffle outside in the corridor. Before we had a chance to open the door, someone crashed against it. As we opened it the figure of a soldier slumped into the room with blood pouring from his forearm as he lay unconscious at our feet. Although he wasn't tall he was extremely stocky in stature. With great difficulty we managed to drag him into the room having sent someone to obtain medical assistance. Upon inspecting his arm we found a substantial jagged wound which required urgent attention.

As the wound was bleeding freely we managed to drag him out into the corridor and into the bath room where we tried to staunch the flow of blood prior to the arrival of the 'Field Ambulance Service' who patched him up and took him to the Royal Army Medical Corps hospital.

Later we heard that he had been playing cards with another Scotsman who had accused him of cheating and in his drunken fury had smashed a beer bottle and tried to stab his fellow card player in the face. Fortunately the injured man had been able to fend off the broken bottle with his arm in an effort to protect himself.

Almost every soldier in the Brigade liked to have a drink but quite a number made a habit of getting drunk, often with injurious consequences either to themselves or to others.

Being a garrison town there was quite a number of brothels. Many girls used to hang around the numerous bars plying their trade. Apparently, at weekends some of the girls used to do the rounds of the barracks although none frequented our room, at least, not to my knowledge.

Luneburg was renowned for its unspoiled heath land and one Sunday a few of us decided to walk the five or so kilometres to the Luneburger Heide or heath. Although situated on the outskirts of town, the heath was comparatively unspoiled, being clothed with heather and other attractive ground covering vegetation. I would say 'comparatively unspoiled' because the British had erected a monument on the heath on the spot where the Allies had received the German surrender on 7th May, 1945. However, once the Allies had left Germany, the monument was shipped to Britain and re-erected in the grounds of the British Military Academy at Sandhurst. It seemed strange to me when, years later I visited Sandhurst, to see the monument in its new home. It crossed my mind that on visiting Sandhurst, the casual observer might have wondered how the German surrender could possibly have taken place at Sandhurst, England.

Men serving in the regiments were required to undertake guard duties on a roster basis. This was a very important part of their duties in view of the existence of what was termed 'the cold war' at the time. Although Joseph Stalin, the communist Dictator of Soviet Russia had died a few years earlier, there had developed a very uneasy peace in Europe. The Russian government had subjected most of the East European countries they had conquered in the war to its autocratic rule and were trying to devour even more countries in their quest for world domination. For the people of East Germany, the evil dictatorship of Adolph Hitler had merely been replaced by the equally brutal dictatorship of Stalin's Russia.

Luneburg was a mere 15 kilometres from the Communist Eastern Zone in Germany and the barbed wire fences and armed guards in watch towers on its borders was a testament to the subjugation of the East Germans. Many East Germans had tried to escape to the west, only to be shot within sight of freedom by communist border guards.

Sometimes Russian spies tried to infiltrate NATO military installations and we were constantly warned to be vigilant. Although official Russian motor vehicles were allowed access through the British, French and American sectors of Germany, they were not allowed to stop and snoop around. If we saw such a vehicle we were under instructions to report the sighting to our brigade headquarters by using a special code word.

Whilst my work did not include guard duties I was required, along with four other soldiers, to undertake the alternative role of 'Duty Clerk'. However, before becoming eligible to do so I had to satisfy the 'Field Security Service,' an Arm of the Royal Army Intelligence Corps that I did not pose a security risk.

Accordingly I was required to complete a very long and searching form to enable them to establish my bona fides. Questions about my family background, parents, grandparents and siblings etc were included. I was also interviewed by the F.S.S who explained that the duty could involve classified secret information.

After a few weeks I was called in and advised that I had been cleared for confidential and sensitive work and was required to read the 'Official Secrets Act' plus sign an acknowledgment that I had read the document and was fully aware of the consequences if the rules of secrecy were broken.

It all sounded terribly important although in essence the role of duty clerk mainly involved receiving envelopes containing despatches derived within Brigade HQ which had already been sealed, and then entering them into a register before placing them into a plain envelope which was then collected by a specially assigned security courier.

Sirens and Grey Balloons

Security of the Brigade Headquarters itself was undertaken by the nightly contingent of soldiers on rostered guard duty. These guards patrolled the high steel railings around the Brigade's perimeters but the actual Brigade Headquarters Office Block was occupied by only three soldiers outside office hours, namely the duty clerk, the cipher corporal and the orderly officer who usually arrived at about 11 pm following his final patrol and visit to the guard room.

The cipher corporal was locked away on the third floor of the building in a heavily protected strongroom. Being close to the East German border his job was to eavesdrop on Soviet Russian ciphers and report any useful information to the Intelligence Corps.

The duty clerk's work involved emptying waste paper baskets into a large bin the contents of which were burned the next day. He was also responsible for locking each office in the building. As all the offices had different types of keys, these keys were then placed on a key board which was then securely locked away.

One of his more onerous duties was that of answering the 'secured' phone line from BAOR Headquarters in Verden. From time to time there would be a mock alarm drill whereby the BAOR HQ in Verden would send a message via the secure line to our Brigade HQ by mentioning a pre determined code word. The duty clerk's duty was to advise his own duty officer who would call each battalion HQ in the Brigade. Having done this our duty officer would advise BAOR HQ that all parties had been advised of the alarm. I suppose the idea was to ascertain the response time in the event of a real emergency.

However, if our duty officer was not around, it fell to the duty clerk to take the place of the duty officer and having contacted each battalion in the brigade, confirm the responses to the chiefs at BAOR in Verden.

Thus it was always a relief when, late at night the duty officer arrived at the Brigade HQ allowing the duty clerk to relax and climb into the bed provided in the office.

Many months later I was engaged as duty clerk and at about 10.30 the duty officer, a Warrant Officer II, arrived and asked if everything was present and correct. I advised him that nothing untoward had happened during the evening. However, in the morning I was called in by a high ranking officer who accused me of not being in the office when the 'hotline' had been activated. I denied that the phone had rung during my time on duty. The duty officer was then interviewed and it was subsequently ascertained that the timing of the call was just after he had arrived at the duty clerk's office. He verified that no call had been received and that was the end of the matter. The frightening aspect as far as I was concerned was that had I been on my own when the alleged call had been made, my word would not have borne as much weight as the duty officer's word and I may well have been court martialled for an offence I hadn't committed.

Having worked for the BOWO for three months, Mr Davis called me into his office and invited me to take a seat. He then said "Peter, I've decided to give you your first stripe". "From tomorrow you will appear on orders where the C.O. will officially advise you of your promotion to Lance Corporal."

I was amazed for two reasons. I had not thought of promotion but the fact that he had referred to me by my first name came as a great surprise as it was so unusual. He must have noticed my look of amazement as he said "I know you would never take advantage and you will be discreet". Thus, only in his office and later at his home with his wife and two boys did he refer to me by my first name. But for me he was always Mr Davis.

I had been in Germany only a couple of months before I woke up to the fact that being a non drinker at the time was quite an asset as my services were much sought after in the role of baby sitter and house sitter.

Married couples and particularly those with children apparently felt more at ease with a baby sitter who would not be tempted to help himself to the drinks cabinet during their absence, thus compromising his ability to look after his charges.

It was a great side-line for me as it gave me extra money, usually a pound an evening, plus the added bonus of a meal left in the kitchen for my consumption during the evening. The extra pound was invaluable as by that time I was only earning less than two pounds a week which included an extra seventy pence for being a lance corporal. In fact there were some weeks when my earnings from babysitting and house sitting amounted to more than my weekly army pay. Sometimes a couple, usually an officer and his wife, would ask if I wished to bring another soldier and if such an occasion arose I would ask Jimmy Kelly to come along as he was such great company.

After a few months the regiment nearest to our Brigade HQ left Luneburg for repatriation to England. The Royal West Kent Regiment had caused very little trouble with other battalions or the local population and were well regarded by everyone. However, their replacement was the Welch Regiment whose rowdy and inconsiderate behaviour immediately became a source of concern and annoyance not only for the other regiments in the garrison but also for the local German population and especially for the German youths.

The Welch Regiment had always shared a hostile relationship with the Highland Light Infantry and although both regiments were renowned for their military prowess in battle, they unfortunately didn't know when to stop fighting.

Shortly after the Welch Regiment moved to our garrison it was rumoured that the Scottish Highland Light Infantry would also be coming to Luneburg. However, most of the older regular soldiers opined that this would never happen as the two regiments were 'daggers drawn' and always left ill will and pandemonium in their wake. Apparently both regiments had been stationed in Cyprus some years before and their soldiers had clashed whenever they met.

Nevertheless the British Military hierarchy in their infinite wisdom decided that the HLI should be posted to Luneburg. The decision was catastrophic, particularly for the local German population.

The good behaviour and neighbourly work of the previously Luneburg based Royal West Kent Regiment became a distant memory as the two regimental newcomers quickly earned a name for drunkenness, rowdy behaviour and hostility to the locals.

The Welch Regiment's mascot was a rather fine looking shaggy billy goat whose behaviour was considerably more acceptable than that of some of its human peers. One night members of the HLI stole into the Welch Regiment's barracks and managed to make off with the goat, much to the chagrin of the proud Welshmen of the regiment. The poor goat must have harboured feelings of extreme apprehension as men dressed in drag spirited him away into the night.

Not to be outdone, some members of the Welch Regiment managed to steal the HLI kilt rumoured to have belonged to that regiment's Commanding Officer, and ran it up their flagpole.

However, by far the most serious confrontation of the two regiments came at the time the Welsh soldiers were celebrating St. David's Day. Soldiers from both regiments clashed in the streets of Luneburg. Rioting broke out with the streets resembling a war zone and it took a joint operation of the military police and German civilian police to move in and eventually restore order.

The logic of sending these old adversaries to share yet another garrison is beyond belief and the top brass who made that decision would have made even Field Marshall Sir Douglas Haig look mildly intelligent.

True to his word, my boss, Mr Davis encouraged me to work with him as a team and he often included me in some of his trips to different garrisons within the British Zone of Germany.

Whenever a regiment or Brigade Group required new or replacement equipment, they had to show cause for their request. Usually it was for clothing or webbing equipment which had passed its use by date (referred to as U/S or unserviceable). The protocol was that the regiment concerned would arrange for the U/S equipment to be displayed so that Mr Davis could inspect it and authorise the necessary replacements. Such inspections were referred to a 'boards of survey'.

I always enjoyed accompanying Mr Davis on trips to different parts of the British Zone, usually in an army Volkswagen car driven by a German civilian employed by the army. It still felt surreal to me as we drove through German towns and villages whose inhabitants only a decade before had been engaged in a bloody war with the rest of Europe. I sometimes felt as though I was in the middle of a dream and that I would soon wake up to find that we were still at war.

On our first such trip I recall parking the car at Hameln (Hamlin) where the Pied Piper had initiated his famous march leading the local children out of the town. It was never clear whether he was marching them away from the clutches of the great plague or whether he had other less altruistic motives. Over the years his deeds have been embellished to include his prowess at ridding the town of rats as well.

There was a British Army base near Detmold and on a couple of occasions we took time to view this beautiful town in North Rhine Westphalia. A little way out of town stands the magnificent monument of Hermannsdenkmal. The monument commemorates the victory by the war chief Herman and the local Germanic tribes over three Roman legions in the year 9 ad. The massive copper statue of Herman is mounted atop a large stone tower and is visible from many kilometres around. During the war it was an ideal marker for Allied aircraft and it was rumoured that British pilots used the statue for target practice although I saw no evidence of this.

The Welch Regiment's barracks were quite close to our Brigade HQ offices and one day I came across the BOWO chatting to a Company Sergeant Major from that regiment. Mr Davis called me over and introduced me to this CSM. He was a most interesting person and told us about some of the incidents which he had witnessed when fighting in the Korean War a few years before.

It so happened that the Welch Regiment's barrack square was close by and a couple of very young looking Second Lieutenants were drilling a company of burly looking soldiers. The two junior officers looked as though they were hardly out of adolescence with their fresh complexions and slim figures. The scene struck me as being quite incongruous given that these two young commissioned officers were in command of not only battle seasoned privates but also non commissioned ranks up to the quite senior rank of staff sergeant.

I commented to the Warrant Officer that the second lieutenants looked very young and inexperienced and somewhat out of place. He told me that whenever youths were called up for national service in a regiment, the public school boys were usually given an opportunity to go before the War Office Selection Board (WOSB) with a view to becoming officers, purely by virtue of the schools they had attended.

I also asked how such men fared in real wartime situations such as the Korean War and he said that such inexperienced officers relied very heavily on their non commissioned Warrant Officers for advice even though the warrant officers were of a lower rank.

Having served in an army corps where soldiers undertook a trade as opposed to service in a regiment, my experience was that in an infantry regiment, one's education at public school was recognised where promotion to officer status was concerned. However, in a corps such as REME (Royal Electrical and Mechanical Engineers), specialists had their pre service qualifications taken into account when it came to promotion.

It struck me at the time that the British Army had progressed very little since the late 1800's when a member of the gentry could purchase his rank in the army although he may have never set his eyes on a firearm or even seen a real soldier in the flesh before.

In the 1950's Europe was a powder keg of unrest with the Allied Powers scrutinising every Soviet Russian move which had the potential to ignite Europe into yet another military confrontation.

In June, 1956 thousands of factory workers in Soviet occupied Poland staged demonstrations complaining about working conditions and poor living standards in their country and the groundswell of discontent and hatred of the Communist regime spilled over into rioting. Unlike the democracies of the Western nations, Soviet Russia was run by a dictatorship where the apparatchiks could make decisions without the necessity of gauging the feelings of their own populations.

Within a short time the Russians had sent in 400 tanks and 10,000 soldiers to quell the riots in which over fifty civilian demonstrators were killed.

Similarly in October, 1956 news came through that people in Hungary had risen up against the Russian rulers and had started a revolution against their Russian Communist rulers. Hungary had been overrun by the Germans during World War II and had been released from German tyranny by Russian troops in 1945.

However, following the surrender of the German forces in 1945, the Russians, instead of allowing the Hungarians to rebuild their lives within the framework of a self ruling democracy, subjugated them with a dictatorship no less brutal than Hitler's sadistic regime. Sadly, yet again the Nazi jackboot had been replaced by the cruel and inhumane rule of the 'Hammer and Sickle'.

By October 1956 the Hungarian people had reached a point of desperation and there rose up a spontaneous nationwide revolution. In Budapest the huge statue of Joseph Stalin was toppled and some members of the dreaded Communist secret police had been killed. By the end of October the Russians agreed to withdraw and the Hungarians selected Imry Nagy as their Prime Minister.

However, the Hungarians respite was short lived. The Russian government went back on its word and sent in the army with troops and tanks, crushing the uprising and killing 2,500 civilians in the process. Their new Prime Minister who had been guaranteed immunity from prosecution was tried by the Russians and subsequently executed.

At our Brigade HQ these events had been viewed with alarm, particularly as Russian occupied Eastern Germany was but fifteen kilometres away from our barracks and the Allies were aware that Russia harboured aspirations to take over the whole of Europe, having previously gained influence over Yugoslavia and taken possession of Poland, Hungary and Eastern Germany.

Our Brigade HQ advised all personnel that we could be mobilised at any time should the Russians display any further aggressive military intentions. Leave was cancelled and our kit was packed for any possible emergencies. Also the Brigade's motor vehicles were to be fuelled up at all times.

Fortunately, Russia's lust for power and new territory eventually withered and countries like Hungary, Poland and Eastern Germany were eventually relieved from Communist tyranny although it took many decades to achieve.

By the end of 1956 I had well and truly settled in to army life and with over half of my period of national service completed felt as though 'civvy street' had been but a bygone dream. Army life was certainly not the sort of life I would ever have chosen but the comradeship of my fellow soldiers was something for which I was very grateful. Also I was enjoying working with Friedl and Mr Davis and often chatted with many of the local German civilians who worked in the barracks. At that time many English people had the impression that Germans had no sense of humour but in my experience I found this to be a complete fallacy.

Shortly before Christmas I was chatting to my boss when he quite nonchalantly told me that I should 'bull up' my kit as I was to be required on C.O's orders the next day. Upon my enquiring why, he told me that I was to be formally promoted to full corporal by the new Commanding Officer, Major Hawkshaw-Burn.

Shortly after my promotion my boss received a phone call from the CRAOC (Commander of the Royal Army Ordnance Corps) in Germany. He advised Mr Davis that he required him to contact the Commanding Officer of the Scottish Cameronian Rifles Regiment as that regiment was to leave BAOR and be deployed elsewhere. The matter was so urgent that they required the BOWO's assistance. Mr Davis accordingly rang the quartermaster of the Cameronians who asked him to drive down to his headquarters straight away.

Next day a driver picked us up, packed our luggage into the front luggage compartment of the Volkswagen and we were soon on our way south to the town of Detmold, near to the Cameronians' Regimental Headquarters.

Having arrived, Mr Davis left me and called on the Regiment's Quartermaster, a Lieutenant Colonel, to be briefed on the situation. The Quartermaster instructed the BOWO to organise the recording and packing up of all necessary equipment required for the move. Four other men from the Cameronians were consigned to work with Mr Davis and me although the next day Mr Davis was called back to Luneburg for another urgent assignment.

The four Scots privates from the Cameronians with whom I worked were wonderful company. They seemed to enjoy working together, nothing was too much trouble to them and it became apparent that their helpfulness was a product of their great morale. It was later that day that I started to realise why. On that first day we carried out the BOWO's instructions, counting stock, entering the details into the necessary manifests and packing equipment into boxes ready for despatch.

By 10.00 pm we still had a way to go to complete the day's tasks so we decided to award ourselves a short break for a 'smoko'. Having settled down on boxes to drink our mugs of tea, the Lieutenant Colonel Quartermaster walked in. Mugs in hand we bolted to attention. The moment he saw us he said "Sit down, boys, you deserve a break – where's my tea?" One of his men hastily poured him a large mug of our brew.

Seldom does one meet a person who appears to have been imbued with a sense of natural leadership. However, this man immediately inspired a feeling in me to the point where I felt I could follow him to the ends of the earth, such was his charisma. He chatted amicably for a while, asked questions about how the job was going and after he had finished his tea he departed into the night.

I asked my companions what they thought of him and they said that they and everyone else in the Cameronians shared the same feelings about him. Apparently he had joined the Regiment as a young man and had worked his way from the rank of private, through all the non commissioned ranks until becoming a Lieutenant Colonel.

For the next ten evenings he came into our store and sat with us over a mug of tea and was interested in keeping up-to-date with our progress. He also told us that he had cleared the normal channels and should we need anything we should approach him direct.

A fortnight later the job had been accomplished; we had worked eighteen or nineteen hours a day and such was this man's leadership qualities that we had all looked upon it as an honour to have served him.

After returning to Luneburg Mr Davis received a dispatch from the Colonel thanking us for all the hard work and long hours we had put in whilst with the Cameronians. Regrettably I am unable to remember his name but his memory certainly lives on in my mind over fifty years later. He was a true leader of men.

Whilst I was not required to participate in guard duties which were particularly unpleasant during the severe German winter, nevertheless the role of duty clerk occasioned more than a few surprises from time to time.

One night a Royal Army Service Corps corporal was duty clerk at Brigade HQ. He went to bed in the duty clerks' office that night doubtless feeling relieved that the 'hotline' from Verden had not been activated and thankful that the duty officer had arrived and was in his room.

However, when the occupants of one of the Brigade HQ offices arrived in the morning they found that the office had been broken into overnight.

The Field Security Section swung into action and interviewed all five of the duty clerks. They dusted the office desks, drawers and other items for fingerprints and pursued every available avenue in an attempt to find the culprit but as far as we could ascertain, all to no avail. In the end we were none the wiser and it was assumed that a thief looking for classified information had somehow broken into the office or had secreted himself on the premises although that particular office apparently contained no documents likely to have been of any use to a hostile power.

GHOSTS

I had been engaged as a duty clerk role for only a few weeks when I experienced a most unusual happening. A little before nightfall, having emptied the wastepaper bins and secured the offices, I decided to write my weekly letter home to my parents. The Brigade HQ building was locked, the windows secured and the only other person in the building was the cipher corporal in his windowless strongroom on the third floor.

After settling down to my letter writing I heard a loud knock on the duty clerks' office door. I was quite startled as I walked across the office and opened it. There was nobody to be seen. Thinking that I may have been mistaken I went back to my desk and continued writing but the moment I picked up my pen there was another knock on the door. This time I crept over to the door and waited. As soon as there was another knock I opened the door and rushed into the corridor but again there was no-one to be seen. Picking up a box of matches I made my way down a flight of stairs to the cellar but again found nothing in the darkness there.

Sirens and Grey Balloons

On another occasion some weeks later I was sitting in the same office having locked the daytime offices and the outside door when the door leading to the corridor opened. Thinking that I hadn't fully secured the door I pushed it shut. The door in question was half glazed with the lower half being of timber and the upper section being of fluted glass. Having shut the door I watched as the door handle moved downwards and the door opened again. This seemed very strange, particularly as I could see through the glazed portion of the door and could perceive no figure on the other side.

Again I pushed the door shut and made sure that not only the latch clicked but the door was locked as well. The door handle went down again several times. I then unlocked the door and waited. The handle went down a third time whereupon I rushed out into the corridor and found nothing. I became quite perplexed by these events but did not want to tell anyone else.

Another similar event occurred a few weeks later when the cipher corporal saw me one morning and asked what I had been doing on the third floor the previous night. He said that someone had been walking along the corridor of the third floor and had opened the door of the BOWO's office and had come out a little later. He looked at me rather quizzically when I told him that I hadn't been on the third floor all that night.

One morning many months later all five soldiers engaged in the duty clerk's role were standing in that office when the familiar 'knock knock' was heard on the door. We all looked at each other and breathed a sigh of relief as we then realised that we had all often experienced the same spooky happening. Oddly, none of us had ever felt scared, although none of us could come up with a logical explanation for these weird events.

Although much of the time at Brigade HQ revolved around administrative tasks and clerical duties, we were constantly reminded that we were soldiers first and foremost, particularly as Communist East Germany was almost on our doorstep.

Soldiers in the infantry regiments were required to practise rifle and foot drill on an almost daily basis and had to regularly attend the rifle range where their performance with the Lee Enfield rifle was strictly monitored. They had to maintain a high standard of accuracy. Some talented soldiers who were exceptionally accurate shots could become snipers with the benefit of extra pay to compensate for their truncated longevity on the battlefield in the event of war.

Although most men had specific duties working at Brigade HQ, they were nevertheless required to attend the rifle range from time to time. Accordingly, one morning we were issued with rifles and then driven to the nearby rifle range.

Having made a perfunctory inspection of the rifle which had been issued to me I found that unlike most rifles where sights could be adjusted to the distance of the target, mine possessed 'battle sights' where only the target distance of 300 or 600 yards could be selected. This obviously meant that firing at a target 200 yards away, my 300 yard sights would make the shot land 100 yards further on.

I mentioned this to the sergeant in charge who merely suggested that I select the 300 yard option and attach a bayonet to the end of my rifle, the weight of which would lower the barrel and also the trajectory of the bullet. As I was not remunerated on my accuracy with a rifle, a poor score on the range didn't worry me unduly.

On the range I attached my bayonet and being the only soldier thus equipped looked conspicuously warlike as I settled down for my first shot. Amazingly, each shot I fired was signalled in the butts (the area of the targets) as being a good shot, in fact after my first session I was feeling that the bayonet attachment had managed to produce a most salutary effect upon my marksmanship. Alas, my moment of glory was short lived when it was discovered that the person beside me had been firing at the wrong target and my battle sights had completely missed my target on each occasion. Happily I was being paid quite well for the shorthand I had never written and transcribing it onto the typewriter I had never touched.

Next time on the rifle range I was issued with a 1917 vintage Lee Enfield with three sights which provided more accuracy than the 'improved' later models which possessed only two sights fixed along the barrel.

Sirens and Grey Balloons

In an attempt to keep us physically fit we were taken on several 'forced marches' the first of which stood out in my mind as the most memorable. By now my size 9 working boots had been overworked to the point of being discarded and I had resorted to wearing my 'best boots' which were a size smaller. With ordinary wear these boots were reasonably comfortable but on this first forced march I was to discover their limitations.

The idea of a forced march was to cover the maximum possible distance with the minimum amount of effort by marching eighty paces and then running eighty paces alternately. This proved to be an excellent tactic for speedy mobility and we all seemed to adjust to the pace quite well and without any undue stress.

Unfortunately, as my feet began to swell the boots started to rub until I could feel the blood lubricating my socks inside my boots. At the conclusion of the march I hobbled back to my barrack room and took off my boots in order to survey the damage. My socks were soaked with blood and having bathed my feet I could observe large blood-filled blisters covering my toe nails like over ripe haemorrhoids.

As I was unable to put my boots back on I slithered my feet into my gym shoes and went to the RAMC hospital carrying my offending boots with me. The doctor took one look my feet and proceeded to cut off the unbroken blisters. As my feet had swollen to be larger than my boots, I was excused boots for a couple of weeks. He also gave me a 'prescription' for a new pair of boots which I obtained after the swelling had gone down.

The vast majority of national servicemen kept a 'demob chart' which recorded the exact number of days they were required to serve in the forces until the great day arrived when they were to become civilians again. These charts came in a variety of forms but the favourite was a large piece of paper on which the shape of a dart board had been drawn. On the perimeter of the dart board was a small box in which was printed the number '729' representing the number of days to be served before his day of demobilisation. Similar boxes were drawn with each box representing a day of service done until eventually after two years the 'bullseye' at the centre of the chart was reached and he was free to leave the service. Most men could tell you at a glance how many days they had to serve until their return to 'civvy street' was to be achieved.

Rather than devise a record showing a daily tally, I purchased a wooden pencil and decided to cut a notch in the wood after each month so that after twenty-four months my time in the army would be over. I still have that pencil.

September, 1957 arrived and as I cut another notch out of my demob pencil I mused that it would now be a little less than two months and I would be a civilian again. However, a lot can happen in two months and there were rumours that we were to be engaged in a NATO Military Exercise sometime in the near future.

Every so often our brigade undertook small scale military exercises which were commonly called 'schemes' in normal military parlance. Although we were part of the 7th Armoured Division, tanks were not used on these exercises as the expense of deploying tracked vehicles such as tanks involved very high costs. Tank regiments usually held exercises in designated open areas close to their own headquarters.

NATO EXCERCISE

Up to this time I had never been called upon to be engaged in the schemes as I was required to be part of the skeleton staff at Brigade HQ when they were taking place. However, when it was announced that there was to be A NATO exercise in Denmark involving NATO troops from Britain, USA and Canada, I was told that my services were to be required. It struck me at the time that my selection could not have been a reflection on my ability with the Lee Enfield rifle or requiring the services of a stenographer in the heat of battle in the muddy trenches of Denmark. I was therefore at a loss to know what my role was to be.

However, a couple of days later all was revealed. Because I was one of the few non alcohol drinking soldiers in the brigade group, I was to look after the officers' grog whilst it was being transported from Germany to the 'battlefield' in Denmark.

As the proposed exercise was to be held over a two week period one could hardly expect the commissioned officers to 'rough it' like the men over whom they had control. Officers required roomy tents, sleeping quarters, carpets and other accoutrements which the ordinary British soldier could only have dreamed about. But above all, no officer could have been expected to function well without his evening discourse with fellow officers conducted over the odd gin and tonic. Thus, I was put in charge of a three ton truck, which was loaded with a cargo of wines, spirits and cases of beer, not to mention various other victuals. Presumably the powers that be felt that these items of refreshment would pose a temptation beyond most men's ability to resist and thus had to be protected. I was therefore destined to be the only soldier on that exercise never to be confronted by 'the enemy'. Rather, I was to be called upon to defend the officers' copious supplies of refreshment from plunder by marauding troops from our own side.

In mid September the convoy was ready to get underway. I had checked the items in my care placing the more attractive cargo such as wines and spirits at the front of the truck and stowing the less attractive articles like carpets and tents further to the rear, leaving a small space for my blankets near to the canvas opening at the back.

A short time later the convoy was ready to move and I climbed into the cab of an ex World War II Austin three ton truck. It was an ancient piece of machinery even by 1950's standards and possessed a few idiosyncrasies not least of which was that when the driver double declutched to change to a lower gear, there was a blowback from the carburettor which found its way back through the air filter situated in the cab, smothering both the driver and passenger with acrid fumes. Additionally, if the speed of the vehicle exceeded more than 40 miles per hour, the engine tended to billow smoke which found its way inexorably into the cab as well. However, I was yet to experience these glitches as we drove through the gates of the barracks to meet up with the rest of the troops.

Having driven north for a couple of hours we reached Hamburg where we stopped for a short time for any men who required a pee. This gave me an opportunity to take a better look at the composition of the vehicles involved. There was an assortment of small trackless armoured scout cars together with a few large Saracens. The Saracens resembled tanks but instead of tracks were equipped with six large tyres, presumably made of solid rubber. There was also a plethora of small vehicles in which the officers rode including American Willys Jeeps dating back to the 1940' plus a number of British Austin Champs. These chunky looking cars were equipped with Rolls Royce engines and were quite powerful compared with the Jeep although roughly the same size but considerably heavier and obviously more expensive. The British had just started to be equipped with the latest Land Rovers which were quite popular. However, most of the vehicles were large and small trucks used for the cartage of army equipment and items of ordnance.

To enable most mechanical repairs to be carried out in the field, REME (Royal Electrical and Mechanical Engineers) were equipped with mobile workshops and also possessed a large Scammell tow truck.

As our motley array of vehicles made its way through Hamburg and around the huge statue of Otto von Bismarck I wondered what the great man would have made of it had he still been alive. He fortunately lived to see his country lose only one world war not two.

From Hamburg we drove north to Lubeck and thence off to Kiel where we spent the night in an army barracks where Erwin Rommel's Panzer Divisions had been stationed only eleven years before. Part of our contingent was given barrack room accommodation here but many men in charge of valuable equipment stayed with their vehicles overnight. As my three ton truck contained many items of valuable luxuries I made up a bed in the back having first dragged a carpet onto the floor upon which I spread my two blankets. The driver slept in his cab but found it rather cramped as the two front seats were separated by a large gearstick.

Next day we were off again and soon reached the Danish border. After passing through Flensburg we motored north to Odense before crossing a causeway at Nyberg, thence further east until we ended our journey at Store Heddinge where, apparently we would be spending most of our time whilst in Denmark. After reconnoitring the area our detachment was instructed to set up headquarters in a large wood not far from the sea.

There was enough space for tents to be erected and vehicles to be parked so we busied ourselves unloading the trucks, erecting officers' tents after which I handed over the crates of liquor to be housed in the officers' mess tent.

Sirens and Grey Balloons

Having set up our camp and a field kitchen for the Royal Army Catering Corps, we were instructed to dig our trenches close to where our vehicles were parked. As we were part of the Brigade HQ our trenches were not to be the conventional long slit trenches one associates with the First World War. We were required to dig a small trench to protect just an NCO and driver or in the case of the catering corps, a trench to accommodate the cooks. The driver and I took some time to dig our small trench but were quite happy with the result having dug it down to the standard depth of four feet six inches (roughly 140 centimetres). This depth allowed a soldier to enter and leave the trench quickly in the event of an emergency but more importantly it allowed the occupants to look over the parapet to sight the enemy and to aim firearms whilst in a standing position.

Feeling quite pleased with our efforts we were about to undertake other tasks when a sergeant, having inspected our trench told us that it must be six feet (180 centimetres) deep. Naturally we asked him why the depth of army trenches had suddenly changed only to be advised that there was a new regulation the logic of which appears to have been that were an atomic bomb to be dropped, we would have been afforded greater protection.

We shook our heads in disbelief and pointed out that were a nuclear bomb to be dropped our lives might be extended for just a few seconds but no longer. Also, incarcerated in the bowels of the earth we would not be able to see the enemy let alone shoot at him and should he lob a hand grenade into our dugout we would be unable to escape. Although the instruction was the epitome of military lunacy, we accepted the fact that the sergeant was merely carrying out his instructions so we nodded our acquiescence and continued digging.

Our next task was to camouflage the vehicle by covering it with a 'scrim net and then fastening branches and foliage to the net to hide it from the enemy. Having completed the task we then erected our small khaki bivouac tent which completed our housekeeping duties in preparation for the exercise whenever it was to commence.

The depth of the trench still worried us so we decided to find some item to place on the floor of the trench to elevate us to what had hitherto been the normal combat height. I have no idea how he managed to obtain them but after rummaging around the driver managed to get hold of a couple of empty ammunition boxes which served our purpose perfectly. Having installed them at the bottom of our trench we felt much safer as we could now leave the trench in a hurry and escape the danger of a thunder flash (firework used in exercises to simulate a hand grenade) should the enemy lob one in our direction.

Having chaperoned and delivered the most important item of the whole NATO exercise in the form of the officers' grog, there must have been a perception by the officer in charge of our unit that the driver and I should be put to some other use until we eventually struck camp and escorted the remnants of the officers' libations back to Brigade HQ in Luneburg.

Wherever the British Army served it was rightly perceived that there existed no greater stimulus to the troops' morale than receiving mail from home. It therefore fell to my lot to be put in charge of the delivery of mail for the whole of the 7th Armoured Division. Each morning we were to drive to the central sorting depot, pick up the sacks of mail and deliver them to each regiment stationed in the area.

We welcomed this appointment as it gave us a chance to get away each morning and to explore the countryside. As we were a considerable distance further north than our home base of Luneburg, the air felt very cool driving along winding country roads each morning. We saw rabbits, hares and quite an array of birdlife including pheasant which took off as the truck sped by. Even when we alighted from the cab to stretch our legs we were often startled by pheasant taking off a few metres away.

A few days after arriving in Denmark we were advised that the exercise would commence in two days time. We had expected to be briefed by the officers with an outline and purpose of the manoeuvres and to be given orders as to our exact duties, but no such briefings were forthcoming. We were only told that there would be an allied landing by paratroopers and a beach assault by the Welch Regiment as part of a joint ground force attacking Denmark. Presumably the paratroopers and infantry had been given details of the battle plan but although our HQ was in hostile territory, our orders were sketchy to say the least.

Sirens and Grey Balloons

Although this was not a live ammunition exercise we were ordered to wear our small packs complete with ammunition pouches. Unfortunately, we were not allowed to remove our boots at any time during the 'conflict'.

I was instructed to collect and deliver the mail as usual although I was told to take special care not to be taken prisoner. However, we had heard that the British were very popular with the Danes particularly following the Second World War, and as we drove around the countryside we were hoping to be captured. Five days away from our atomic trench and the promise of a real bed with sheets seemed to have a lot to commend it at the time. In spite of our driving slowly and me exposing my head and shoulders through the three-tonner's canopy, we never once sighted the enemy.

The British Army for some reason held the view that were an enemy attack to take place it would usually be either at first light or at dusk. For this reason we had to obey the order to 'stand to' each day. This involved standing in our trenches (on purloined ammunition boxes) with rifles at the ready, making sure that total silence would be observed. Thus, an enemy force would have difficulty in pinpointing the location of their ever vigilant foe.

On the first day of the exercise the driver and I delivered the mail to the troops scattered about the Store Heddinge region of Sjaelland and had returned to our own camp in the evening. The truck was duly parked under the camouflage netting which allowed us enough time to grab our rifles and drop into our trench just as the last glimmer sun drifted over the horizon. Not a sound could be heard and as no torches were allowed to be switched on the woods were in almost total darkness within a few minutes. Notwithstanding the order for total quiet, we heard the major in charge of our contingent calling "Where's Corporal Hurdwell, where's Corporal Hurdwell" but not a sound did we make. Although we could not see him we knew that he was getting nearer and nearer to our trench and then it happened. He was suddenly beside us in our atomic trench having toppled in, ending up splayed out at our feet amongst our ammunition boxes. Having told him that I was in the trench with him he sounded quite annoyed and said "Why the bloody hell didn't you say something!" However, I advised him that it was 'stand to' and was unable to respond. This placated him somewhat as we hoisted him out of our trench and into the night. I never did find out what he wanted of me and the occurrence was not mentioned the next day.

That same evening we were ordered to remain in our trenches as there was the likelihood of a possible enemy offensive that night. Some members of our unit had already collected empty food cans from the Catering Corps and having threaded string through them they were attached to a trip wire along the perimeter of the wood. A pebble was then placed in each tin. In this way we would be able to hear the enemy as they tripped the wire and rattled the empty cans.

All night we stood, leaning over the trench parapet, rifles in hand, as every tin in the neighbourhood was rattled by rabbits, hares, owls, wind and just about everything except the enemy. At the sound of each tin rattling our edgy nerves jangled and we could only have speculated as to how Allied troops must have felt fighting the Japanese in the jungle campaigns of the Second World War.

Army food during manoeuvres consisted almost entirely of canned 'combo' food which was surprisingly tasty and easy for the Army Catering Corps to prepare. In fact, all that was required was for a large 'dixie' (saucepan) to be filled with water and brought to the boil before the cans of combo were immersed for about twenty minutes. Gourmet meals such as steak and baked beans or sausages and beans were delicious although somewhat volatile when coming into contact with ones gastric juices a little later. We seldom emptied these meals into our mess tins as we found it easier to prise the can open and eat the contents with a spoon.

Prior to the five day exercise we did have fresh bread and milk delivered by the local shop keepers but once the 'hostilities' were under way deliveries ceased.

On the second day of the exercise the driver and I left at the normal time but on this occasion were required to drive to the battle zone where the Americans had been deployed. We found the Americans very outgoing and friendly and appeared to be more casual and less structured than their British counterparts. However what struck us with more force was their equipment. Whereas the ordinary British soldier had to make do with a couple of blankets for his bedding on cold nights, the U S soldiers had luxuriously padded sleeping bags. They also had hot showering facilities and their motor vehicles appeared to have been the latest models with some of their trucks even boasting automatic transmissions.

Whilst we were there we suddenly had to take cover as a couple of fighter jets swooped down at rooftop level in a mock attack on our position. The noise of a jet plane at low altitude was worrying enough but when we found out that they were a couple of British Hawker Hunter planes attacking us it prompted me to the conclusion that in the event of a war I hoped I'd be on the other side.

Having left the Americans we felt ourselves to have been very much the poor relations after visiting our rich overseas cousins.

Whilst we had no complaints about the food during the exercise and mugs of tea were in copious supply, after three days without normal ablutions we felt grubby and ill-kempt. We had been allowed only a very limited ration of water for washing and shaving and my annoyance was exacerbated by being reprimanded by a major for having a tidemark on my neck where I had failed to wash properly. Had I not been in the military it would have been easy to remonstrate with the officer and to complain about the inadequate facilities, particularly as officers had no problems with matters of personal cleanliness. Officers were not expected to wallow in the trenches or undertake duties such as ensuring rifles were well maintained or that camouflage netting was adjusted each time a truck was moved.

Being forbidden to remove our boots was unpleasant and after three days our socks had become lubricated with sweat which made our feet feel clammy as they slipped around in our boots. I longed for a strip wash with hot water and oodles of soap.

As we drove off the next morning for our usual mail run we were therefore looking forward to the end of the exercises and the chance to wash and put on fresh clothing.

Upon our return to camp we were told of a very successful raid on our unit made by the Danes. Apparently, unbeknown to our officers, the baker and milkman had been members of the local militia and during their 'peacetime' deliveries to our camp had reconnoitred our unit's layout. Using this covert intelligence they led an invasion of our unit throwing thunder flashes into our HQ and the surrounding trenches. However, the main worry for us was that they had also thrown thunder flashes into the POL (petrol, oil and lubricant) dump as well. Given that this was only an exercise it had been a rather reckless act to say the least. Fortunately no flammable liquids were ignited.

However, a few days later and after the completion of the exercise, a potentially serious event involving the dump did occur. Two Military Police soldiers were refuelling a Willys Jeep by the light of a kerosene lamp. The petrol tank on this type of vehicle was situated under the driver's seat. As they lowered the lamp to assess the level of the petrol, the tank ignited shooting flames into the air and threatening to spread fire throughout the whole camp including the POL dump.

Suddenly a very quiet and unassuming private seconded from the Welch Regiment, rushed out of the darkness, sat on the flaming driver's seat and drove the vehicle out of the woods. Fortunately for all concerned but more particularly for this self effacing national serviceman, sitting on the flames actually excluded the oxygen to the fire and extinguished it. Although his battledress was singed he was none the worse for the experience.

It was quite a relief when the NATO exercise was finally over for we could strip off our soiled clothing and perform our normal ablutions again. There was a pebbly beach nearby and we grabbed our soap and shaving gear and walked down to the water. Although sea water and soap seemed to harbour a natural antipathy to one another we nevertheless soon felt reasonably human again particularly having washed our feet and donned fresh socks, underclothes and shirts.

Although we had spent only five days under mock battle conditions, it did enable me to gain a minuscule insight into what it must have been like for the millions of gallant men who had fought in campaigns on the Western Front in World War I and in the deserts and jungles of later conflicts.

Sirens and Grey Balloons

Copenhagen was only an hour's drive away and we were very pleased when word was passed around that anyone wishing to visit the Danish capital would be transported there for a day trip.

I possessed only a schoolboy's knowledge of Copenhagen up to that point and so it was a wonderful experience to actually walk the streets of that beautiful city. My first impression having jumped down from the army truck was the huge number of Danes who appeared to rely on bicycles as their primary mode of transport. Hundreds and hundreds of bikes were lined up along the road waiting for a swing bridge to open following the progress of a steamer along the intervening canal.

We walked some distance towards the open sea and, as directed by one of the locals, came across Hans Christian Andersen's Little Mermaid statue reclining on the sea shore. It somehow felt unreal to me to be actually standing in front of the beautiful statue which had resided there since 1909.

Looking out to sea I tried to imagine the famous battle of Copenhagen of 1801 during which Horatio Nelson ignored his Fleet Commander's signal to withdraw, choosing to put his telescope to his blind eye pronouncing that he had seen no signal. Against all the odds, Nelson won the battle.

It would be seven years before I would see the statue again and under vastly different circumstances.

After a trip to the famous Tivoli Gardens we returned to our truck at the appointed time and drove back to camp very much indebted to the army for making it possible to see some of the sights of Denmark's wonderful capital.

Next day we struck camp, packed our belongings and started our journey back to Luneburg.

We broke our journey near the Danish border with Germany and our unit was directed to a farm where most of our number camped in a field. However, as we still had a depleted amount of valuable alcohol on board our Austin, we were ushered into a barn where we were to stay the night. At one end of the barn was a large haystack so we took little time to lay our blankets in readiness for a good night's sleep. Having spread clumps of hay between our two blankets to fashion makeshift eiderdowns, we slept soundly although disturbed once or twice by the rustling of the odd rat running over our feet.

It was a strange experience as we drove into Luneburg. I had come to like the town and its environs very much and had certainly enjoyed the civilians whom I met. Inexplicably, I felt quite saddened when I pondered that although I had been looking forward to my demobilisation for almost two years, Luneburg had become home to me and I would miss it very much.

Once inside our barrack room I stripped off my dirty clothes and made my way to the bathroom where I slid into a lovely, luxurious, warm soapy bath. I could almost feel the adhesion of a fortnights dirt and grime releasing its grip on my skin as I lay there semi comatose for almost an hour.

It was back to work on the following day. Although the BOWO had been on the NATO exercise, our paths had seldom crossed so it was great to see him again and to learn of his impressions of the trip.

CHAPTER XII FAREWELL

The last few days of my army service ticked by and the day that I would say farewell was rapidly approaching. Whilst I would never have chosen a career in the army, nor would I have volunteered for two years national service, I must say that it proved to have been so worthwhile. I had been exceptionally fortunate in the bonds of friendship which had been forged during those two years.

I was truly sorry to say 'farewell' to Mr Davis and Friedl and as the Volswagen Kombi bus took me to Luneburg station I counted my blessings, particularly when, just before I boarded the train, Friedl phoned the station and spoke to me to say farewell again.

There were no displays of Dutch tulips on that October day as the train sped towards the Hook of Holland. I boarded the 'Empire Parkeston' an even older vessel than the Empire Wansbeck that had conveyed me to Holland seventeen months before. As I lay in my bunk I started to ponder when my next overseas trip would take place.

On a beautiful sunny Sunday afternoon I arrived home in Chingford carrying my kitbag just as the family was sitting down to a roast lamb Sunday lunch.

Two unforgettable years were over but what next? Little could I have imagined that the next chapter of life's journey would prove to be as eventful as the first twenty years of my life and that I would end up living on the opposite side of the globe.

GLOSSARY

BAKELITE	Thermo setting plastic
BATMAN	Soldier assigned to an army officer for servants duties
BEAU JESTE	Soldier fighting in the French Foreign Legion
BRYLCREEM	Hairdressing cream for men
CATHERINE THE GREAT	19th century ruler of Russia
CSM	Company Sergeant Major
DAG	Wool on a sheep's rear quarters sullied with excrement
DICTAPHONE	Instrument for recording dictation
DOMESDAY BOOK	1086 survey on life in England undertaken by William the Conqueror.
KING'S SHILLING	British conscripted soldiers were paid a shilling a day plus extra emoluments if they had families. Empire soldiers received higher pay, Australians receiving six shillings per day.
LEDGERING EQUIPMENT	Fishing line equipped with lead weight to ensure hook reaches the sea bed.
NAAFI	Navy, Army and Airforce Institute
PALLIASSE	Mattress of straw
RAMC	Royal Army Medical Corps
RMP	Royal Military Police (often called 'Red Caps)
RAOC	Royal Army Ordnance Corps
RASC	Royal Army Service Corps
SCRIM NET	Open weave linen netting used for camouflaging

www.ingramcontent.com/pod-product-compliance
Lightning Source LLC
Chambersburg PA
CBHW062204080426
42734CB00010B/1778